The Woman
Who Loved Paul

By Frances F. Neilson

THE DONKEY FROM DORKING
MOCHA, THE DJUKA
GIANT MOUNTAIN
THE TEN COMMANDMENTS IN TODAY'S WORLD
LOOK TO THE NEW MOON

By Winthrop Neilson

THE STORY OF THEODORE ROOSEVELT

By Winthrop and Frances Neilson

DUSTY FOR SPEED
BENJAMIN FRANKLIN
BRUCE BENSON: Son of Fame
BRUCE BENSON: Thirty Fathoms Deep
BRUCE BENSON: On Trails of Thunder
EDGE OF GREATNESS: A Day in the Life of Benjamin Franklin
VERDICT FOR THE DOCTOR: Dr. Benjamin Rush
SEVEN WOMEN: Great Painters
WHAT'S NEW—DOW JONES: Story of The Wall Street Journal
THE UNITED NATIONS: The World's Last Chance for Peace
LETTER TO PHILEMON
THAT LYDIAN WOMAN

The Woman
Who Loved Paul

A novel by

Winthrop and Frances Neilson

A DOUBLEDAY-GALILEE ORIGINAL

DOUBLEDAY & COMPANY, INC., GARDEN CITY, NEW YORK 1978

ISBN 0-385-13190-9
Library of Congress Catalog Card Number 77-12868

To
Kathryn Galbraith
"Lux in tenebris"

CONTENTS

The Woman
Who Loved Paul

I
CORINTH

1

I, Priscilla, wife of Aquila, am writing of the events through which we passed, tragic yet glorious. Especially I write of that dearest and warmest one whose voice must reverberate through all ages to come but who could be so gentle and understanding with me, a woman.

Indeed I am certain now that no woman during his lifetime could have been closer to Paul of Tarsus than I have been.

As I begin this story, I see again through the eyes of memory all that we went through together. I feel again the emotions of my heart. Those shared hours of discouragement, onslaughts of hatred and violence, dread foreboding and terror, as well as our times of joyful work and accomplishment, remain sharply with me. Gruff, reticent, blunt with others when he wished, Paul opened his inner self to me, as I did mine to him.

Paul claimed me as his disciple. He was my master, and my friend.

The beginning was on that day when we first approached Corinth, Aquila and I, on the great ship that brought us from Puteoli, in Italy, to the shore of Greece. I stood alone on the foredeck with the strong south wind whipping out my hair, the hot sunlight sparkling on the blue blue water, nearly blinding my eyes. I was startled when my husband quietly came up behind me and put his arm around my waist.

"I know what you are thinking," he said. "I am thinking too."

The mast of the vessel creaked under the pressure of the huge sail overhead; the ship swayed gently over the soft waves. Already we saw small fishing boats out across the Bay of Corinth. The wharves of the port and the vessels at their moorings grew larger as our own ship drew nearer. Beyond, the city rooftops and buildings appeared to the right under a slight haze. Farther away, a huge rock rose up from the country around the city itself, the Acrocorinth mountain, buttressed on its slope by the overpowering Temple of Aphrodite.

"I am frightened." I clung to Aquila. "I feel— well, already lost."

"You need not be," he reminded me. "We have our introductions here, the prospect of starting up a good business, and we have each other. What else would we want?" He paused. "So . . . I am frightened too; it is all so new. . . ."

I threw my arms around his neck. For a moment we hugged, each giving the other reassurance. Here we were—two young people, in our early twenties, facing a most uncertain future. My husband and I have often been told we are alike. Yes, we are in many ways, even in our physical appearance. We are about the same height, our bodies are thin and lithe. We both have brown eyes, and both brown hair although his is not as dark as mine.

We had left our home in Rome after the expulsion of all Jews by edict of the Emperor Claudius. The Caesar had been angered that dissension had arisen among us of the Jewish faith in the capital city of the Empire. A number of us had heard and believed the words of the stranger who came to Rome to tell us in our synagogue that Jesus of Nazareth was indeed the Messiah so long awaited in accordance with the scriptures. We were baptized in our belief, and the Holy Spirit of God came upon us.

Others of the Roman congregations could not believe that the Messiah promised by the prophets would be a lowly man, not a king with armies to free our nation from the servitude of Roman rule. They argued that no one who claimed to be the Son of God would allow himself to be crucified as a common criminal. God himself would not have permitted such a thing. The Law of our fathers decreed that a man hanged to death was a man accursed by God. As for the Resurrection, they scoffed at the story. These people warned that to dispute the Law was heresy.

We who accepted the Way of Jesus were therefore vilified and condemned by many of our friends of the synagogue. The Emperor Claudius was displeased when he heard this, and ordered

4

that all Jews should take their conflicts elsewhere, to preserve the peace of Rome.

I, who was born and married in Rome, had never traveled except to my father's summer villa at Antium, on the Tyrrhenian Sea below the city. For my parents to retire to the villa from Rome was not a hardship. Likewise, Aquila's family lived at Pontus, in the Campagna near the Appian Way, south of Rome, and the Emperor's edict did not affect them. Aquila and I were terrified at the prospect of leaving home, family, and friends to live in a strange place.

Aquila, in accordance with Jewish tradition for young men, had been taught a manual trade, that of tentmaking, which included awnings and sails for ships. Already he had set up a fair business in Rome. Now, at my young age of twenty-two and Aquila at twenty-five, in our third year of marriage, we were forced to go elsewhere to earn our living.

It was my father, an experienced traveler on business throughout the Roman world, who advised us to go to Corinth, in Greece, a growing and important city of the Empire. . . .

When I descended from our ship and stood on the solid wharf, I felt it was rocking beneath me. I swayed dizzily. Aquila, beside me, had a peculiar expression on his face. He seemed to be swaying too. My instant thought was of an earthquake, but I dismissed that as too coincidental.

"You feel the solid earth rocking?" Aquila asked. "I've been told it always happens after being on a ship for a time. The sensation will go away."

I felt it until the next day.

After our baggage came ashore with our small amount of clothing, personal possessions, and the sacks with Aquila's working tools for cutting and sewing canvas, we hired a wagon to take us into the city of Corinth itself. On the way, we were astonished to see small boats being lifted by dozens of slaves and placed on enormous flat wagons for transporting across the narrow Isthmus of Corinth between the Gulf of Corinth on the west and the Saronic Gulf to the east. We had already been told that Corinth, lying between the Peloponnesus, the southern part of Greece, and the mainland to the north, was at a crossroads of the Empire, with

5

every nationality of the known world represented by sailors, business travelers, scholars, and ordinary vacationists. It had the greatest reputation of any city for sin and sexual license, a fact we were soon to know.

We were taken by the hired wagon to the address of Gaius Titus Justus, a friend of my father, who had already written letters announcing our arrival. Once we knew him, we simply called him Gaius. He was wonderfully helpful to us. Gaius is a short, plumpish man with a slight, clipped beard, and he wears a Roman toga as a symbol of his status in Corinth. Before our first meeting, we knew that he had been converted to belief in our God of the Jewish faith.

"I have already found the house for you," he told us. "It is in the potters' quarter of the city; I hope you approve. You know Corinth is, famous for its beautiful porcelain ware. I chose this place for you, thinking of your occupation. The houses in that area have sheds behind them as studios, good for your work. Shall I take you to see it?"

On the way, Gaius said that he had instructed one of his servant girls to put the house in order and make supper for us. Her name was Bendis, and she was to be with us for a few days to help me become settled and find my way around. Gaius explained that all the houses in Corinth were relatively new, as, only a hundred years before, Julius Caesar had ordered the ancient city to be rebuilt on Roman lines after its previous destruction in the Greco-Roman wars.

"The rebuilding is still continuing," Gaius remarked with pride. "We are now a city nearly a million in population—almost half of the two million in Rome itself."

Our house was perfect for us. It was two floors in height with a small attic room under the eaves reached by a ladder. The front door opened directly into an atrium, quite large for the size of the house. It was a room for every purpose of living and entertaining. Next to it was a study, or gineceo, or if need be, a guest room. The back room had a stove for cooking and heating water. On the upper floor were two rooms, one for ourselves and the other for any purpose we wished. Lead pipes along the walls from the stove carried hot water upstairs to the rooms and to a bathing room for warm baths. Plumbing and water supply in Corinth was even more

6

advanced than in most of Rome, Gaius assured us. He was right. Though the house was smaller in size, the facilities were better than in our own Rome home. Even the shed behind the kitchen provided more space for our work of measuring, cutting, and sewing.

As Gaius left us, he suggested, "When you are settled, come to see me. I think I have work for you. No one in Corinth need be idle."

Both Aquila and I thanked him enthusiastically. He replied, "Priscilla, I know your father well. I will do everything possible for his daughter and her husband. Having met you now, I see that I will do as much for your own sakes as for his."

Impulsively I leaned forward and kissed his cheek. I knew it was wrong, but I am guided by impulse. Aquila knows that. Gaius was startled, but he smiled and shook Aquila's hand as he took his leave.

The girl Bendis had welcomed us on our arrival. Praise be, both Aquila and I had learned the substance of the Greek language in our school studies. At least we could communicate with Bendis. She helped us to unpack, and served us our supper. She was a pretty girl, dressed in the usual short white tunica of a slave.

When she had prepared the supper for us and put it on the table in the atrium, Aquila asked abruptly, "Does she know our laws about food? Is this meat proper for us to eat?"

I reminded him that Gaius had adopted the Jewish faith, which meant going through the rite of circumcision and education in the Law. Bendis belonged to Gaius, and must understand.

"Anyway," I added, "I am hungry. I am not going to ask questions on this first night."

After our meal, while Aquila unpacked his tools and set up his shop behind the kitchen, I took time to become familiar with everything in the house. It was furnished completely; I found nothing lacking. And Bendis told me that on her master's orders she had bought necessary kitchen and house-cleaning implements.

Our atrium was equipped with divans, couches, and tables for our dining, relaxing, and entertaining. A vase of fresh flowers stood on a small table. In the small gineceo, everything needed for use as a study had been provided, as well as a sleeping couch for use by a guest if desired. Facilities for an overnight visitor were the last things I thought would be useful.

Impossible for me to anticipate at that time was the arrival of a guest. Nor could I have foreseen how many evenings I would spend in our comfortable atrium listening to Paul of Tarsus explain to me the gospel of the Way of Jesus.

But I think I remember now our small house in Corinth best for the countless afternoon hours with him in the gineceo, in which Paul lived and worked for so long. Here I sat at a table writing down his dictated letters as he paced back and forth across the floor, thinking out his next phrases. These letters went to friends, to the headquarters of the Christian Church in Jerusalem, and to the churches he had founded in Asia and Macedonia. Listening to him as he planned his texts opened my mind to the deep recesses of his philosophy, and to his infinite dedication to teaching the Word of God.

One cannot be so close to a man of such great power without being drawn to him in respect, admiration, and devotion. But I am far ahead of my story. . . .

After inspecting my new house in the foreign city of Corinth, I was very content.

We retired early that evening. As we lay together on the double-size couch in our second-floor room, I leaned over Aquila to say, "I am no longer frightened. Everything is going to be good for us."

He nodded, yawned. "Yes, I believe so. Go to sleep, Priscilla; tomorrow is our day."

With Bendis as guide, I learned quickly where the Agora, the central point of the city and marketplace, was in relation to our house. I discovered quickly that the synagogue stood next door to the house of Gaius. Bendis showed me the public library, the public baths, and the theater. She kept pointing up to the Temple of Aphrodite, where a thousand girls acted as priestesses of the goddess to perform the religious rituals. In the Corinth theater, at all times a thousand seats were reserved for them; such was the respect in which they were held. Without her saying so, I understood that Bendis really envied the position of those girls, all in slavery, who had such glamorous positions compared to hers as a household domestic. I restrained myself on comments—unusual for me, who can be very outspoken.

I released Bendis as soon as possible in order that the household of Gaius should not be disturbed by her absence. Within several days, Gaius sent an invitation to us to dine at his house. He assured us that, although he was a native Corinthian Gentile and for most of his life had been a follower of Aphrodite, he had turned entirely toward the God of the Jews. Nothing forbidden by Jewish law such as meat from idolatrous temples would ever be offered at his table. To avoid any such question, we were served with fish freshly caught from the Gulf of Corinth.

After our meal Gaius told us much about Corinth, its people, and its feelings. The patron of the city is Poseidon, god of the sea, obvious for this seaport. Yet the favorite, among the many Greek and Roman deities, is Aphrodite with her temple on the rock. Gaius, with a humorous smile in retrospect to his own earlier life, said that the goddess was especially favored because of the beautiful young priestesses whose services went along with the religious rituals.

The Jewish colony in Corinth was quite large, he told us. The synagogue next door was very active, and usually filled each Sabbath day. At this point I brought up to Gaius something that had been on my mind.

"In Rome, Aquila and I have been baptized in the Way of Jesus of Nazareth as the true Messiah," I said. "We believe he was the Son of God and rose from death in promise of eternal life for those who do believe."

Gaius was surprised. He looked from one of us to the other. "You are both Christians?"

"Christians?" Aquila did not understand. "We are Jews who believe Jesus was the Messiah. Many of our Roman friends do not believe this."

"Then, you are called Christians. This term is new. It comes from Antioch, where those who follow Jesus Christ are known as Christians. I was in Antioch not long ago, and I understand there are many there. In Corinth?" Gaius paused. "You are probably the first here."

Gaius sent three customers, two for awnings and the third a

fisherman who needed a new sail for his boat. We were pleased that we had work to do so promptly. Aquila found where to buy the strong coarse cloth of hemp required, and brought home several rolls. He had taught me how to do the lighter sewing and binding of our products, so that we worked together. Also, I was in charge of our accounts: the expenses and bills of sale. So, quickly we were busy.

Besides going to the market each morning, I took time to enjoy walking along the streets of the city. I like the crowds of people and the varied manners of dress from so many parts of the world. There is always a feeling of intensity and excitement in Corinth, where everyone walks fast, as if on important business. Even the horses and mules pulling wagons of goods and carriages with passengers seem to move with unusual urgency. Boys making deliveries with pushcarts often run, turning and twisting their heads through the congestion of traffic. It is exhilarating to see.

One day I found myself in a part of the city where I had not been before. It was an area closer to the two seaports at each end of the isthmus. The streets were quieter, with few people. Those persons whom I passed were men in rough clothing, and they turned to look at me critically. Even the houses were not as well cared for, and most windows were covered. I noticed several women staring silently down at me. Suddenly I realized I was lost.

Every one of the narrow streets and alleys now looked alike. I tried to find the wide Lechaeum Road, running between the docks and the central city, along which we had come on our first arrival. I was not sure whether it was to the left or the right. As I hesitated, I became aware of a group of men coming along a street toward me. They were singing, walking unsteadily.

As they approached, they saw me. I turned to walk away quickly, but I heard shouts and exclamations in a language I did not know. My heart was beating now. I remembered what I had heard about the sins of Corinth.

They overtook me and surrounded me. There were five or six of them, clearly sailors in from the sea. Their beards were matted, their clothes stained, feet bare. They all spoke at once, and I didn't understand a word. I saw only gleaming eyes. Their intentions were only too clear.

I screamed as one reached out to touch me. I must have shaken the neighborhood, but the only person I saw was an old woman's face at a window, grinning down. One of the men pointed at a narrow, dark alley between two houses. With roars of laughter one man took my arm. Another snatched off the shawl covering my head. A hand pulled loose the heavy coils of my hair so that it fell full length to my waist. I felt myself being lifted. . . . I can only believe that God was with me at that moment. A sella came around a corner. From the tears of fright in my eyes I did not see it at first. I was only aware of a sharp, commanding shout. The sailors paused; I heard their protestations, more angry words from the voice. I was released; my attackers were in full flight, and I was standing alone.

The sella, a single-seat vehicle carried on poles by two slaves, one front and one back, was resting on its four legs in the middle of the street. A tall man was coming down from it, frowning. He was dressed in the white Roman toga with purple border, signifying rank of importance.

My body shook from fright. What my appearance must have been I don't want to think. My hair was down, my ankle-length tunica awry. The shawl lay in the dust of the street.

The stranger came up to me. He was clean-shaven, with close-cropped hair and an eagle-like face.

"Who are you?" he demanded. "What is this?"

I was helpless as a child. "I am Priscilla," I answered incoherently. "I was walking, and I'm lost."

His examination of me was stern. He was wondering what kind of a woman I really was. "How did you happen to be in this neighborhood? Where do you live?"

I told him our house was in the potters' quarter, that my husband and I were tentmakers, and that I was a stranger in Corinth. I liked to explore the city, I said.

He believed me. When I added that we had come from Rome, he seemed impressed.

"I must tell you that you strayed into the worst part of our city," he exclaimed. "Every one of these houses is a brothel, or worse, of the cheapest kind. At night these streets are places of terror. If those men had raped you, they could not have been punished, for any woman here is expected to be out for only one purpose. Look up; you see their faces at the windows."

11

It was true. Now we were objects of curiosity from nearly every window in sight.

"Most likely, they would have killed you afterward," the stranger continued. "Murders are commonplace here. Cleanup crews come in the mornings; they take the bodies they find and throw them into the sea, down there. That's all they are worth. You are a very lucky girl—especially with the beauty you have."

"My deepest thanks are to you for saving me."

I straightened my tunica, picked up my shawl, and shook out the dust. Using the shawl, I was at least able to tie my hair back and cover my head. The stranger watched me, with a slight sign of amusement.

"Now," he ordered, "get into my sella and I will take you to where you are safe. I will walk beside you."

I protested, asking him only to point out the way toward home. He would not hear of it. He explained that he had come through this area as a short cut to see a man near the docks on business. He was not that hurried.

So I did as I was told, with relief. In the sella I was lifted up by the slaves, and with my rescuer walking beside the vehicle we left the place. As we proceeded, he asked more of my life in Rome. He was curious about me. I told him my father's name, Joshua Marcus, the dealer in grains, now retired.

"Ah!" he exclaimed. "I know his name; he has used my ships. So you are his daughter. I am more than happy to have been of this service to you. My name is Stephanas, shipowner of Corinth. When you write to him please say that we have met." He looked up at me, smiled. "I suggest that you do not tell him of the circumstances of our meeting. He would be quite worried about the foolishness of his daughter."

I had recovered from my scare. I smiled too. "I will take your advice. Not only for my father but also for my husband."

"Wise girl." He lifted his hand to touch mine. "Consider me your friend. It would give me pleasure if you and your husband would come to my house to dine with us. My wife can be of help to you in Corinth."

I turned my head. For the second time that morning I faced a sudden crisis beyond my control. Lord God, I thought. I turned back to Stephanas.

12

"Thank you for your goodness. I cannot accept. Aquila and I are Jews. It is forbidden for us to sit at table with Gentiles."

This time I put out my hand to his. For a moment he ignored it, staring ahead. Then he took my hand, and his smile was of the greatest friendliness.

"I did not know. Forgive me. I honor you all the more. Is it forbidden that we can be friends?"

"No, I am sure that is acceptable. So it will be."

Of course he took me to the door of my house. There was so little more that I could say. He climbed into his sella, and the two bearers carried him off.

I told Aquila only that I had been accosted by a rude man on the street, and a man named Stephanas, clad in a Roman toga with purple border, had chased him away. Had I said more, Aquila would have forbidden me to go out alone.

"Stephanas?" Aquila was startled. "There is a Stephanas . . . . I have heard of him. One of the most powerful men in Corinth."

"He is a Gentile," I said.

2

Late one afternoon, we were together in the work shed while Aquila measured and cut sections of cloth to fill an order for five travelers' tents, each to be large enough to provide shelter for four persons. I was busy binding edges on pieces already cut.

Our business had grown so rapidly that I had to reduce my daily walks after marketing. We needed every hour of the day to keep up with the work.

Someone knocked at our door. I stood up, sighing. A vendor to turn away?

But when I opened the door I found Gaius standing outside. With him was another, a man in a worn brown robe, a sack hanging from his shoulder. He was of average height, with broad shoulders and long arms. He had a full beard and hair receding above the forehead. His head jutted forward, giving him an appearance

13

of intensity. What character was this? I looked at Gaius with an unspoken question.

"Priscilla, this is Paul of Tarsus, a Christian. He is looking for temporary work in Corinth as a tentmaker." Gaius glanced at the stranger doubtfully. "He came to the synagogue; they sent him next door to my house for lodgings. But when I told him of the two of you, who are Christians as well as tentmakers, he said, 'Take me to them.'"

Gaius seemed to be apologetic. No wonder. Yet the name Paul of Tarsus . . . something rang in my recollection, something I must have heard in Rome; I could not remember what it was.

I turned back to the stranger, and all at once caught the expression in his eyes. They were deep, fiery, piercing, as if his gaze went through me. I was held by them, transfixed.

"Yes, I am Paul of Tarsus." His voice rumbled up from that great chest. "Apostle of the Lord Christ Jesus, Son of God, by command of our God in Heaven. I ask of you shelter for the night. I will repay by the work I do for you."

Faintly I replied, "Come in, master; you are welcome."

Still I was caught in the spell of those penetrating eyes. I can never forget them.

Gaius took a step backward. "I must return to my house, Priscilla." He said to Paul, "I will see you in the morning, master; I am sure I can help—"

Paul raised his hand. "Later I will need you. I am grateful that you brought me here."

Gaius hurriedly walked off.

Paul followed me into the house. As he lowered the sack from his shoulder I told him I would fetch my husband.

"Aquila," I whispered to him in the shed, "come quickly. Gaius has brought a stranger who claims to be an apostle of Jesus. He wants to work for us—and he wants to spend the night here!"

"What are you saying?"

I tried to explain further.

Aquila frowned. "I don't understand; what does he look like?"

"An ordinary workman. But—there is something different about him."

"I'll talk with him." Aquila laid down his cutting tool. "Another delay in our work. . . ."

14

He left the shed and went into the atrium, where Paul waited. I followed close behind.

"Sir," he said to Paul, "we have very poor accommodations here. If you would find something more comfortable—"

"Nothing is too poor for a Christian," Paul replied. He smiled. "My credentials? I come under the cross of Christ."

Both Aquila and I caught our breaths. No charlatan or imposter would have dared make that statement. Crucifixion, symbolized by a cross, is anathema, despised and feared. We looked at each other. I nodded.

"We have a couch in the gineceo," I suggested.

"Master," Aquila said, "we will share what we have with you. You have been traveling?"

"From Athens. A wagon coming this way overtook me on the highway and brought me here. I am covered with dust from the road."

I showed Paul the couch in the gineceo, the first-floor room next to the atrium, while Aquila brought in the heavy sack. I took our guest to the bathing room and assured him of hot water. I handed him a clean towel.

Fortunately I had brought home from the market that morning a plump chicken killed and dressed in accordance with Jewish custom. For our evening meal we would have enough for three. Paul appeared after his bath much refreshed, and while I prepared the supper Aquila showed him the workroom and equipment.

When we sat together on the couches around our table in the atrium, I looked across at Paul before serving. He bowed his head, as we did also.

"God Eternal, our praise and thanks go to Thee. We thank Thee for our safety and for the presence of the Holy Spirit in this house. May Thy grace and peace be always upon us here, and on those others who work with us, in the name of our Lord Christ Jesus. Amen."

As we ate, Paul asked questions about ourselves. Between Aquila and me we told him our story, as I have related it on these pages. He knew about the edict of Claudius expelling Jews from Rome.

"One day you will be free to return," Paul seemed to believe.

"How can you think that?" Aquila asked.

15

"The commands of men pass away," Paul answered, "but the Will of God remains forever."

He told us he hoped to establish a Christian church here in Corinth, as he had in a number of other cities in Asia and Macedonia. He would begin his teaching in the synagogue, proclaiming the facts about Jesus and describing in plain words the evidence that Jesus was the Messiah and Redeemer. But, he added, the more traditionalist Jews would surely not accept his teaching. Sooner or later, the elders of the Corinthian congregation would rise against him, accusing him of heresy. It had already happened in Thessalonica and in cities of western Asia. Then, Paul said, he would try to form the beginnings of the Christian Church. He would be free to evangelize the new Way of Jesus to Jews and Gentiles alike, without impediment.

"Separate from the synagogue?" I asked, surprised.

"Yes," Paul declared.

"Then, Gentiles would become Jews and abide by our Law? Otherwise they would not be acceptable to God."

"The Way of God and his Son as the Messiah is open for all people everywhere," Paul replied. "To the Lord there is no distinction among those who believe in him, whether Jew or Gentile, rich or poor, man or woman, free or slave—all are equal in the sight of God. Through his death on the cross and his redemption from the grave, Jesus fulfilled the Law and confirmed God's promises of eternal life as told in the scriptures. The Gentiles, who do not know the Law of the Jews, must be a law unto themselves, in their own hearts and consciences. To meet God's judgment there is only one requirement: for each person to live within the Holy Spirit, whom the Lord has now revealed to us."

Aquila interrupted here. "As Jews, we have been brought up to obey the Law of our fathers. Although we believe that Jesus was the Messiah, we are still Jews. Certainly we must obey the Law or lose God's favor?"

Paul leaned forward over the table. That intense look returned to his eyes. "The Law was given by God as commandments as to what we should *not* do. Jesus, the Son of God, has told us what we *should* do: accept the Spirit received in baptism in our minds and in our hearts. This is a new creation for all people, not alone for us who are Jews. The Law says that those who are hanged are

16

cursed. Was Jesus cursed after God himself raised him from the dead? Let those who abide by the Law be judged by it. To find and to do through God's Spirit what God desires of us will gain our own Resurrection. This is the message of Jesus Christ."

Aquila and I listened intently. I could not guess what was in Aquila's mind. I knew that mine was in confusion.

"What of circumcision?" Aquila asked. "Every male child of the Jews is required to be circumcised on the eighth day after birth. What of the Gentiles?"

"Circumcision is nothing," Paul said definitely. "Circumcision or not, it is the same to God when a man accepts the Holy Spirit through faith. True, circumcision is not a mere act, it is a symbol of belonging to the faith of the Jews. We speak now of a larger faith, in God our Father through Jesus Christ, for all nations of the earth. Baptism may be a symbol too, as a sacrament, but, again, more. Baptism in the name of Jesus is an acceptance of the Holy Spirit, which comes upon us and becomes a part of our whole being." He paused a moment. "There are some who falsely call themselves Jewish Christians but demand circumcision and adherence to Jewish Law by Gentiles. They do so only to subjugate Gentiles and prove their own superiority. They are liars, who reject the essential truth and are among those who stir up trouble, even to violence and riots. Better, when they were circumcised, that the rabbis had gone all the way and made them eunuchs!"

"By what right can you say these things?" Aquila demanded. "They are against everything we have been taught."

Putting his hands on the table, Paul said in his most gentle voice, "The Lord Jesus revealed himself from Heaven to me, as he had before to his apostles in Jerusalem and to many others as well. God himself gave me the apostleship to carry his gospel to the people of all nations, especially to the Gentiles. Peter, whom I call Cephas, the leader of the apostles in Jerusalem, and those who are with him are taking the Way of our Lord to the Jews, the circumcised. I am charged by the Lord God to do the same for the uncircumcised."

All along, I had wondered what stirred my recollection when I heard his name. All at once I knew. I cried out, "Paul of Tarsus! Saul . . . Saul of Tarsus! I remember now, I heard of you in

Rome! *You are the one who stoned to death in Jerusalem the man named Stephen because he believed in Jesus!"*

"I am the one," Paul said.

How I carried out the plates and empty cups from the table after our meal I do not know to this day. My scalp prickled, I felt faint, I was terrified. My first thought was that this man was an agent of the Emperor, come to find us out as the only Christians in Corinth. He would call soldiers to take us to prison as by reputation Saul had done so viciously to men, women, even children. I stood in our kitchen reasoning with myself. Such supposition was scarcely possible, only a woman's alarmed response.

But otherwise, what?

Aquila and I had been brought up by our respective families in the strictest faith. Even after the unknown evangelist in Rome convinced us the Messiah had come and that we should be baptized in the Way of Jesus, our customs of life did not change. The idea of Jesus as Messiah seemed especially intriguing to adventurous young. When dissension broke out among the Roman Jews, we kept aloof.

On that night when I stood alone in the kitchen after hearing the words of Paul, I felt that a cataclysm had struck us. I had a premonition that all we were and had been could never be again. At my feet a precipice fell off into a great unknown space before me. I trembled, my body shook. Nothing had ever hit me so hard. I had to sit on the bench against our kitchen wall, I shook so much.

I tried to put together in my mind what Paul had said to us so briefly. He was talking about an entirely new religious creed, not a mere difference of opinion between Jews. His God was the same, but his interpretation of Jesus as the Son of God and Messiah went far beyond anything I had even contemplated.

An entirely new faith—the Christian Way—with its own churches and congregations! A new way of belief in God that might even endure through the eternal centuries! I felt that it was happening right here, in my own house, that the walls were expanding, the roof rising under the pressure of something so important that it was beyond imagination.

I knew that I would be caught up inevitably, inexorably, in the new church of Jesus Christ. How I knew this is impossible to explain, except that I remembered that strange light in Paul's eyes when I first saw him at our door. I was afraid.

Slowly I pulled myself together and walked back to the atrium, carrying a bowl of fruit. I found Paul and Aquila discussing the merits of the various kinds of cloth for making awnings. I put the bowl on the table and sat on the couch opposite Paul.

He took an orange from the bowl. "Yes, that new flax linen from Egypt is good for light use," he was telling Aquila. "It does not have the strength to take strong winds, but it is easy to cut and sew. For small tents or awnings for litters and the like it reduces carrying weight."

"I should try it, then," Aquila said.

"Best you tell your customers of its limits as well as advantages," Paul suggested.

Paul peeled his orange.

I broke into this interlude with my customary blunt directness, which I cannot help.

"How did it happen," I asked Paul, "that you are now an evangelist for Jesus when once you stoned a man to death for believing him to be the Messiah?"

Paul sat back in his couch. "I was waiting for your question, Prisca," he said. (From that moment, Paul always called me by the nickname Prisca, never Priscilla.) "I want you and Aquila to hear things I have to say."

"I have heard things about you, if I remember. But—"

"I will tell you many things you have not heard," he promised. . . .

Paul talked to us long through that night. Aquila forgot the urgency of the work waiting for him. I forgot everything except what I was hearing. I cannot use Paul's words, but I can put down the essence. By the time he finished I knew for certain that our future would be changed enormously.

Paul, or Saul then, named for one of the great leaders of his ancestral tribe of Benjamin, was born in Tarsus, in Cilicia, western Asia near the Mediterranean. His father, wealthy business man, strict Pharisee of the Jewish faith, held also the rank of Roman citizen, a special distinction that Paul himself received through family lineage.

When he was twelve, his father took him to a meeting of the elders and members of the Tarsus congregation. A fierce argument broke out among Pharisees, Sadducees, and Hellenists, leading to near violence. On the way home, Saul asked his father how men could worship the same God but at the same time fight so over different ways of interpretation.

"Our Jewish nation does not have a leader to bring us together," Saul's father told him. "These times are troubled, and we have no one to take us from the darkness of differences into the light of unity."

Next morning at dawn, Saul crept from the house and walked through the empty streets to the deserted synagogue. Kneeling, he pledged his life to God and asked the Lord to help him to be that leader of the Jewish faith. He returned home to tell his father he wanted to be a rabbi.

Young Saul was placed in the school of Gamaliel in Jerusalem, a place world-famous for its education in the Jewish Law. He grew to be Gamaliel's leading student, qualified as rabbi. He attracted the attention of the Sanhedrin, the council of elders of the Jerusalem Temple, and of Caiaphas, high priest of the Temple and of Judea, for his outspoken zeal in defense of the ancient Law of the Jewish people.

Saul became a bitter opponent of the cult of Jesus of Nazareth. In spite of the crucifixion of its leader, the cult grew in numbers to the thousands in Jerusalem. Stephen, one of its vocal adherents, was arrested, tried before the Sanhedrin, and condemned to death for the heresy of profaning even the Temple itself. Saul concurred in the conviction, was officially present at the execution.

"I regret what happened; I can never forget it," Paul told us that night. "I feel remorse, but I cannot feel guilt, for I did only what the Law required. I was zealous in protection of the Law. Afterward I asked Caiaphas, chief priest, for authority to stamp out the Way of Jesus in Jerusalem. In raging fury I attacked those who were believers, and sent many of them to prison, men and women. I cast my vote against those being condemned to death. I went into the synagogues and tricked others into blasphemy. Many fled from the city, and I followed them to other cities to persecute those whom I could find. Caiaphas sent me with a squad of soldiers to Damascus to bring back in chains some who had escaped me."

Paul stopped talking for a time, with his head in his hands. Aquila and I waited, literally holding our breaths.

Then Paul continued. "I am the least man whom God should have called to be an apostle for the Lord Jesus. But on the road to Damascus it happened. We were approaching the city, the soldiers and I. Suddenly, about midday, a light appeared, so great I fell to the ground. The light was beyond that of the sun, beyond understanding. From somewhere a voice came to me. . . ."

Paul rose from the couch. He spread his arms, gazed upward. "The voice said, 'Saul, why do you persecute me?' I asked in reply, 'Who are you, Lord?' I heard him say, 'I am Jesus of Nazareth, whom you persecute.' And in that blaze of light shutting out all else, I saw a man standing, the Son of God. 'Stand up,' he ordered; 'go into the city and you will be told what to do.'

"I rose to my feet. The light faded into darkness. I could see nothing at all; I was blinded. Around me I heard the frightened soldiers talking together. Some had also fallen to the ground in fear, but, unseeing, I did not know. Some claimed they had seen the light, others that they heard the voice. In my own confusion, I did not know.

"They led me by the hand into Damascus. I was taken to a house on the street called Straight, and did not eat or drink. I prayed incessantly for forgiveness and guidance. All I knew for certain was that Jesus had come to me as he had after death to his apostles in Jerusalem and to many others. All my accusations against him were wrong, all the injustices I had piled up against his followers were false persecutions. I had much for which to pray."

As he described these things, Paul's rumbling voice rose and fell. The uncouth man who had appeared at my door earlier with Gaius was transformed now. To me, he was a giant of truth, of faith, in what he said. I could not disbelieve.

He sat again on the couch. After three days, he told us, a man named Ananias, a follower of the Way, came to him. Already Paul had, in his blindness, received a vision that this would happen.

Ananias placed his hands on Paul, and his sight returned. Then Ananias gave Paul the message he was to receive from Jesus: that he was chosen as God's instrument to carry the name of Jesus Christ to the world of Gentiles as well as Jews. He was baptized at once, and the Holy Spirit came upon him.

That was as much as he told us that night. More was to come later. Paul was ready to go to his room. I picked up a lamp and led the way. As he came into the gineceo, I noticed for the first time that he limped.

"Your leg, are you hurt?" I exclaimed.

He grimaced. "No, it's nothing. I hope I have not spoken too much for tonight."

I put down the lamp on the table. "No, no, master. . . ."

Embarrassed, I could not express what I wanted to say, that we were so honored by having one with us who had seen Jesus himself.

He shook his head. "Dear girl, I am not master. I am Paul, the humblest of men. I am humble because of what I have told you. I am the one honored, that you and your husband have accepted me into your house."

"You guessed what I wanted to say." I laughed, and so did he. I gestured at the little room. "But we have so little. . . ."

"You have so much. You will help me in this city of Corinth."

"It will be very difficult to speak of the Way. It's a— a sinful city."

Paul nodded. "Jesus found it difficult to teach his Way. That did not deter him. God bless you, Prisca."

Thoughtfully, I left him. Aquila and I went up to our room, carrying another lamp with us.

As we prepared to sleep, Aquila said to me, "I have been thinking. This Paul plans to look for lodgings tomorrow. He seems to be well experienced in our work. We are pressed for time and extra help. Do you think we could keep him here with us for a bit, temporarily, so that he could work with us in return for his board?"

"I think he would like that," I replied. "It is a good idea. We will ask him in the morning."

I had been thinking too, but in a different direction from

Aquila. We were not the ones who needed Paul's help. He needed ours, to help him bring the message of Jesus Christ to the sinful city of Corinth.

3

In the morning, we spoke with Paul, inviting him to stay on in our house for a while and help us with the tentmaking. He accepted gladly. After an unrewarding visit to Athens on his way here from Macedonia, his finances were depleted. He expected two of his associates, Silas and Timothy, to meet him shortly in Corinth. They, too, would be coming from cities of Macedonia in the north, bringing contributions from the Christian churches already established there. This assistance would enable him to carry out his work in our city.

He was also expecting Luke, another associate, to follow him from Athens in a day or so. Luke, a physician from Antioch, had been one of Paul's early converts of uncircumcised Gentiles to the Christian Way. Traveling with Paul, he had remained in Athens longer to ask questions on certain medical developments.

Paul told us that he had a number of assistants—he called them disciples—to help him on his evangelical journeys. Some were Jews, some Gentiles, but all faithful to the gospel of Jesus.

He set to work at once to help Aquila with the order for tents. On my way to the marketplace I stopped at the house of Gaius to let him know that Paul would be lodging at our home.

"Yesterday I was afraid of imposing this stranger on you," he commented. "I could not be sure who he was, from his appearance."

"He was dusty from the road," I replied. "Last night he told us many things we had not known. Paul is a very great man, a man of God, and he plans to start a Christian church here."

"He told me that," Gaius said. "Priscilla, I think he should be warned: the elders of the synagogue are extremely traditional in their views, perhaps more so than in other places."

"I think Paul will understand their viewpoint better than any of us. Last night he described how at one time he was so violent in defense of the Jewish traditions against heresy that he sent believers in Jesus to prisons by the hundreds, even to death. Until Jesus, from Heaven, came to him and revealed the truth."

"Oh." Gaius looked at me oddly. "Perhaps so. Perhaps I have not been long enough of the Jewish faith to understand. There is one more thing that greatly concerns the elders here. For many years the Caesars in Rome by custom have allowed the Jewish people throughout the Empire to worship God in their own way, as long as they did not commit subversion against the Roman authority or break the peace by dissension. Our elders are aware of the ever-present danger of dissension among us."

"I know what you mean, after our experience in Rome," I reminded him. "And Paul did mention it too. I will certainly tell him what you think." I put out my hand. "Thank you, Gaius. We have so much to thank you for."

He took my hand. "My reward is to have you in Corinth, Priscilla, and Aquila. I wish no trouble to come to you."

"I am sure it won't." I smiled with confidence.

Actually, I knew that Gaius was right. Since our first arrival in Corinth, we had attended regularly the synagogue services on every Sabbath and on Holy Days. We had made some friends among the congregation, had been asked several times to homes of older members, and had returned their friendship by having them in our own house. But whenever we mentioned Jesus Christ as the Messiah, they quickly changed the subject. We did not press our belief, not being in any position to do so. Nor did we have the knowledge.

The average types of the Corinthian Jewish congregation were quite different in style of life from our friends who lived in Rome. These men were local tradesmen or artisans, not wealthy as compared to so many Gentiles in Corinth. They were plain, sincere, God-fearing people, and, with their wives, not given to the social ostentation around them. The Jewish population lived to themselves in small houses on quiet streets. Corinth itself was filled with great villas and private gardens, especially around the outskirts.

As I left Gaius, I noticed that the door of the synagogue next to his house was open. I took the opportunity to go in to say a prayer, circumspectly kneeling by a bench in the rear, as a woman should. I prayed to God first for the welfare and work of Paul of Tarsus in this city of Corinth. And—after a moment of thought—I asked God to show me how to help his apostle Paul in the service of Jesus Christ. Why I did this at that moment without remembering that I was a woman—and a very young one at that—I have never quite understood.

Leaving the synagogue, I ran into Crispus, leader of the elders. He was coming in.

"Good morning, Priscilla," he greeted me. "And how is your fine husband?"

"Thank you, he is well. He is working hard. We are blessed with many orders for our products, unknown as we are in Corinth."

He laughed. "Your reputation for good work is spreading. God blesses those who work well."

That evening, after our meal, I repeated to Paul the warning from Gaius about the traditionalist elders of the synagogue. The three of us were sitting around the table and I had not yet cleared away the dishes.

Aquila nodded agreement. "Most of the people seem to follow the elders," he added. "We found this soon after we arrived in Corinth. They resented our speaking of the Way of Jesus."

Paul listened carefully. Then he explained to us things we did not know. The synagogue elders were influenced by Asian and Macedonian "Hellenist" Jews, who were far more intolerant of Jesus as the Messiah than even the Jews of Jerusalem. But it was necessary for Paul first to approach the Gentiles through the Hellenistic synagogues, whose congregations already contained some Gentiles converted from paganism to the true God of the Jews. Converted Gentiles without ancestral traditions were usually more receptive to receiving the Way of Jesus, and through them Paul could hope to reach pagans, despite Hellenist opposition.

The path was difficult and dangerous; he knew that. We should know it too, he told us.

Paul glanced at me and Aquila. With a half-smile he added, "You are taking a risk with me in your home."

Aquila stood up nervously, lips compressed. Without a word, he left us to go back to his workshop.

Troubled, I watched him depart. "Paul, I understand what you have said to us these several days; I do understand. Tell me what I can do. I am only a woman, but I am strong."

Paul stared at me as that strange light grew in his eyes. "The time will come. I will not have to tell you, you will know." Then he relaxed. "Prisca, do not worry, nor Aquila either. But I do thank Gaius, too, for his concern."

Luke arrived in Corinth several days later, on schedule. He did not attempt to find Paul until he had arranged to give assistance to a Corinthian physician. Luke worked professionally as much as he could on his travels, to pay his own expenses. As Paul's disciple he kept notes, and told me that he expected to write a narrative on Paul, as well as on acts of other apostles.

I liked Luke at once. He was young, cheerful, and spread confidence among those whom he met. I have never heard a word said against him.

He had supper with us that first evening, after securing his lodgings. Then he asked, "Has Paul told you of his experience in Athens?"

"Do not speak of it," Paul growled. "There was no gain in it."

"Not so," Luke replied. "How much dent could you hope to make in that city, still living in past glory? I kept a record of what you said to those wise men. Let some mock you, there were others who believed."

Paul hunched himself up on his couch. "Wise men are wise in the sight of men. What is their wisdom compared to the wisdom of God?" His eyes suddenly blazed. "I reject the wisdom of those who call themselves wise. I rejoice in being a fool in their sight!"

Disregarding him, Luke described to us how Paul had been called to speak of God and Jesus before the Athenian Court of Areopagus, the ancient council responsible for interpreting Greek religion and morals. The meeting was on the west side of the Mars Hill, in the shadow of the Acropolis. As I listened, I understood for the first time how tremendously difficult it must be to bring the Way of Jesus Christ into the Gentile world of pagan idolatry. This lesson opened my eyes.

The Athenian Court, as Luke explained, contains both Epicureans and Stoics, followers of two systems of philosophy developed in Athens nearly four hundred years ago. Both systems believe, in different ways, in the existence of gods. To the philosopher Epicurus, all substance, including gods themselves, was created from invisible atom-like particles in space. When these particles collide, they form the realities of life until dispersed once again into atoms. New collisions regenerate life and matter, causing eternal being.

But, Luke went on, Epicurus taught that the greatest human attainment is the pleasure of peace of mind coming from an honest life. Over many years, his followers lost his original ideals and now believe that pleasure is the only end, in itself.

Neither Aquila nor I were acquainted with Greek philosophies. We heard with fascination Luke's explanations, as Paul listened in silence.

Stoics, on the other hand, Luke continued, believe that the immortal god Zeus created mortals in his image and governs all destiny through universal reason—that all events are inevitable fulfillments of the laws of nature. The mortal people who did not accept the fixed reasoning of nature were doomed to be miserable wretches.

As he talked, Luke kept looking at Paul, rather than at either of us. He was implying something, more than just an explanation to us, but a message for Paul himself.

"Our friend Paul has a sharp eye and a sharp mind." Luke laughed. "But he came into Athens to bring news of a way of knowing God to a city where the great gods of Olympus were born. How can an unknown evangelist be so bold as to speak thus to the learned body of critical men? I'll admit I was nervous for him. But Paul can face down lions, of the human sort."

I stared at Luke incredulously, hearing this kind of comment. Was he joking?

"Paul," Luke went ahead, "you reminded that Court of the Areopagus of a shrine in their own city inscribed TO AN UNKNOWN GOD. You told them this god whom they revered was in truth the supreme God of Heaven and earth, who gives everyone life, who has no need to dwell only in man-made temples."

He pressed ahead. "You had them in your hand, Paul. They

27

were excited when you told them that God overlooked their igno-
rance of him for so long. Now God had revealed himself to all
men by sending Christ Jesus to live on earth as his Son. They
heard you. Am I telling this correctly?"

"Yes, except for the end. When I spoke of the Resurrection of
Jesus from death, they began to laugh. First one, then another,
then others, until all laughed at me. . . ." Paul covered his face
with his hands. "The bitterness of mockery! I wished I could reach
out, to say something—"

Luke reminded him, "Do you remember the Greek poet Aes-
chylus, who in his play *Eumenides* quoted the god Apollo as saying, 'When the dust has drunk up the blood of a man, there is no
recalling to life that one who is dead'? These wise men of the
Athenian Court believe the imagination of a playwriter, saying that
Apollo denied the fact of Resurrection. You cannot blame yourself, master, for what happened in Athens."

Paul jumped up from his couch, agitated. I noticed again that
he winced as from a pain in his leg. He stamped across the room
and back. "Blessed be the fools who believe in the Lord Jesus
Christ!" he burst out. "Let the wise ones who believe in their own
wisdom be judged accordingly!"

He stopped. "Prisca and Aquila, there is another story that you
must hear. Luke, I believe you will hear it for the first time, for I
have seldom if ever told it, for fear of appearing to boast.

"I know of a man of Christ who, some years ago, was caught up
to the third heaven—whether in the body or in the spirit out of the
body I do not know. Only God knows. And I know that this man
—whether in the body or in the spirit out of the body I do not
know, God knows—was taken into Paradise and heard forbidden
words that no man is allowed to speak. For this man I can be
proud. For myself I have no pride except for my weaknesses.

"To keep me from being exalted beyond my measure because of
the great revelations allowed me, I was given a sharp pain which is
always with me. I call it my thorn. Three times I have asked the
Lord to remove it from me. His answer is, 'My grace is sufficient
for you. In your weakness is my strength.' So I take pride in my
own weakness, that the power of Christ will possess me."

As Paul stood before us saying these things, he seemed glorified.

The strange glow in his eyes appeared again. His stature appeared to increase beyond his shabby brown robe.

I felt at once another Presence in the room with us: the Holy Spirit of God. My spine tingled in awe. I whispered to myself, My Lord God too, my Christ!

On the Sabbath after Paul's arrival, the three of us attended the synagogue service together. This was to be his first public announcement to Corinth. Paul wished to be there early. To be certain he knew the way through the city streets, I walked with him. Aquila followed shortly after us.

I was worried again, since the evening in our house with Luke. "Paul, you have said that, after starting with the Jewish synagogue, you would preach to the Gentiles. If those Gentiles of Athens rejected what you said, why won't the Gentiles of Corinth do the same?"

"Perhaps they will," he grumbled as we moved along the street, "but I must try."

"You know the reputation of Corinth."

"I do." Paul walked a few more steps. "Corinth is one of the great cities of the Empire."

I could not press him; I should not have mentioned this just before he spoke to the Jews.

But he continued, "Prisca, the Lord has chosen me to bring the Way to the Gentiles, as you know. The apostles and disciples in Jerusalem are charged with bringing it to the Jews. I live in Jesus Christ. If I fail in my task, my life is for nothing."

"You won't fail—" I noticed that his face was tense and his hands trembled. "Paul, are you all right?"

"I am nervous, yes." He made an attempt to laugh. "I must confess to you that I am always nervous before I speak—unless I am very, very angry. I am not a good speaker; I have been told so and I know it. Feel my hands."

They were too cold on a warm day. "This is foolish," I told him. "You have been speaking in public most of your life."

"I cannot put my own convictions as clearly as I should before groups of people who resent me."

"Paul—" I tried to think of an answer to this—"talk to the people this morning as if you were telling me."

29

"There will be too many, and they won't be receptive like you."

"Then, next time, practice on me, and I will give you arguments."

"I would only get angry at you."

"Good!" I cried. "You will forget yourself."

Paul laughed genuinely. "Prisca, it would be impossible to get angry at you. I would feel silly if I tried to. However, you have made me feel better."

We approached the synagogue as a few people began to arrive. Inside the door I had to leave Paul to go to my bench in the women's section, at one side to the rear of the building. I pressed his hand as we parted.

From my place, I saw Paul find a seat and kneel to pray. Aquila came immediately afterward, nodded at me, and went to his own, customary location with the men.

As the congregation entered, I noticed Gaius; then Crispus, leader of the synagogue, coming in with his usual cheerfulness. Behind him appeared Sosthenes, the deputy leader. He was a big, solemn man, greatly overweight, who had never shown any friendliness toward Aquila and me. Perhaps he had heard of our acceptance of the Way of Jesus.

Then a friend took her seat beside me. She was Chloe, a widow with children, who was first of the congregation to invite us to her house. I had not realized for some time after we met that she was a Gentile converted to the faith of the Jews following the death of her husband. She found great comfort in her belief.

Waiting for the service to begin, I became nervous myself. Our synagogue rabbi appeared, spoke the call to worship, and led the prayers. The first lesson, from the Law, was read by Crispus, and the second lesson, from the Prophets, by Sosthenes. The customary time had come for visitors to speak to the congregation if they wished to do so. . . .

Paul rose. "I am Paul of Tarsus, recently arrived from Antioch and Jerusalem and other places in Asia and Macedonia. May I have the privilege of saying a word to you?"

Crispus replied, "We will be pleased to hear what you have to say, Paul of Tarsus."

Paul turned to face the congregation from his place. In his

30

brown robe, twisted rope belt, with matted hair and beard, he startled the people. He certainly had their attention.

He paused before speaking. Then he began:

"People of Corinth—those of Israel, and others who worship the God of Abraham and Moses, listen! I have come among you to bring a message. The scriptures which you know well as read to you Sabbath by Sabbath foretold the coming of the One of whom I speak now. His name is Jesus."

Paul's resonant voice carried through the synagogue. His hearers suddenly sat straighter.

"Christ Jesus was sent to live among men by God Almighty, as the Savior for mankind. The people of Jerusalem and their rulers, without understanding what they did, in fact fulfilled the prophecies of old, which you have often heard." Paul lifted his arm. "They crucified Jesus! They took him down from the cross, and laid him in a tomb." He lowered his arm and pointed a finger over the heads of the people. "But on the third day after, God raised him from death, Jesus appeared alive to his apostles and many others, who are now witnesses to the truth of what I am saying."

Chloe, the Gentile widow beside me who had accepted the Jewish faith, gasped. She must not have heard of Jesus before. Among the congregation, the reaction appeared mixed, but the shock of Paul's words was evident.

Once again he paused before continuing:

"Through the death of Christ Jesus, our Father in Heaven has given forgiveness of sin to all people who will believe in him. By the Resurrection of Jesus, Almighty God gives promise of eternal life beyond death to those who follow his commandments. For our Lord Christ Jesus is indeed the living Son of God! This is the message I bring to you today, my brothers and sisters. I speak to you in the Name of Jesus."

Paul took his place on the bench and bowed his head.

The silence throughout the synagogue was a non-sound in itself. For a time, no one moved. Then Chloe looked at me, puzzled. The service of worship resumed normally until it was concluded by the rabbi's benediction.

For me, the sound of Paul's voice and his words kept ringing in my ears. I was thrilled, and awed.

Even on the way out, the congregation was subdued, some

31

whispering to each other. On the street Luke met Aquila and me.

"Paul spoke well," Luke commented. "It is a good beginning."

Paul joined us, and we congratulated him.

He glanced at me. "My hands were warm."

We walked home with Aquila on one side of Paul and me on the other. Many people watched us as we left.

Later in the day, when I was in the kitchen preparing the evening meal, I heard what sounded like a voice in another part of the house. Aquila, I knew, was on the upper floor taking a nap in the heat of the afternoon. I went into the atrium and listened.

All was silent. Paul's door was closed; I supposed he was sleeping too. I was about to return to the kitchen, believing I must have heard someone on the street.

Suddenly a loud cry came from the gineceo. It was desperate, a cry for help. . . .

"Lord Jesus, O Christ! Listen to me, I pray to Thee. Come to me with Thy strength, O Lord, in my weakness—"

Paul! A chill ran down my spine. I stood still.

"My Lord, my Jesus, I am afflicted with my burden. Give me of Thy strength that I may do Thy Will. I am weary, Lord Jesus, and in pain. Intercede for me with Almighty God, our Father, that he may renew in me the power and the strength to go on against these obstacles. . . ."

For a moment there was silence. I thought I must run, anywhere, not to hear.

Paul's voice was not as loud then, more like a plea.

"Christ Jesus, Thou hast placed upon me that which I feel I cannot do. Release me, O Jesus, if it can be Thy Will. I am weary, I am weak, I am but a human on this earth. What Thou hast asked me to do is beyond my strength of body, not of heart. Take me to our Father, O Christ, before I fail Thee. . . . May this be the Will of God in Heaven. . . ."

His words ended in a sob.

My own heart went out to Paul. I tiptoed over to his door. I raised my hand to knock softly; I would go in to kneel beside him and pray. . . . No. This was between Almighty God, the Lord Jesus, and Paul himself. I let my hand fall. I could not intrude.

So I knelt on the floor outside his door and silently added my prayer to his.

As I knelt with head bowed, eyes closed, I felt something happening. Yet there was no sound. I opened my eyes. A light seemed to be coming through from under Paul's door, a light that a hundred of our lamps could not equal.

I stood up hastily. On tiptoe again, I fled back to the kitchen. There I collapsed on the bench against the wall.

I could not think, I could not feel—I was numb.

In the house there was only silence.

4

Two days later, a note came from Gaius inviting us and Paul to the opening of the Isthmian games, three days away.

He was asking other friends, too, he wrote, and wanted the three of us to join the group. It would be a great occasion, which happened only once every two years. We would enjoy the company as well as the games, he thought. And he would send his carriage to pick us up.

I had heard a good deal about the games, probably Corinth's greatest celebration. Especially lately, near the opening day, banners had been flying everywhere. Around the marketplace, little else could be heard in conversation except of the competitions.

The Isthmian games of Corinth go back into antiquity. They are modeled after the famous Olympic games of Athens, except that here they are held every two years instead of four. Unlike Roman games, in which gladiators fight to the death against wild beasts or other gladiators, the Greek games are true athletic contests.

But the Isthmian games are in honor of Poseidon, legendary god of the sea. To attend them might be construed as homage to a pagan god.

I talked it over with Aquila. At first he was enthusiastic, but then he, too, thought it might be in violation of the Law as an acknowledgment of a false deity.

I took Gaius's note to Paul. To my surprise he was delighted. "Of course we'll go," he responded. "I wouldn't want to miss these games; I've never been to one. Certainly accept the invitation, and for me also."

"They're in honor of Poseidon, god of the sea, patron god of Corinth," I said doubtfully. "Wouldn't it be a sacrilege in the sight of God?"

"Do you believe in Poseidon?"

"Of course not! He doesn't exist—"

"Then, how can you commit a sacrilege against God through something you know does not exist?"

I accepted the invitation from Gaius.

Gaius and his carriage arrived in front of our house by midmorning. The four-wheeled vehicle, a carruca, was pulled by two white dappled horses driven by a servant; the sides of the carriage were painted, as by custom, in yellow and blue with bands of violet. An awning overhead kept off the hot rays of the sun.

"Good morning," he called out and jumped down from his seat in front. "All ready for a holiday?"

"We're ready," I shouted in return. "One moment—"

Inside the house I called to Paul and Aquila, "He's here." I picked up the basket I had prepared for refreshments: bread, goat cheese, and a flask of wine, with fruits. The others had been waiting, and we came out to the street in joyful mood.

I saw that Gaius wore a white Roman toga. Paul was in his usual brown robe with the rope belt. Aquila had a white woolen tunica tightly bound around the waist with a leather belt, as was correct for a Roman of his status.

For myself, realizing that this would be an "informal formal" occasion to meet new people, I used a long-sleeved white stola reaching to my ankles. I wore white sandals, and a white shawl over my head reaching down to tie under my chin. A married Jewish woman must never appear bareheaded in public, according to tradition. (I did not realize how soon I would violate the rule.)

Aquila suggested that he sit in front by the driver so that Gaius, Paul and I could be together in the back of the carriage. Our horses were fast, yet it was still close to an hour before we left the city of Corinth behind and followed the road through the countryside to Isthmia, the place for the games, near the eastern end of the Corinthian Isthmus.

"We are meeting my friends at the bath house there," Gaius explained at the beginning of the drive. "It is a social gathering place for the games—a new building erected by the Romans. Be sure to look at the mosaic floor in the main hall. I know of nothing like it in all of Greece."

Gaius said that among those we would meet were the most prominent of the Greek community of Corinth. The opening of the Isthmian games, every second year, brought every other activity to a halt. Visitors as well as athletes from all over the Empire would be there. In fame the Athenian games at Olympia exceeded the Isthmian celebration, Gaius admitted. But in very ancient times the two cities had fought wars for supremacy of each other's games.

As we came closer to Isthmia, the traffic on the way to the games grew heavier. There were hundreds of carriages, litters carried by slaves, people on horseback and thousands on foot. The whole of Corinth seemed to be on the way. Our carriage had to stop repeatedly for the congestion.

At last we reached what was called the bath house, a huge structure of white marble. We went inside to the great hall, now filled with people. To look at the mosaic floor as Gaius had suggested was impossible for the number of feet standing on it. I had glimpses of black and white chips of mosaic stones with pictures of sea animals: fish, shelled creatures, and dolphins, and of geometric forms. The tiny fragments glowed between the shadows of so many people.

Gaius's friends were waiting in a group. There were a number of them, all Gentiles, and they greeted us with the enthusiasm of a holiday. We were introduced all around, and some I do not remember to this day.

It was then I met Antonia and her husband, Cyrus of Corinth. I could not know at that moment that Antonia would become one of my closest friends, or that Cyrus eventually would give Paul so much trouble.

Antonia is of about the same age as I am. If I have ever thought vainly I am beautiful, Antonia is more so. Her face is softer than mine, her nose blunt, her mouth smaller and rounder. Her black

35

hair she keeps in rolls on top of her head. She wore that day a long sleeveless tunica, white with gold trim, more formal than my dress. Her head was uncovered.

It happened that we walked together, with the rest of Gaius's group, across the lawn that separated the bath house from the stadium. Antonia learned from me that we had moved only recently from Rome to Corinth. She told me that her grandfather had come here to settle nearly a hundred years before, as an ex-soldier in Julius Caesar's army, at the time when Caesar was rebuilding the old destroyed city. Her husband's family were Hellenes originally from Macedonia. Antonia and Cyrus lived in a villa at the northern edge of Corinth.

Later that day, when we talked again and became more confidential as women do among themselves, Antonia said that the great sorrow in her life and her husband's was her inability to bear a child. She had miscarried three times, and the physicians had told her she should not try again. In turn, I admitted that I had never been able to conceive at all, and the doctor in Rome believed I never would. This knowledge between us became an immediate bond.

Another Gentile with whom I talked was Melas, a young Greek who looked at me with an eye that I can only call lustful. He had with him a woman named Laodice, whom he introduced as his mother. This surprised me, as she was far too young to have Melas as a son. I learned later that she was the second wife of Melas's father, an elderly man who had divorced his first wife. Laodice was blond, by nature or by intent I don't know. She had blue eyes which seemed half closed under heavy lashes. I never did meet her husband, Melas's father, whose name I cannot recall. At that first meeting I had a feeling of distaste for Melas, for no reason that I could sensibly define at the time.

There were others in the group, too numerous to mention here; but some of the women I came to know well later.

Gaius led us to a reserved space in the portico facing the stadium, where we sat on benches to watch the games. Under the portico we were sheltered from the sun, but on two sides of the stadium were high earth embankments covered with grass. There thousands of people were already sitting in the blinding sunshine.

36

A small temple dedicated to Poseidon took up the center space of the sports area.

Trumpets blew. A parade of the athletes passed before us. Each participant carried a banner proclaiming the city or region or nation he represented. Competitors were divided into separate groups: boys, adolescents, and men. Among the divisions for sports, runners for races were the most numerous, each clad in the briefest white loincloth, with ribbons of his banner colors attached. Boxers followed, with clenched fists held high. Heavily muscled wrestlers came next, naked except for a temporary string around their waists holding their color ribbons. Then there were jumpers, discus and javelin throwers, gymnasts, acrobats, and even trumpet players for their own competitions. Other small groups, toward the end, were poets carrying sheaths of parchment in their hands, dancers, and musicians holding lyres.

By now the enthusiasm of the great crowd reached its highest. Cheers for individuals, localities, for groups, and the whole of the events rose to a roar. Everyone stood at this point. As the competitors passed the Temple of Poseidon, each one paused a moment, and moved on.

Gaius explained everything to the three of us as the march went by, so that we were fully aware of what was going on. Looking about, I noticed Stephanas, my rescuer from the sailors, under the portico at a distance. He recognized me and waved. On the other side, beyond our group, a number of girls in the shortest tunicas were jumping up and down cheering for the Corinthian athletes.

"Priestesses from the Temple of Aphrodite," Gaius told us. "They always have the places of special honor."

The moment the procession ended, the stadium erupted into activity. The races began, wrestlers and boxers took places on special platforms, jumpers ran and leaped into the high and broad jumps. The whole area was alive with sunburned bodies already gleaming with sweat.

Paul was entranced. He liked the running races. "Select the one beforehand you think will win," he called out. "See which one of us chooses best!" Paul won that competition, hands down. I'll admit that my choice of runners as I saw them mark time at the starting gates either came in last or after the average.

Aquila sat beside Cyrus, Antonia's husband, at times in deep conversation, then both at times leaping to their feet shouting encouragement to particular athletes.

These games were of the centuries-old Greek spirit, of individual strength and endurance, of daring and skill. Unlike the games of Rome, no one thought of contempt or death to the losers. Glory went to the winners, with wreaths of oak leaves placed on their heads amid cheers from their supporters. I found myself shouting for Corinth over my native Rome athletes, and for Rome over the cities of Macedonia and Asia. It was a wonderful day of achievement, enthusiasm, and enjoyment.

When the afternoon began to fade and the cooler breezes of evening arose, the trumpets sounded again. The games were over until the morrow.

We took leave of our new Gentile friends, including Antonia, who promised, "We will see each other again soon." Cyrus, her husband, shook hands with Aquila and Paul, and bowed graciously to me. As the group broke up we smiled and waved at the others, and all were quickly lost in the crowd. I found myself walking from the portico beside two of the Aphrodite priestesses. They were pretty girls in their teens, talking excitedly about their heroes of the games.

With difficulty the four of us found Gaius's carriage again. On the way home Paul led the conversation about the runners, who should have won and who should have lost. The races meant more to him than I realized—until much, much later.

It did not occur to me at the time how much the simplicity of our lives was changing, Aquila's and mine. Perhaps Aquila did know, but he did not speak of it yet. Events seemed to move swiftly.

We had become accustomed to Paul's presence in our house, working as he did in the shop. In the evenings, after work, he told us more and more of the new Christian faith. He described his meetings in Jerusalem with Peter, whom he called Cephas, and James, the brother of Jesus, and what he had learned from them of Christ's life, teachings, and death. Paul had talked to no other apostle but these two, except incidentally.

He told us how unimportant the span of one's life can be, in riches or poverty, in fame or obscurity, when earthly life is

compared to God's eternity. The ultimate result of life can be only
—these are my words—the testing of the human spirit with the
Spirit of God.

This idea, of the Holy Spirit, opened a new vista to me, however
little was given to me to understand. The prospect of my life—my
self—enduring through whatever eternity might mean, was difficult
to comprehend. Probably God meant it to be so. What Paul knew
from his own experience with God he was forbidden to tell us.
Could we have understood if he had? Paul openly admitted he did
not understand all things.

What Paul taught sank deeply into my heart. As he spoke to us
of Christ and his brief life on earth, I came to wonder how any
person, Jew or Gentile, could doubt that Jesus was indeed the Son
of God.

So, subtly, everything in my life changed. Some of the external
events proved it.

One morning, while Paul and Aquila were both out of the house
buying new rolls of canvas, I had a most unexpected visitor. It was
Stephanas, who had waved to me at the games. He came to order
some awnings for his house. He explained that his own sailmakers
for his ships were so busy that he did not want to disturb them
with personal requirements. He dared to presume on Aquila's
time, if that was in order.

When I told him that Aquila was out for the moment and would
need measurements for the awnings, Stephanas said that he already had the exact measuring. He produced a piece of parchment
with figures written on it and handed it to me.

He spoke at once of having seen me at the games but not otherwise since that dreadful morning when I had lost my way and
ended up in the terrifying brothel neighborhood. Ever since that
morning, he said, he had wondered about this religion of the Jews,
whose faith in their God was so great they would refuse to eat at
the table of any who were not Jews. Now he had heard rumors
that we were also Christian Jews and harbored in our house a man
who preached of Christ. Who was this Christ? He himself was a
follower of Apollo, but he said he was curious about the new God
of the Christian Jews.

I told him as much as I could about Jesus. Stephanas listened
carefully, thanked me. After he left I was worried. Had I said too

much to a stranger? Stephanas was an important man. Could he have been looking for trouble, for something to report to the Roman authorities?

I was concerned enough to tell Paul about the episode as soon as he came back with Aquila.

He appeared pleased. "How otherwise can we spread the Word of Christ?" he asked.

But Paul went on to give me a special warning: every disciple of Christ Jesus who taught his Way placed himself or herself in the greatest dangers—of contempt, rejection, physical harm, possible imprisonment, torture, even death.

"Prisca, as a disciple of Jesus, you will be exposed to these severe perils. Founders of the churches of Christ risk every kind of opposition. Yet the Christian Church of God will endure."

I went upstairs to my room and sat on the edge of the couch. I felt frightened. Paul had told me I was a disciple of Christ and what it meant to be one. He accepted me, even though I was a woman. Then a warmth of peace filled my body.

On the following Sabbath, Paul talked again at the synagogue. This time he was more specific. He told the congregation that Jesus was indeed the Messiah promised by the prophets. Through his Resurrection, Christ proved that he was the Son sent by the Lord God to fulfill the Law for all nations and all people through baptism in his Name.

"For in Christ sin is dead," Paul cried out. "In Christ is life eternal."

At the end of the service as everyone stood to leave, I saw that Stephanas, the Greek pagan, had been sitting on the last bench of the synagogue. I was surprised, then alarmed that he disappeared quickly.

Gaius stopped Paul on the way out to say that he had received that morning a great deal to think about. While they talked, I noticed that four or five of the synagogue elders had gathered together impatiently. As Gaius turned away, the group moved in. I guessed from their expressions that they were questioning Paul sharply on his views, but I could not hear what they said. I could not hear Paul's quick answers either, but the group of elders retreated angrily.

The three of us walked home together again. But Aquila remained very quiet for the rest of the day.

Before going to sleep that night, Aquila and I had an argument. All along, Aquila began, Paul had been saying things he could not understand. Especially so, he added, during that morning's service at the synagogue.

"We were brought up to honor and obey the Law. We are Jews, God's selected people, according to the scriptures we have learned since we were children. The Law tells us what we must not do to keep from sinning. No one who believes in Jesus has any sin. Does that mean we can do what the Law says is sinful?"

I suppose I was tired that evening. I snapped back, "What sins do you want to commit?"

"That's not the point," Aquila protested. "I don't want to commit any. But if I do not follow the Law, how do I know what is sinful? I do not think I am a sinful man. What should I do differently?"

"God guides you into the Way of Christ," I replied. "We received his Spirit when we were baptized in Rome. This is what Paul has been teaching."

"No one in Rome told us that God's Spirit took the place of God's Law."

"Paul has not said anything to us against the Law. He says that Jesus completes the Law." I was grasping at straws myself, I knew so little. "The Law isn't necessary. Otherwise, how could Paul convert to Christ Gentiles who know nothing of the Law? For us who are Jews there is nothing wrong if we wish to continue acceptance of the Law. It is good. But Christ goes further than the teachings of the Law."

Then I remembered something Paul had said to us, and I paraphrased it: "When we were children, our parents told us what we must do, as discipline for our own good. Now that we are grown up, we have the knowledge to decide for ourselves. So it is with God and the Law. As the Jewish people were the children of God, he gave us the discipline of the Law for our own welfare. But he sent Jesus to give us the knowledge to decide for ourselves with the guidance of the Holy Spirit, and freed us from the Law's discipline. It's as easy as that."

"It isn't easy for me," Aquila grumbled. "I guess I am still a child."

"To follow Christ is not meant to be easy," I told him. I put out my arms to Aquila.

"I feel so tired," he murmured. "Forgive me for always doubting. Let's go to sleep."

5

Several days later, Silas and Timothy arrived in Corinth from Macedonia. They brought with them the long-awaited contributions from the churches in Philippi, Thessalonica, and Beroea, which freed Paul to carry out his evangelical activities.

Paul came at once to Aquila and me. "You have been generous and kind while I waited for these contributions. I have much to thank you for. Now I can release you from the burden of my staying here. I can move into the lodgings that my friends expect to find today," he told us. "Aquila, may I come as much as possible to help you in the shop? Perhaps part of each day. A man can think better when he uses his hands as well as his head."

I interrupted. "Paul, you are not a burden to us. This is only the beginning of your work in Corinth. I had hoped I could be part of it by having you stay with us."

Aquila joined in with me. "Don't leave us for any reason unless you feel you would be more comfortable elsewhere. You have taught me a great deal about tentmaking that I did not know. I have a lot yet to learn."

Paul smiled. "You make me very content. Of course, I would rather stay here than anywhere else. I can rest better with you through the long work ahead." Then he chuckled in that deep chest. "Prisca, you are the best cook, and a patient listener to my many thoughts."

Paul remained in our house for all of his eighteen-month stay in Corinth, to the pleasure of both Aquila and me.

On their first night in Corinth, I had Silas and Timothy at our house for the evening meal. I also asked Luke to come. I prepared fish fresh from the sea that morning, with lemon juice to flavor it. I discovered small artichokes in the market, and served fruit afterward including figs, then coming into season.

The six of us at the table celebrated the Lord's Last Supper, as Jesus had asked his apostles and followers to do. Paul blessed the bread and cup of wine, thanked God for it, and passed both among us. As we shared them, Paul repeated Christ's words which he had learned directly from Peter in Jerusalem: *"This is my body which is given for you. Do this in remembrance of me."* Then, *"This cup is the new covenant in my blood, which is being shed for you."*

Paul bowed his head and thanked God for the safety of the travelers, for the churches in Macedonia, and for the results so far in Corinth. He asked the Lord for his own continued strength, of which at times he felt failure.

I added my prayer in a low voice. More for Aquila and for me than for the others, I asked that we be shown how we could help Paul, the apostle of Christ, and how we should keep our faith strong and from ever doubting. Paul's strong hand closed over mine at the end.

During the evening meal and long afterward, the two newcomers kept up a steady conversation with all of us, bringing Paul and Luke up to date on the events and people of the Macedonian churches that Paul had founded. Silas told Aquila and me of an amazing, chilling experience that he had had with Paul while they were both in Philippi. It began with a painful beating of Paul and Silas ordered by Roman authorities in front of a shrieking mob because Paul had exorcised an evil spirit out of a very ill slave girl who had been profitable to her owners by prophesying. They were then chained and imprisoned in a dungeon with their feet in stocks. That night a mighty earthquake came to the city, shaking the buildings and the prison. The chains of Paul and Silas were pulled apart and the stocks broken. They could have easily escaped, but they waited until morning, when Paul commanded the Roman authorities to come to the prison formally to release them and apologize for beating a Roman citizen unlawfully, without a trial.

As they left the prison, after the authorities' frightened apology, the captain of the prison guards knelt before Paul. "Master, I believe."

In the morning a wonderful thing happened:

Stephanas, the Gentile, came to the house to examine his awnings, which Paul and Aquila had already prepared.

"First, though, is your friend Paul here?" Stephanas asked me. "I would like to speak with him, and with you."

I held the door for him. "Of course, please come in. Paul is still in his room. One moment—"

Paul appeared at once. I introduced him to Stephanas.

"I am a follower of Apollo," Stephanas said. "I have worshiped in his temple since I was taken as a boy by my father. But I have wondered about many things, such as death for mortal humans. This young lady has told me of the Christ of the Jews, and I listened to you in the synagogue. I would like to know more of your God, otherwise unknown to me."

In reply, Paul related the story of how in Athens he was invited to speak to the esteemed Court of the Areopagus, and what happened there with the reference he made to the shrine for the Unknown God.

"Then, when I told them of Christ's Resurrection, they laughed at me," Paul said. "They replied that, long ago, Apollo had said there could be no life after death."

"Even though I have followed Apollo, I assure you I will not laugh. May I ask you to come to my house to teach me?"

"Certainly," Paul agreed. "This is why I am in Corinth."

Stephanas looked at me. "Once before, I asked this lovely girl if she and her husband would dine with us. I understand that all of you are of the Jewish faith, and such an act is forbidden to you because we are Gentiles. Do I dare to ask once more? I would like my wife and our family and household to hear what you say."

"We will come," Paul promised. "In the sight of God, all people are equal and open to receive the Word of Jesus."

I caught my breath. To sit at a Gentile table to eat?

Stephanas bowed. "Good. I will send you the invitation. Now, for the awnings—"

I showed him the way to the shop and introduced him to Aquila. The awnings were ready to be folded for delivery.

44

I hurried back to Paul. "I don't understand. We cannot eat unclean food of the Gentiles—"

"Prisca dear, do you have reason to think the meat is not fresh?"

"It is fresh, yes, but it comes from sacrifices to the idols in the pagan temples."

"If idols are nothing, is there any difference between what is butchered on a pagan altar and what is butchered by other means? If you bring home a chicken alive and butcher it at your kitchen door, is that different from a fowl whose neck is cut on an altar for a god who means nothing?"

"But to associate with Gentiles in their home, at a meal where their serving is unlike ours—"

Paul said sharply, "To serve the Lord our God, I will go anywhere."

When I told Aquila of this, he refused. He could not go so far in breaking the Law as to sit at table with Gentiles and eat unclean, idolatrous food.

"Go with Paul if you must," he told me. "I cannot do it."

Then Paul spoke to Aquila. "When we teach of Jesus to the Gentiles and they accept the Way through baptism in Christ's Name, is it not right that we ask them to share with us the bread and wine of the last Passover supper, as Christ commanded us to do?"

"I suppose so," Aquila answered.

"Then, in justice, is it right that we refuse to eat with Gentiles who are seeking Christ—provided what we eat is in Christ's Name and for his purpose, not for the purpose of idolatry?"

Aquila bowed his head with hands over his face. "I will come with you to the Gentiles."

Two days later, a servant from Stephanas arrived with a note addressed to me. Stephanas, his wife, and his family would be pleased to have Paul and his friends, and my husband and me, for midafternoon dinner the next day. The time should be four o'clock. "Please come," he added in a postscript.

I asked the servant to wait until I wrote a return note to Stephanas accepting his invitation for all of us. I put in the note that, since the arrival of two of Paul's disciples from Macedonia, there were six of us. I hoped this number would not be too many.

And later that same morning Gaius appeared at my door. I was finishing my housekeeping, sweeping the floor of the atrium. Paul and Aquila were out in the work shed.

"Is Paul here?" Gaius asked. "I have a request to make of him."

"He is here, but working. I will call him."

"No, please don't disturb him, it can be done later." Gaius paused. "I wish Paul to baptize me in the Christian faith."

I dropped my broom and clasped his hands. "I am so happy and so will Paul be," I cried.

"I do not do this for Paul, much as I favor him," he said. "I am satisfied that Jesus is the Son of God, resurrected for my sake."

I felt tears in my eyes. "May I tell him now?"

"Please don't; he is working. Tell him later. There will be a better time soon. I will not change my mind."

That afternoon, Paul went to the house of Gaius, with Silas and Timothy, and baptized Gaius into the faith of Jesus Christ. He was the first in Corinth to accept the Christian Way.

The Villa Stephanas was in a section of Corinth unfamiliar to me, not so far away we could not walk to it. We found it in a quiet neighborhood of beautiful houses. But the Villa Stephanas dominated all the others. I was astonished by the size. Accustomed as I was to the great buildings of Rome, this villa appeared more like a miniature palace. Built entirely of marble, it was four floors high and designed in the simplest form of contemporary Greek architecture. Rows of windows across the front were all protected from the sun by lines of awnings, as Aquila and I both noticed.

Set back from the street, the building was surrounded by a high wall intercepted by an imposing grilled iron gate. A gatekeeper opened it for us and we were shown the gravel path that wound its way between clipped lawns and banks of flowers to the villa portals—I could think of the huge doors only as portals. They opened as we approached. A servant bowed, and we were led to a large reception room.

Stephanas met us there, with his wife, Dorice. She is a demure and unassuming little woman, with black hair twisted into a bun at the back. She smiled her welcome as her husband introduced us along with Aquila's introductions of Luke, Silas, and Timothy. Stephanas himself seemed to have grown beyond my memory of him as tall, clean-shaven, eagle-faced. In his own surroundings, he was like a king in his palace, clad in purple Roman toga.

Their children came in to meet us, two teen-age boys and a younger daughter. The boys bowed and shook hands with each of us. The girl held back and smiled.

We were taken into another equally large room where a table was spread with foods. I looked at the remarkable mosaics on the floor of each room and the hallway between, in colors of blue and violet. Designs showed ships large and small, sea creatures, nymphs, and dolphins.

Four couches, each for two persons, were set around the square table. I was placed on the couch beside Stephanas, Paul with Dorice. The three children sat at another table. Suddenly there was a silence, everyone looking at Paul. His hands were raised as he asked God to bless the room, the food, and all who lived under the roof of the Villa Stephanas. Stephanas seemed startled, but kept silent. Dorice stopped in the middle of a gesture. No one said anything except for the "Amen" from the five of us.

Activity began again. Servants seemed to appear from everywhere. The meal was elaborate. First we were served with tiny shrimps, boiled and sprinkled with olive oil and garlic. Neither Aquila nor I had ever eaten shellfish, forbidden by the Law as unclean. I hesitated, looked at Aquila who frowned down at his plate. Paul ate with relish, and so did the others. Tentatively I tasted them; they were good. In fact, the more I ate the better they were, and suddenly the plate was empty. I did have a feeling of guilt. Aquila made a show of eating, that was all.

For the main course—inevitably it had to be—came roast lamb. I visualized the animal as one of the sacrifices on the altar of Apollo, cut apart to ritual prayers by robed priests of the cult. I had frequently bought lamb but only from one special butcher's stall, where all produce was certified to be clean by our synagogue rabbi. The slices of lamb in front of me may not have been from the temple but they certainly had not received a kosher approval.

Nevertheless I ate it. I dared not glance at Aquila again. Meanwhile Stephanas talked to me about Rome, and once more of my father, which made me a little homesick. I asked him about his travels. He knew every corner of the Roman Empire from the farthest boundary of the Orient to Spain and north through Gaul to Britain. How many ships did he have? I asked. He laughed; he had not counted them, two or three hundred perhaps. There were other owners with more, for shipowning came naturally to Greeks.

When the meal was finished, Stephanas waved to the servants to clear the table. He signaled to the children to bring up their couch. By ones, twos, and threes, servants appeared through the back quarters of the villa and lined themselves against the far wall, standing.

As Stephanas asked Paul to teach all those present about the Lord God in Heaven and the Lord Jesus Christ, Dorice moved over to sit with the children.

Paul spoke very simply to the Stephanas household. Primarily, he had in mind the younger ones and servants to whom the subject would be new. He was not nervous. It was my first time hearing Paul teach. I can remember many of his words.

He began his message slowly: "Most people in this world worship gods and goddesses. Probably all of you do, as you have here in Corinth temples and shrines for Poseidon, Aphrodite, Apollo, and even more. Your parents worshiped them, and their ancestors in turn for many generations. But, from the beginning, stories and legends about gods and goddesses were conceived by men. Indeed, many philosophers and writers of Greece described them too, and their writings have helped to convince you."

Paul had complete attention. Stephanas himself kept his gaze fixed on him.

"I come to tell you of the God in whom I believe. He is the one and only God, who created the earth and all things on it, including ourselves. From the beginning all nations of the world have sought this God, but only the prophets and people of the Jewish faith were ready to receive him. Other civilizations and nations made their own gods and worshiped them in the form of idols. Can anyone believe that lifeless images of stone and metal could create the world and living things? Hardly."

One of the sons scratched his nose uneasily. Two of the servingmen standing against the wall of the room exchanged dubious glances.

48

Paul went on to tell them of the gospel of Jesus. His listeners did not move; they heard it, for the first time ever, with the closest interest. Then, as Paul described the Crucifixion, their shock was apparent. One of the serving girls broke into tears. I noticed the hands of Stephanas opening and closing in twitches.

Then Paul raised both arms and looked upward. He was carried away himself. I was as much moved as though I had never before heard the Word.

"But God raised the Lord Jesus from death. After three days he rose from the tomb and came before his apostles and disciples. So God our Father through the Resurrection of his Son promised eternal life to all those who believe in him and keep his commandments."

Paul let his arms fall.

"How can you trust what I am telling you? Why should you believe what I am saying? As a young man I did not believe in Jesus, or the Resurrection. I did not believe he was the Son of God. One day, as I traveled on the road from Jerusalem to Damascus, the Lord Jesus Christ appeared to me and spoke to me in a light so brilliant I was blinded for three days. Then I knew I had been wrong; Jesus was indeed the Son of God our Father in Heaven."

Stephanas, beside me, leaned forward, listening to every word. Dorice stared in wonder as her daughter clutched her hand. All who heard were quiet.

"I had sinned grievously against the Will of God, as all men and women are tempted to sin in one way or another. But I was baptized into faith in Christ, and through baptism received for myself forgiveness of my sins and the gift of God's Holy Spirit, which now guides my life. And God gave me a command, that I was chosen to carry this message to all people everywhere: that those who receive baptism in the Name of the Lord Jesus Christ will receive forgiveness of their sins, the promise of eternal life with God in Heaven, and the gift of his Holy Spirit to protect you.

"This is my message to you."

Then Stephanas cleared his throat. "Master, when I asked you to come today to speak to us, I expected to consider your God against the god Apollo, whom I have worshiped. I thought there must be something in a belief as sincere as that shown by your disciples here—" he glanced at me—"but I wished to take time. Now I deeply believe what you have said. I am convinced that my worship of an image all these years has been worthless. I believe with all my heart in your God. If he will accept me, I wish to be baptized in the Name of Jesus." He turned to those around him. "But I wish for each member of my family and of my household to decide for themselves, in their own consciences, as they have the right to do. There is to be no coercion."

Every one in turn asked for baptism. We had a group sacramental ceremony, with Stephanas, his two sons standing erect, the young daughter, somewhat frightened, holding her mother's hand as she received the blessing of Christ and God's Holy Spirit. In all, there were eighteen baptisms, including even the gatekeeper.

And Paul promised that Silas and Timothy would come to the villa to teach them more of the Way of Jesus.

On the way home, I asked Paul if he thought that they would keep to the Way of Jesus. He believed that some would stand, and some would fall.

Aquila admitted that he could not eat the food served to him. The thought of it made him ill.

"You did not trust the Lord," Paul reproached him. "God does not care what a man puts in his stomach; God cares for what a man puts into his heart."

We bade Paul good night at the house. Without saying anything to him or Aquila, I took a tray of bread, cheese, and fruit up to our room. I knew Aquila must be hungry.

News that Stephanas had forsaken worship of Apollo and had accepted the Unknown God of the Christians spread quickly through Corinth. Not only had Stephanas himself been baptized in the new faith, but his family and whole household. The shock throughout the city must have been enormous, from the echoes we kept hearing for some weeks later. Nothing could have helped Paul more. Stephanas was, after all, as prominent as any other Corinth citizen.

Reaction among the Jews in the synagogue was something else. Murmurings against Paul became loud. They said that he, with his group, not only spread heresy among the public but as Jews had associated with Gentiles and eaten of their unclean food. Crispus, head of the synagogue elders, came to our house several days later to warn us of impending trouble. He assured me that he was not a part of it. I told him that Paul expected trouble; he would face it when it came. Crispus admitted that he believed Paul's teaching was right. He had almost persuaded himself to become a Christian.

On the morning after the Villa Stephanas conversion, Antonia's letter was delivered to our door. It had been written the day before, so I could be certain its arrival was only coincidence. Antonia wrote:

> *From Antonia, to Priscilla: My dear friend, I have waited for an opportunity to invite you to our villa since our meeting at the games. This opportunity has arrived. My husband, Cyrus, and I are asking some of our close friends for next Friday evening, and we wish you both to come. We will have a late dinner and then the entertainment which Cyrus is arranging. I want to introduce you to our friends, for now that you are in Corinth you must join our social group here. Compared to Rome, we may seem provincial, which we are. Yet I believe you will enjoy yourselves. Your friend in Corinth, Antonia.*

I kept the letter for most of the day, thinking about it while I brought our accounts up to date. This invitation was different from the one from Stephanas, which had a direct religious purpose and ended happily. Now to associate so closely with Gentiles merely for enjoyment gave me pause. But I confess I longed to go, to see what the life of wealthy Corinthians was like.

In the afternoon, I went into the shop to help Aquila with sewing. I told him about the invitation, and my own doubts. Aquila was more reasonable than he had been before the Stephanas event.

"It would be good for our business," he said. "All our orders are coming from Gentiles. But business is not an excuse for joining Gentile pleasures. Let's ask Paul."

I agreed with that; I was sure of the answer.

When Paul returned that evening, after spending most of the day with Silas and Timothy, we discussed the invitation with him.

He told us it was not a sin to be social with others. "You may be of great influence in showing them the Way. Do not hide your beliefs, let your light shine. I myself will go anywhere, if by doing so I can help in the work of the Lord."

So I wrote a return note to Antonia, accepting her invitation for Aquila and me.

Once the decision was made, my excitement grew. I was determined not to let those Gentile women put me in second place in my appearance. In the morning, I bought enough heavy white oriental silk to make a new formal tunica, sleeveless, to be cut low below the neck, with gold braid for shoulder straps and a sash to fit tightly around my narrow waist. I also bought a new mamillare, the leather belt to go around my ribs under the tunica in support of my breasts, and new sandals.

At home I took out my small collection of jewelry, which I seldom used: the pair of gold pendant earrings, a family heirloom from my mother, and gold bracelets with turquoise, worn one on each arm, above the elbow, the only color with the white and gold. Aquila's mother had given them to me on my wedding day.

I fashioned my tunica to fall in soft folds from the waist to just below the knees. I dared not show it to Aquila until the night of the party.

But my anticipation increased each hour before that night.

6

Antonia's party was not as easy as I had expected it to be.

There were times later when I regretted that we had gone. Then, over all, I realized it had to be so that Aquila and I could grow into what we are. We heard, saw, and felt—yes, felt—things otherwise restricted from the experience of young Jews. Because of that party and all that followed, we were better able to understand the people of the Roman Empire and—if I may go so far—the people of life itself.

Aquila had arranged to hire for the evening a sedan chair with seats for the two of us, carried on poles by four strong young men.

They took us to the villa of Cyrus and Antonia, and waited to bring us home after the party.

The villa, on the northern edge of Corinth, seemed to be half in the country, half in the city. It was all on one floor, surrounding a large atrium in the center open to the sky—a type of dwelling in the Asian style, placed among trees and gardens.

As we entered a large reception hall I caught my breath. I suppose I had expected a party of several dozen or so people. There must have been several hundred. The hall was filled, most of the guests young people. They were the truly elite of Corinth. Most of the men were clad in the privileged togas, some with the honored purple borders or even in the full purple cloth of highest rank. I was more than glad for my own silk tunica—which surprised Aquila when he saw it earlier—for the women were dressed in the richest clothing. Many of the formal tunics were held by only one shoulder strap, leaving the other side curved tightly over a breast two-thirds revealed. Hair grooming was spectacular, some with towering masses under gold circlets so high the hair must have been false. A number of girls used more cosmetics and wore more revealing tunicas than most of the other women. They seemed to be something special, as if a line were drawn between them and those of Antonia's special friends. I wondered if they could be of the hetaerae, the courtesans of Greece whose paid duty was to entertain the men.

Antonia and Cyrus met us in the crowded hall as other people pushed around us. Antonia hugged me and kissed my cheek while Cyrus greeted Aquila.

"I am so happy you are here." Antonia had to raise her voice over the sounds of the throng. "I want you to meet my friends."

She turned around and pulled women over to be introduced. "This is Priscilla, my friend from Rome," she kept saying. I had no idea of their names or who they were; all was lost in the confusion. I lost Aquila completely. Looking over my shoulder, I saw him being taken off by a man in purple-bordered toga to a room that seemed to be full of men only. I did not have time to see more; Antonia continued introducing me to one woman after another. Then even Antonia was lost in the milling crowd of people.

Slave girls in brief white tunicas were passing around wine cups on trays, somehow squeezing between packed bodies. I took one offered to me.

I found myself talking to one woman who looked at me with the greatest curiosity.

"I have heard about you from Antonia," she remarked. "You are from Rome? I've never been there, but I know I would love it. My name is Druda. If you didn't hear it, it is no wonder. Antonia tells me that you are a Christian. Is that so?"

"Yes, that is so." I smiled.

"I've never met a Christian," Druda was saying. "It's something new, isn't it? Do they come from Rome?"

"Some of them," I replied. "Before long you will meet many of us."

"How interesting—" she began to say. Someone pushed in between us; that conversation ended.

A man and a woman came up to me, a young, stocky man and a very blond, blue-eyed woman. They seemed familiar, but at this confusing moment I could not place them.

"Priscilla of Rome!" the man exclaimed. "How good to see you still in Corinth." He turned to his companion. "Mother, you remember meeting Priscilla at the games?"

Of course—Melas, the one who had given me an uncomfortable feeling of distaste, and his impossibly young mother. Her name—yes, Laodice.

"Thank you," I murmured. "I enjoyed those races."

Melas grasped my hand; his thumb began caressing my palm. His glance went over me, head to toe, his lower lip protruded. Quickly I pulled my hand away. Laodice was smiling, an empty sort of smile.

I liked the man even less, and now the woman, too. Something was wrong between them. Fortunately, before the conversation went further, Antonia arrived with another friend to introduce. Melas disappeared, and Laodice drifted off into the crowd.

For an instant I had a chance to whisper to Antonia, "Who is she? Too young to be the mother of that man. . . ."

"She's older than she looks," Antonia whispered back. "Second wife of Melas's father. He's too old to know what they do—I'll tell you later."

Someone had interrupted.

54

Many others spoke to me, but after what Antonia had said I almost spilt my wine. A serving girl handed me another cup.

All at once the men from the neighboring room poured out into the hall, mixing with the women. A hand grasped my elbow.

"Shall we sit together?" a voice said in my ear. "I know just where to go so that we can see the entertainment later."

Before I could reply, the man with the firm grip and I were being carried by the stream of people out into the atrium. The one at my elbow was a young man, not quite as tall as I am. He was in a white toga, but without the purple. He steered me relentlessly through the atrium entrance and to a divan nearby and told me this was it. I had no choice. Both of us were almost forcefully pushed down onto the divan by the pressing mass of those moving farther.

I worried about Aquila. I needn't have. In the distance across the atrium I saw him being moved along by a girl who held his arm.

"We are going to have a wonderful evening," the one beside me was saying. "Every party these people give is wonderful, don't you think so?"

I was about to say this was my first, but a girl's hand appeared over my shoulder with a fresh cup of wine. She took my half-empty cup away.

"Do you know Antonia well?" my new companion asked. "She and Cyrus are wonderful people. They make Corinth the delightful city it is."

He had been given a new cup of wine too. He raised it in salute.

"Thanks to them for the wonderful evening we will have," he said softly. "Do you know, I find you to be the most beautiful girl here. How fortunate I am to have discovered you! I am usually fortunate in finding girls, but tonight—"

He placed the emphasis on the last word, at the same time looking into my eyes. What does a girl do under this kind of approach, with the third cup of wine? She begins to forget. . . .

Lights in the atrium came from flaming torches placed on poles. The night was warm, and a slight breeze came out of the open sky above. Divans around the atrium were filled now by couples, the scent of flowers in the center of the open space was heavy, splashing fountains among them sent out coolness. Male servants dressed

55

only in loincloths dashed about, placing a table in front of every divan. The girl standing behind me held out another full cup of wine over my shoulder. This time I said no. My companion accepted his. I could not see across the atrium to the people there.

Where was Aquila, my husband? I decided I was in a dream, a fantasy of some kind.

The man beside me touched my hand, just briefly, as if by accident. He continued the conversation, leaning toward me.

"I am from Athens," he said. "I've come to Corinth because I love this city, it has so much to offer. Are you a Corinthian?"

"No, I'm quite new here."

He nodded. "I thought so; you have a different quality. Not that I don't admire Corinthian girls, but—well, the difference in quality shows."

The time had come to stop this, I thought. "I am from Rome. I live here with my husband."

"You have a husband? I don't have a wife. To be truthful, I have never wanted one. I prefer this feeling of being free, to meet with girls who attract me—as you are doing."

One of the male servants placed two bowls of soup on the table in front of us.

"So you are from Rome," he was saying. "I love Rome, such a beautiful city. I studied there, I am an architect, you see. To be truthful, I am in Corinth for work."

He picked up his bowl of soup, drank from it. I did also. It was a fish soup with herbs; I drank it all. The hand of the girl behind our divan held out a new cup of wine. I put it on the table. Music was coming from somewhere.

My companion was telling me of his work as an architect. He was quite talkative. He said that he was engaged now in designing a new section of houses on the edge of the city, complete with a small marketplace, a building with baths and library combined, and a temple dedicated to Venus, Roman goddess of love and beauty.

"You see," he explained, "there is Roman money behind this development, necessary for a growing Corinth. So I am trying to devise a combination of architectural designs using the triangular façades and classic columns of Greece with the new, grand arches of Roman origin. I envision a long vista—" he gestured with a sweep of his arm "—behind the Greek entrance, a succession of Roman arches forming a wide promenade, roofed over, with shops on either side, an arcade in fact."

"It sounds most impressive," I told him. "And original."

A girl servant took our empty soup bowls; a man replaced them with platters of chicken breasts covered by white wine sauce. I began to eat with enjoyment, and sipped from the cup of wine along with the food. My friend almost gulped his, in the excitement of describing his project.

"My project will be most unusual, a meeting place for two cultures, Greek and Roman, symbolic for Corinth, the meeting place of the Empire, between the ancient and the new. My Roman employers will be pleased. Rome, the world revolves around it."

The next course for dinner was roast lamb with gravy on grape leaves, and vegetables. The male servant in the loincloth took his place behind our divan with the girl. She never allowed my wine cup to be empty.

Between bites the young man went on. "My Temple of Venus will be modeled like yours in Rome, but I will make ours better. I see it now, inhabited with girls dedicated to love—not chaste, like those of the Temple of Vesta, who must preserve their virginity on pain of death." He leaned toward me. "I am in love already with beauty and love, like yours. What are you doing in Corinth? Not just visiting—"

"No, we are living here, my husband and I."

"Good," he murmured. "Corinth is even more enticing to me."

A trumpet sounded with a blast. Instantly four large torches sprang into fire around a platform beyond the atrium, in full view of the guests. Our plates were removed and a large bowl of purple-red figs placed on the table.

"Figs, the most sexual of fruits," my companion said, handing me one. "Now the entertainment; I hear it will be excellent tonight."

A young man jumped onto the platform. He carried a scroll, and after waiting for silence began to read. Clearly he was a poet. What he read must have been his own work, and popular, for he was interrupted by frequent applause. I heard little of it, for I realized all at once that the architect's arm was moving around my shoulders, slowly, pulling me back against him while he moved one leg up on the divan.

The serving girl behind us filled our cups again. I noticed that most of the girls on the divans around us were reclining in the arms of the men beside them. I took a sip of wine, the pressure of the arm around my shoulders pulled on me. Inadvertently I relaxed. As the poet read his verses, I felt the warm tongue of the architect caressing my ear. The poet finished to applause; I sat up quickly.

"No," I whispered, "I've had too much wine. Please excuse me—"

I tried to stand but he held me. "You cannot go now, you will disturb everyone, see?"

Three men strumming lyres stepped on stage, singing as they came. Guests around the atrium shouted and applauded.

"You know who they are," the architect said. "They call themselves the Corinthian Trio, very popular. You must not upset the show."

I saw that this was true. To cross over to where Aquila must be sitting meant passing in front of the whole assembly. Everyone would see me, and gossip.

His hot breath was close on the back of my neck. With my elbow I pushed against his arm, his hand fell on my thigh, squeezed it.

I turned my face to him, whispering again, "Please, I cannot—"

With a quick move he pulled me close, kissed my mouth, his tongue flicked across my lips. For one instant I closed my eyes, a shock went through my whole body, his hand touched me. I felt a dizzying convulsion—

I pulled back so hard I bumped the feet of the couple on the next divan lying flat in close embrace.

"Please, please," I begged, trying to keep my whisper low.

"But you are my Venus tonight. My beautiful one for love—"

"No." I almost cried out. "Your Venus doesn't exist, I'm not— I don't believe—please don't," I pleaded.

He released me. "Forgive me. I didn't think— this is a party, you see— I forgot you are a stranger in Corinth— but in Rome, too, you have parties—"

The musicians had been playing loudly, but now their songs

were softer. Many of the torches around the atrium had burned out. Couples in the shadows lay close on the divans, obliviously entwined together.

I was in a panic. "I am so sorry; it is my fault. In my faith we do not have parties like this; I did not know. I am a Jew, and a believer in Jesus Christ. I cannot do—what you want. I should have told you, but . . . I didn't realize. . . ."

I took his hand. Words were difficult in this situation.

"For us it is a sin to love a man unless one is married to him."

"I don't understand your meaning of sin," he said. "Is it wrong if I promise to give you my love tonight?"

"We are in separate worlds." I smiled. "You have your Venus, I have my God."

The music of the lyres was slow now, insinuating, sensual. The darkness deepened.

"I will tell you a secret," the young man spoke close into my ear. "I believe in no gods. Just now my preference is Venus, because of my work to build the temple. If I said this aloud, I would have no work. I believe only in my work."

"Your work is temporary. It could be destroyed by an earthquake or by conquerors. Corinth was destroyed once; it could be again. But belief in Jesus Christ is forever."

He laughed softly. "My life is more temporary than my work. I make the most of life by love with beautiful women. If I have offended you—"

"No." I shook my head. "I should not have been here in the first place. I am the one at fault. May I thank you for your compliments? I must look for my husband."

He restrained me for a moment. "Don't go yet, your voice is like music. My name is Dino, the architect. I live close to the marketplace. My office is there. You can find me there, if only to talk again. Please, what is your name?"

I made a mistake which I regretted immediately. .

"I am Priscilla, wife of Aquila, the tentmaker. Antonia is my friend."

"Then I will find you. If Venus did exist and promised what you say of your own God, you would be that goddess."

I put my finger to his lips. "That sounds blasphemous; you never spoke it."

59

When I stood and put out my hand to him, he kissed it. I left him and quickly crossed in front of the atrium to where I hoped I would find Aquila in the darkness. Everywhere I looked, couples were in tight contact, some silent, others talking in low voices.

Then I saw Aquila sitting upright on a divan, wine cup in hand, eyes glazed. A girl was stretched out with her head on his lap, her hands reaching up to caress his face.

"Aquila," I said softly, "it is time for us to go."

He staggered to his feet, pushing the girl aside. She looked up at him and laughed. "I'll wait for you," she promised.

I took his arm and led him from the atrium into the entrance hall. His feet seemed to be in his way. Neither host nor hostess were around to say farewell. Outdoors, I signaled for our sedan chair to take us home. On the way, Aquila fell asleep.

Then or later, I said nothing to Aquila about the party. There was nothing I could say.

7

On the following morning, the Sabbath, Aquila and I accompanied Paul to the synagogue as usual. As soon as we entered, I knew that something was different.

All was routine on the surface. But the congregation so far seated were restless. Many turned their heads as the three of us appeared, then quickly looked away. The group of elders were standing together at the front, near the altar. As they saw us, some whispered and nodded to each other.

I went to my usual seat in the women's section, finding my friend Chloe already beside me. We exchanged morning greetings, but her eyes were round and wondering. ·

As Paul walked up to the bench he had used before, he turned to glance at me. With one hand he made a slight gesture of reassurance. He, too, realized something was pending, the crisis he had foretold. He took his place and kneeled in prayer, remaining longer than usual.

Aquila sat in his own place in the men's area, farther ahead than mine. Luke was off to one side, Silas and Timothy in the midsection. Looking about, I noticed Gaius and Stephanas sitting together.

The synagogue was filled to capacity that morning, with some latecomers standing in the back. At the exact time, the rabbi appeared and approached the altar to issue the call for worship.

At that moment, Sosthenes stepped forward from the group of elders.

"Hold!" Sosthenes cried aloud. "There is a matter that must be settled before we begin our worship. I, Sosthenes, deputy leader of this congregation for Almighty God in Corinth, must speak to you urgently. It becomes my duty to speak, inasmuch as your appointed leader for us all, Crispus, has refused to do so, for whatever reason is not clear. So, as deputy under Crispus, I must do what he will not."

The congregation seemed to hold their breathing. I felt my heart pounding. Sosthenes took a deep breath, his eyes narrowed.

"On these last Sabbaths we have had come into our midst a stranger who has spoken to us peculiar things concerning the God of our fathers and of the Law given to us by Moses and the prophets. He claims his heritage as a Jew faithful to our God. Yet he speaks words in this synagogue that appear to us as heresies, in opposition to the Law itself and thereby in opposition to our Lord. He has uttered blasphemies that stain the walls of this place. Further, we have heard on good evidence that he has entered the house of Gentiles and partaken of their unclean food while preaching lies in defiance of God himself. . . ."

Sosthenes paused to glare down at Paul. "I see that the stranger is among us once again. I have the duty to demand that he recant these heresies, which have brought sacrilege into our house of worship. We, your appointed elders, demand of this stranger that he account himself as faithful to the God of our fathers and the Law and the Prophets—"

Before Sosthenes had finished, Paul stood up, storming with anger. He left his seat, strode up the aisle toward Sosthenes while speaking loudly, "I have come among you these days to tell you of the Son of God, who was crucified by the Jewish elders and men

61

of the Temple in Jerusalem in contravention to the prophecies of old. . . ."

He reached the front of the synagogue and shook his finger at Sosthenes. "You blind one, you repudiate the truth of the scriptures and deny the Son of our God!" He swung around toward the people, many already crying out protests.

Paul held out his hand for silence. "I am a Jew as much as any one of you." His voice shook but he made his best effort to control it. "I appeal to you as a Jew. At one time I, too, agreed with your elders and believed that Jesus preached heresies. But after the Resurrection Christ appeared to me as he did to other apostles—" Jeers and whistles began again, overriding Paul's words.

Now I could see Paul's shoulders hunch forward, his jaw protrude under the bristling beard. He roared. "I testify to you as truth that Jesus was the Christ of the prophets, risen from the dead for atonement of sins. . . ."

The congregation erupted in wild confusion, cries, protests, some men standing up, pressing front. Shouts came from everywhere: "Blasphemy! No Christ! Jesus an imposter! . . ." The group of elders pushed at Paul. Sosthenes attempted to push him back against the people. Men grabbed at him, pulling him away.

I was paralyzed with fright.

Then Paul seemed to rise, grow straighter and taller. He shook his drab brown robe at the people; his voice coming out from his deep chest reverberated through the synagogue.

"Your blood be on your own heads!" he shouted. "My conscience is clear! I will go to the Gentiles. Let those Jews follow me who will! I will always teach those who want to hear about the living God and Christ!"

He shoved away the grasps of the elders, raised his arms high, and with head erect marched through the uproar into the bright sunlight of the street.

Luke, Silas, and Timothy followed immediately. So did I, but I waited a few moments for Aquila to catch up with me. I saw him hesitate as if dumfounded, trying to absorb the significance of what was happening. Then he rose and came to me, and we walked out together.

Gaius went just ahead of us, and so did Stephanas. To my surprise, Chloe, my friend, came close behind. Once outside, I was more amazed when I saw Crispus, the leader of the synagogue elders, come grim-faced through the door. Still others of the congregation left too—several of them Jewish friends from our early days in Corinth, others whom I did not know at all.

We gathered around a disheveled Paul on the street, a small crowd. All together, there were more than twenty persons.

Then Gaius Titus Justus called in a voice loud enough for all to hear, "Paul, my house is here, next door. Freely I offer it to you for your use in teaching for as long as you wish, so that you may continue your ministry for Jesus Christ in Corinth."

Paul clasped him in his arms. "God will reward you in ways I cannot," he cried in a voice that was husky. "I accept in the Name of our Lord Christ Jesus."

So Gaius walked ahead to his house, with Paul close behind. All those who came out of the synagogue followed too. Gaius opened the door and conducted us into the large atrium within. There all gathered together, and Paul led us in a prayer of thanksgiving.

Crispus was first to ask Paul for baptism into the Christian faith. Paul himself carried out this sacrament. Then Silas and Timothy baptized those Jews and Gentiles who had not previously received the sign of the Holy Spirit.

So, on that morning, was established the first Christian church in Corinth, and indeed the province of Achaia, the land of ancient Greece.

Somewhere later I happened to say to Paul, "Those elders at the synagogue that Sabbath were so vicious to you it seemed as if they wanted to tear you apart physically."

"Prisca," he replied, "remember, at one time I was one of them. They are defending the faith of their fathers as I once did, however blindly. I have my own feelings, yes. But I understood them."

Afterward, the daily routine in our house became considerably changed. Each morning, Paul went up to the house of Gaius to teach those who came to him. Many Jews as well as Gentiles wanted to hear more of the Christian faith, and as word spread the numbers of listeners increased. Silas and Timothy performed baptisms for persons ready for it, and from its small beginning the church in Corinth grew.

I found that when I went with Paul I could be of help to him during these teaching sessions, especially in talking to the women who came. I was able to explain much that they did not understand, and to answer questions. At first I was surprised at the number of women who were interested and who eventually became converted. Later I understood why: most Greek women accepted without question their husbands' beliefs, with very little participation in them. The Christian faith gave women opportunity to think for themselves.

After teaching each day, Paul resorted to what I was told by the others had been a favorite way of his to spread his work. He went to the Agora, the center of the city, a large open space surrounded by government buildings, minor temples, and the imposing Temple of Apollo. There he wandered until he could pick up a conversation with one or two or a group of men. He would deftly lead his listeners into discussion of religion, usually pagan, and then introduce the Word of God. Of course this was not always successful, but often it did lead to men coming to Gaius's house the next day to hear him further. That way, he eventually made many converts.

In the meantime I would go off to do the day's marketing. The marketplace itself was next to the Agora. After that I returned to our house to join Aquila for the afternoon in the shop, sewing. When Paul returned, usually toward dusk, he took my place with the work while I prepared the main meal of the day.

Christian churches throughout the Empire were beginning to use the first day of the week—Sunday—as their day for services of worship and rest, contrary to the Jewish custom of the Sabbath on the seventh day, Saturday. Sunday commemorated the third day after the death of Jesus as his day of Resurrection. This was considered more appropriate for Christians.

Nevertheless, it was another sign of the absolute break between the faith of the Jews and that of the Christians.

The growing congregation of the church in the house of Gaius met weekly on Sunday evenings for the time of worship. Paul led the services in much the same way as the familiar Jewish practice. Prayers of thanks and praise to God were the same except for the addition of the Name of Jesus Christ. Scriptures were read, but then Paul spoke of the gospel of Christ's teachings during his lifetime. Before the conclusion we always celebrated the Last Supper of Jesus. To newly converted Gentiles, all of the service was strange.

Another tradition of Jewish worship was broken. Men and women sat together on the benches supplied by Gaius for the atrium, partly because of the informality and small space for a number of people, but even more because of Paul's view that in worship of God there was no difference between the sexes. In Corinth this arrangement did finally lead to difficulties, but Paul's stern words at that time smoothed out certain frictions.

The influx of members into the Christian faith did imply some possibly serious consequences, divided as they were among Jews and Gentiles. Gentile converts soon became the majority. They who had all their lives worshiped pagan gods came to hear about the God who forgave sins and promised eternal life in the Grace of the Holy Spirit.

Many of these were young people who understood eagerly that the faiths of their fathers were false. When Paul told them that idols were made by men and represented nothing but man-made conceptions, they responded at once to the apostle's description of the creation, and then the Resurrection. Some had difficulty in comprehending the meaning of sin, especially older men. To relate that word to the accustomed ways of their lives seemed unreasonable. Others took the opposite interpretation, and thought that to earn life after death meant giving up all temptations and pleasure, retiring to a self-restricting discipline.

Some Gentiles, on the other hand, decided that release from sin meant that they could do anything they pleased, even more freely than had been allowed by civilized custom.

Many Jews believed Paul as he told of his own conversion on the road to Damascus. How, the Jews asked among each other, was it possible not to believe when they heard this from another Jew, like themselves? A few went too much further. They had expected that the promised Messiah would ride as a king and rally his people into a great strength to overcome enemies and conquerors—at this point the legions of Rome. If all Jews accepted Jesus as the true Son of God, would not this be an ultimatum to the non-believers of the world? With God and Christ behind them would not the Jewish nation then be all-powerful against adversaries?

65

Paul's popularity among Corinthians through these misplaced interpretations by only a few came to a point when Gaius and Stephanas together expressed their worries, in my presence, to Paul.

Stephanas asked, "These Greeks, these Gentiles, who for generations have worshiped idols, who have their own rites, many of their rituals involving physical pleasures, are they so quickly to abandon their ways and accept the self-denying commands of a God whom they cannot see even in the form of an idol? Will their faith sustain them?"

Gaius then followed with his question: "Will your converts from the Jewish congregation be able to uphold their belief in a resurrected Christ only by the word of one man who tells them that Jesus lives because he saw him? They have to confront their elders and rabbis, who call them heretics and blasphemers against the Law."

Paul listened to them. "Do not think that I do not have my own fears. My good friends Gaius and Stephanas, and you, Prisca, my faithful one, I have this to tell you. I have told no one else so far except Luke. One night, not long ago, the Lord came to me in a vision and said these words: *'Do not fear, but speak and do not keep silent. I am with you and no one shall stop you. I have many people in this city on my side.'*"

Then Paul looked in turn at the three of us. "What else can I do except what the Lord commands?"

The two men were silent, and said no more.

But I caught my breath involuntarily. I remembered: the light under the door! Paul's vision . . . !

Some of the warnings of Gaius and Stephanas did come true. Then I remembered an old saying that my father often used to repeat: *Out of the chaff must good grain fall.* He had another saying that seemed appropriate: *Out of the fire the iron comes stronger.*

In the end, these things were what happened in Corinth.

8

Although for lack of time I missed my early walks around the city, I loved going to the market with my shopping bag. It was a colorful place, bright with awnings to keep the burning sun off the oranges, lemons, exotic Asian fruits, and vegetables. The whole huge area was filled during the morning hours with carts, wagons, and open stalls arranged in rows according to produce, with each seller crying out loudly that his stock was better than his neighbors'. The aisles were packed with people, mostly women, seeking their supplies. Most buyers were of the tradespeople class. Few of them were poor, for Corinth was a prosperous city of the Empire, but often even women of the wealthier group did their own marketing. These were usually brought to the Agora market in litters carried by servants. Household stewards handled payments and inspection of the goods the lady selected by pointing from her cushioned seat.

I was always fascinated by the diversity of people, nationalities, and languages in this cosmopolitan place. Shopping was finished by the noon hour, and at one o'clock the market was left deserted, unsold produce carried away and no one in sight except the sweepers washing down the pavements under the broiling sun.

I no longer concerned myself over the sources of the meats I bought, only the freshness, such was my change of habits. I was at the fish market one morning when I heard, over the clamor of the crowds, my name called.

Puzzled, I turned away from inspecting the eyes of a fish for quality. A woman hurried toward me—Antonia, my friend. I had not seen her since the night of her party. She approached with delight, followed by a serving girl who carried a large, flat basket on her head.

"To think of meeting you here." She embraced me. "I must tell you, I have a message for you. Dino, the architect whom you met at my party, has asked about you. You must hear what he told me, that you are one of the loveliest women he has ever met, yet one of the most puzzling. I believe Dino is truly fascinated by you, Priscilla."

"I am complimented," I replied, and added with a wry smile, "I enjoyed his company too."

Antonia went on, "He said you spoke of a strange God of whom he had never heard. It has to do with your friend Paul, doesn't it? The man we met with you at the games? Everybody in Corinth is talking about Paul—and about you, too, Priscilla. Your God is the Christian God, isn't he?"

"The God of the Jews and the Christians." It was the first time I had expressed it that way. The phrase sounded strange, but it wasn't strange any more.

"Dino thinks there ought to be a temple to him. He is in that business, you know. Have you any temples for your God? Maybe there should be one in Corinth, and Dino could build it."

"God's temple is on land, sea, and sky. It is everywhere for all creatures—including ourselves. No man can ever build such a temple, and it will never be destroyed."

Antonia drew back a little. "You seem to speak in riddles. I am trying to help Dino by passing along his message."

I was contrite. "I'm sorry to confuse you. Please tell Dino that he can learn more about Jesus Christ by coming to the house of Gaius. Paul teaches there every morning."

"Gaius?" Antonia was surprised. "If he believes this, there must be something to it."

Then she smiled with mischief. "I believe Dino would rather hear it from you than from Paul."

I turned to look at the eyes of the fish I had been examining. I lowered my voice to ask, "What god do you believe in, Antonia?"

"I believe in the god my husband tells me to," she said. "I really don't think much about it."

"You don't care?"

"Sometimes, but I have little choice. Right now he believes in Aphrodite. I wish he did not, for after he goes to the Temple he does not come to me for many a night. The rituals that go on there—"

Antonia's voice broke; her eyes filled with tears.

"Priscilla, you touch me where it hurts, oh, so much! I want my husband, I want—terribly—a child. I hate Aphrodite, who takes my husband from me. I hate all gods who make impossible . . . a baby!"

She bowed her head; one wrenching sob shook her. I put an arm around her shoulder.

"Antonia, easy. Please come with your husband to hear Paul speak; perhaps things could be different. . . ."

She straightened up, wiped her eyes, looked around to see if anyone had noticed, then tried to smile.

"Priscilla, we have become too serious." She looked at me searchingly. "I could wish for more happiness but . . . we are different. Let's always be friends, I do not have many. Why don't you join us at the library? We meet there almost every morning to read plays. Then, afterward, we often go to the baths for massage."

On an impulse I said, "I would like that; I have read very few plays. I will come, soon."

This time I reciprocated her embrace.

"I'm glad you saw me here, Antonia," I told her. "Oh, my fish; someone has taken it!"

Antonia laughed in spite of her emotion, and moved off, serving girl following with the market basket on her head.

For his outdoor public conversations it seemed that Paul came to choose a far corner of the Agora, where several streets of the business section of the city intersected. One day an unusual incident happened there that developed to involve all of us. Timothy told the story first to Aquila and me, really wondering whether anything could be done.

One morning a small group gathered around Paul at the same place. Several men were asking Paul serious questions and Paul was replying. Timothy was standing nearby, and his attention turned to a young girl who remained on the edge of the group, listening intently. He had noticed her before without especially thinking of her. She appeared always in a plain mantle with a hood to hide her hair. Her eyes, dark and large, stared out from a pale face. Curious, Timothy moved around to stand beside her.

"You are interested in what Paul is saying?" he asked.

The girl jumped back. "I mean no harm," she said quickly. "I will go—"

"Wait." Timothy restrained her. "What interested you in what Paul is saying? You have been here several times. Don't be afraid of me; I am a friend of Paul's."

She hesitated. "Is that his name, Paul? I do not know. I have heard him speak of a real God, the only one who exists. Is this so?"

"Yes," Timothy told her. "Paul tells of the God who exists for all people, men, women, and . . . girls like you. He is the one true God of all."

"Not for me," she said solemnly. "I do not know of the things he speaks. I listen only because I have never heard of them."

"Not many people have. This is why Paul speaks to all who listen. What is your name?"

She shook her head. "I cannot say; I must go—"

"No." Timothy touched her arm. "You can speak to me, I told you I am a friend of Paul's. I believe in this God of whom he speaks. What you say to me I will tell no one, except perhaps Paul. Tell me now of yourself."

She looked at him, hesitating. Then she explained, "I belong to Aphrodite, the goddess of love. I am a priestess in her temple."

Timothy was startled. He looked at the girl again. "How old are you?"

"They tell me I am fourteen; I do not know, I only remember that my mother sold me to the priests of the Temple long ago. I belong to the Temple. I am told I will always belong to Aphrodite; she is my goddess."

"Suppose this other God made you free?"

The girl was puzzled. "How could I be free when I am already sold?"

She turned to run. Timothy caught her by the arm.

"Tell me your name, please; I won't hurt you."

She was thoroughly frightened and shook her head. "I would be punished; I would be whipped across my back until I came close to death. I have seen it done to others—"

"Wait just a moment." Timothy tried to quiet her. "You will come to no harm. Tell me one thing: why did you come back more than once to hear Paul?"

"Because he makes me feel that—I could almost—almost love his Jesus more than my Aphrodite."

Tears ran down her face as she pulled away.

"Please, tell me your name," Timothy urged gently.

"Alcesta."

Her voice was so low it was scarcely audible. She fled from the Agora.

Meanwhile I found myself with even less time to spend in the workshop. Business kept growing as it never had in Rome. I managed to keep up with the accounts and handle orders and business contracts but could help Aquila little with sewing and measuring. At one point, a thunderstorm in the vicinity of the Isthmian games was preceded by a sharp, violent wind. A number of the awnings sheltering spectators were ripped to shreds and had to be replaced at once. Every tentmaker in Corinth was pressed into the emergency. I gave up my mornings and worked through the days and evenings. Paul hurried back from his teaching until the rush orders were over.

After that, church pressures grew. Visitors came frequently during the afternoon to the house to see Paul. When he was out, they stayed to talk with me. Then Paul asked me one day to help him write a letter to the apostles in Jerusalem. His report on progress in Corinth was long overdue.

Paul preferred to dictate letters rather than to write them out with his own pen, and I have a good hand for writing. He was so pleased that he suggested I could be useful in assisting him to catch up with all of his delayed correspondence. There were letters to people whom he knew in Asia, especially at Antioch, and he had inquiries, which he had not answered, from a number of churches he had founded. So we spent many afternoons and evenings on this work.

Paul dictated slowly and thoughtfully. I sat at a small table writing out what he wanted in the language he wished. I knew Latin, Greek, and the two Jewish languages, Hebrew and Aramaic. The only trouble I had was with Greek spelling; the complicated symbols for letters at times confused me. Paul helped me when this problem arose.

I must say that I looked forward to writing his letters. To be such a close part of the wide surge of the Christian faith through Macedonia, Asia, and the provinces of the south excited me. And there were so many places not yet touched, as Paul in his own impatience told me. I was happy, too, with this close relationship to Paul. I came to know well every action, every inflection of his great voice, almost his thoughts before he spoke them.

But, as I have said, I had little time left to help Aquila at his work. Neither did Paul, although he did his best to share the time he did have.

Even further, Paul frequently liked to talk after our evening meal about his plans for the future, the problems facing the new faith, and questions that came up during his teaching. I suspected a double purpose: first, by talking aloud he could think out solutions in his own mind, and second, he wanted me to know as much as possible of the reasoning and background for the Christian Way. He told me a great deal of the life and teachings of Jesus that he had learned from Peter and James.

Usually during these evenings Aquila silently returned to his workshop, and stayed there until I called him. I knew him well enough to realize that he was brooding about his work with so little assistance, and about his house with so much unusual activity. I talked to him about it, to convince him that we were both engaged in a world-wide revolution going on throughout the Empire under the guidance of God. Every person converted became another step forward, beyond themselves in importance for the future of a lasting total Christian Church.

Aquila's reply was always a noncommittal, "It's all right; one day we may be able to return to Rome."

In my conscience I had to admit that our normal married life was disrupted. I could not remember how long it had been since we had made love. But all our days were too busy, and at night both of us were too tired to suggest it. In fact, neither of us had spoken about it since before the night of Antonia's party when I found Aquila too full of wine with the girl's head on his lap.

Unaware of any of this, Paul unwittingly added to my burdens by asking me to make friends of the increasing number of women in our growing church. So I stayed longer at Gaius's house, delaying marketing. Also, I went out of my way to call on women in their homes. By now the church membership included women from various circles: tradesmen's wives, wealthy matrons of the villas, workers' women in the poorer sections of the city. I was careful never to identify myself with any one circle, which would exclude me from others. I tried to be especially kind to slaves, who had nothing of their own to offer but who had freedom to accept spiritual belief in Jesus as their ultimate liberty.

One morning when I was reasonably free I took Antonia's suggestion and went to the library. I found my friend with three of her friends. One I remembered meeting at the party: Druda. Antonia said I had met the others too, Lida and Cornelia. Among the crowd that night, I could not have known which ones I met.

Druda greeted me with the same supercilious air. The others were very friendly. They were engaged in reading by turns the play *Antigone*, by Sophocles. They were seated on couches in a corner of the large library room, far enough to themselves to keep from disturbing other readers.

Lida moved over on her couch to make room for me.

"Should we start again?" Antonia asked. "We're quite well along with it—"

"Please," I protested, "just keep on. I can read the first part another time."

"It's a sad play," Antonia explained. "The poor girl gave up her life for what she believed was right."

"She needn't have," Druda remarked. "It was family pride; she deliberately went against the king's orders. Anyway, she achieved nothing by sprinkling a little dust on her brother's body; she didn't bury him at all."

"Every time I read the play, I wish the king would arrive in time to save her from the hanging," Lida said. "I hold my breath as I read to see if it might happen once."

"Sometimes you talk nonsense, Lida dear," Druda commented.

Antonia had been reading when I came in. She picked up the parchment pages and continued. Of course, I understood nothing of the story, as I had never read it. I did not tell them.

But the music of the words fascinated me. Antonia's voice was clear and sweet, and she put such pathos into her interpretation. One passage especially struck me for its relevance to our time. I remember it well enough to quote, as later on I bought a copy of the play and read it despite its pagan orientation.

73

But dreadful is the mysterious power of fate, there is no deliverance from it by wealth or by war, by fenced city, or dark, sea-beaten ships.

And bonds tamed the son of Dryas, swift to wrath, that King of the Edonians; so paid he for his frenzied taunts, when, by the will of Dionysus, he was pent in a rocky prison. There the fierce exuberance of his madness slowly passed away. That man learned to know the god whom in his frenzy he had provoked with mockeries; for he had sought to quell the god-possessed women, and the Bacchanalian fire; and he angered the Muses that love the flute.

Cornelia, who had not spoken before, finished reading the final scenes and, with three principal characters dead, laid down the pages.

"I could cry for the poor girl Antigone," Antonia said. "I can see her hanging in that tomblike cell clasped in the arms of her dead lover."

Druda disagreed. "She should have obeyed the command of the king. Then all would have ended happily."

"But the king was a vicious monster," Lida objected. "The gods were right in punishing him so dreadfully."

I still had little idea of what they were talking about. It did not matter, for Druda tossed the next question at me.

"Priscilla, you don't believe in our gods, do you? You believe in the new God of the Christians; you told me at the party."

I did not like the tone of her voice. "How can you believe in your gods when you know quite well they do not exist?" I replied. "There's only one God in Heaven, and he is not new. He created the world, and all of us in it—including you."

There was silence.

Then Lida said, "I must go; I have some shopping to do."

I noticed that Cornelia, the quiet girl, looked at me with a curious interest.

And from Antonia: "Priscilla, I've been thinking since you talked with me before. I would like to know more about your God. You told me I could come to hear Paul—?"

"At the house of Gaius. Tomorrow morning?"

Antonia nodded. "Yes, this is something we should hear."

Cornelia asked quickly, "May I come too?"

"We'll all come," Antonia suggested. "Instead of reading here at the library."

"I'll meet you there," I agreed.

The group broke up. Antonia asked me to wait a moment, that she had something to tell me. And I had something to ask of her. The other three left with proper expressions of pleasure at meeting me, except for Druda, who was angry over what I had said to her. I didn't care; she deserved it.

Antonia asked at once, "Have you seen Dino?"

"No, only that one night. Why should I?"

"He said he would find you." Antonia laughed. "Do you know, I think he's afraid of you."

"Afraid of me?" I laughed in turn. "That's not possible."

"He's afraid you'll convince him to be a follower of your God."

"For his own sake he will have to convince himself. It is God whom he should fear."

"I will tell him that. I'm seeing him tonight. Why don't you go to see him yourself? His studio is close by the marketplace, on that little street that turns off—"

"No, Antonia. I have something else to speak to you about. Perhaps you can help me."

"Of course, if I can—"

"There is a girl who has come often to listen to Paul speak in the Agora. She wants to know more about Jesus Christ, but she is too terrified to ask. She is a priestess at the Temple of Aphrodite."

Antonia stared at me, her face went pale.

I kept on. "I want no harm to come to her, but I wondered if—"

She raised her hand to stop me. "A priestess in the Temple of Aphrodite? You don't know what you are saying."

"We want to rescue her. I hoped that perhaps your husband might intervene."

"A slave girl in the Temple? She belongs to the goddess; she is bound for life, or at least the best part of it. You know why she is there?"

"I can guess."

"There are many of them," Antonia told me. "The priests train them from childhood in all the ways of prostitution, so they know nothing except the rites of the goddess. They are made to smile and laugh and do as the men ask of them as worship to Aphrodite,

goddess of erotic love. She is the mother of Aeneas, Greek hero of
the poems and hymns of Homer, who wrote about the Trojan
War. The Romans identify her with Venus. Leave her priestesses
alone, Priscilla. The men worship them as they do Aphrodite herself."

"I thought maybe your husband might buy her and set her
free."

"You must be out of your mind, Priscilla. Anyway, what would
your Christ want with one of the lowest of people?"

"The lowest are the most blessed in the sight of God."

"I don't understand your religion."

Antonia, in her agitation, rose from her couch and came over to
sit by me. She took my hand in hers.

"Priscilla, I told you of my inmost secrets when we first met,"
she said. "It helped me to talk of them, as I cannot talk to other
friends for fear of gossip. There is one more secret I must tell you
now. I am losing my husband."

I was the one to turn pale. "Oh, no."

"Yes, he has lost his love and interest in me; I am no more than
his housekeeper. Of course, I know that every wife must accept
this when she reaches a certain age. We have joked together about
it—that a wife's fortieth birthday gift is her husband's freedom to
take a young mistress. But I am far from forty, and he is not taking a usual mistress. His mistress is the goddess Aphrodite."

"Now *I* don't understand."

Even before I heard the answer I knew what it would be.

"He goes to the Temple feasts regularly now, nearly every
night. You know how I want a child, Priscilla. My husband no
longer comes to me. We sleep apart."

"I don't know what to say, Antonia, it is very sad."

"There is nothing you can say, but it helps to talk to you. There
is no one else I can confide in. You see why, beyond all other
things, I cannot help with the slave girl. She may be one of those
who keep him away from me, although it would not be her fault. I
hold nothing against any of them. They do only what they are
trained to do."

"A slave's body may belong to his master," I said, "but his or
her belief, or faith, can belong to the god of his choice."

"Under Roman law that is true," Antonia agreed. "But a slave whose body already belongs to a god has no choice. The priests see to that."

"There was a phrase that you read from your play," I reminded her. "It was, *the god-possessed women.*"

"I hadn't thought of that. How true!"

She stood up again. With her back to me, she said in a low voice, "I wonder if—perhaps—your Christ might have an answer for me. I need one."

I rose impetuously from the couch and took her hands in mine. "Listen to me, Antonia: We will pray together to our Lord Jesus Christ."

We bowed our heads, and as I spoke slowly, Antonia repeated the words after me.

"Lord Jesus, Son of our Father in Heaven, Thou hast promised to hear all who come to Thee in sorrow and laden with trouble. Grant that we, Thy servants Antonia and Priscilla, may find comfort and peace with Thee, now and for always, through the blessings of Almighty God. Amen."

She looked at me with eyes growing wide. "Priscilla! I feel stronger already. . . ."

I took her arm, and we walked out of the library together. Antonia went her way, and I did a hurried marketing at the stalls.

9

On the following morning I was up early as usual, with much on my mind. I prepared the morning meal, served Paul, and saw him off. First I told him to expect Antonia and her three friends to come to hear him, and something about each. I said I would be at Gaius's house in time to meet them. Aquila came downstairs grumpy that day. He picked up his bread, cup of goat's milk, and a bunch of grapes, and disappeared into the shop, saying little.

I began a hasty cleanup of the house. A messenger knocked at our door. He handed me a sealed note and left. I laid aside my broom and opened the note.

It read: *I will be at my studio this afternoon at 3 o'clock, waiting for you. Antonia has told you where to find me. I must see you then.—Dino.*

My face flushed with anger. After reading the note twice—three times—I tore it into small bits and threw them into the trash barrel. The effrontery of the man! To summon me like this, as if I were subject to his call!

I returned to my sweeping.

When Aquila came back into the house, I was cleaning Paul's room, folding his blanket from the couch. Sometimes Paul forgot to put things where they belonged.

"Priscilla," Aquila said, standing at the gineceo door. "I'm working on that big sail for the fishing boat. I need help in stretching out the canvas."

"Oh," I groaned, "I have to be up at the church early this morning. Antonia is bringing three friends to hear Paul."

"How long will this go on?" Aquila shouted. "I've held up on that sail for five days now, and neither you nor Paul has been near me to help. The man needs it; how can we keep going like this, with you away all the time?"

"Don't you realize what we are doing?" I'm afraid I shouted back. "This is the critical time for the church!"

"What is the matter with Silas and Timothy? And Luke? Why can't they help with the church? Isn't that why they are here?"

"Aquila, they are working from early morning till late at night. They're out teaching, making calls, baptizing people. Luke has sick people to care for. You don't realize what is going on—"

"I realize they shouldn't ask a woman to do these things. It isn't a woman's place—"

"It's the women I deal with," I cried. "It takes a woman to deal with women! They're just as important to Christ's church as men."

"What would Paul be doing if we were still in Rome and had not come to Corinth at all? What would he be doing then?"

"I don't know, maybe it's God's Will that we are here."

"God doesn't go that far," Aquila snapped. "He means us to do our work, not someone else's—"

"Aquila! How can you say that—"

"All right, I'm sorry. I'll do the best I can with the sail alone. It's just that I don't feel that I have a wife any more—in any way."

He disappeared back into his shop.

"What's more important—" I began.

I stopped myself. That last remark of his cut deeply. Yes, I had failed as a wife in the most important duty. The wrong was with me.

For a few minutes I went back to sweeping the floor. Then I gave up; my mind was not on it. I went upstairs to change from my work tunica to a stola appropriate for meeting the women. I combed out my hair, which had been hanging loosely over my back. I put it into the usual coils behind my neck and tied a light scarf over my head. I had long since abandoned the heavier scarf, which tied down under the chin.

All the time I was trying to think, to no avail. Why did so much have to arise at the wrong moment?

But before I left the house I went into the workshop. I kissed the back of Aquila's neck as he bent over to sew the sail pieces together.

"I'm sorry," I told him. "I'll try to find more time. Leave the sail until later, and I'll help you."

"Never mind," he answered. "I've done what had to be done."

I arrived at the house of Gaius shortly before Antonia. The girl Cornelia was with her. Both of them were nervous, I could see. What brought Cornelia I still didn't know, but there certainly was a reason.

Lida and Druda appeared separately. Lida came only because it was something to do. Druda's purpose was to sneer at the idea of a new God who was suddenly so much in Corinthian conversation.

I remembered suddenly another phrase read the day before from *Antigone: That man learned to know the God whom in his frenzy he had provoked with mockeries.* How easy to replace the word *man* by *woman.*

When all were together I introduced them to Paul. Antonia, of course, had met him at the games. I sensed the surprise of the three who had never seen him. Instead of a tall, commanding presence, there stood a man in a dull brown robe, with beard, long arms, and a great chest. But if they were disappointed, they were subdued by the way Paul's intense gaze seemed to reach in turn into their very beings.

Gaius's atrium was a place of quiet. For Sunday services the room was filled with benches. Other furnishings were gone for lack of space, except for a table at the end of the rectangular area where Paul stood. Other people had come for Paul's teaching. Some knelt in prayer, others simply waited.

I took the four women to a bench and knelt beside them to pray, as I always do in God's presence. Druda was scornful, the others uneasy. At the appointed time Paul began his teaching for the day.

He directed his words especially to my friends. His theme was the love of God. He described the many meanings of love, then added, "But the love of God for us includes all these, and reaches beyond our understanding. It fulfills and glorifies all the others. Christ Jesus on earth gave us the two greatest commandments: Love your God, love your neighbor. In these two are included all other laws."

My friends had listened with the greatest attention and emotion —even Druda. Paul had included in his talk a brief life of Christ, and stressed the meaning of the Crucifixion and Resurrection, facts that much affected his hearers.

He finished, looking at the five of us sitting together: "Jesus said, 'Come to me, all you who have heavy burdens, and I will comfort you.' That is the love of Jesus Christ for you who believe in him. Let us pray to Almighty God."

Paul kneeled, and so did all in the room. Even Druda, glancing about first, followed. Cornelia was crying, Antonia's eyes moist.

"Almighty God, bless those in this room, that they may come into the Way of Christ and receive your infinite goodness for their comfort, in the Name of Christ Jesus. Amen."

He rose and spread out his hands. He was finished for the morning.

Cornelia stood up and pushed past us, blindly. She rushed to Paul and fell at his feet, clutching his robe.

"Master, I believe, I believe! Take me, master, take me to your God! My husband has been incurably lame for a year, he can do nothing; I have two small sons, I am so alone with so much worry! Master, help me!"

She collapsed on the floor, sobbing.

Paul lifted her up. He put his hand on her head.

"The Lord God hears you," he said. "Believe in him and you will receive his strength in your troubles. Come tomorrow, that you may be baptized in Christ's Name and receive the Holy Spirit, which will make you strong and ease your worries."

At three o'clock that afternoon by the sundial in the market-place I stood in front of Dino's house and, after a final hesitation, knocked at his door.

I hope that Almighty God in his mercy may forgive every woman who allows herself through vain conceit and pleasing compliments to be led into temptation.

All day I had told myself, "No, no." I would not be demeaned by jumping at his arbitrary summons. My pride would not let me go. But some spirit inside me whispered, "Perhaps by going you can make him a Christian too. You know what happened this morning for Cornelia. Isn't it worth while to try?"

The nagging by the spirit was only an excuse; I knew it in my conscience. I knew that in reality I was intrigued by the persistent attention from a man with worldly charm who could have had on his couch almost any woman in Corinth. And undoubtedly he already had had many of them, which made his compliments only the more curiously fascinating.

Even as I knocked, the door opened.

"I knew you would come," he said smiling. "I was waiting."

He took my hand, led me inside, and closed the front door. We were in a small hallway.

"You could not have known that," I said. "After the arbitrary note I was exceedingly angry."

"This way." He ignored my remark, still holding my hand. "My studio is upstairs, where there is light."

He guided me up a narrow stone stairway to a back room above. Here the afternoon light poured through a window across a table with drawings on it. The small room also contained a chest, a covered couch—and a small table with a vase of oriental roses.

"Usually my workroom is a tangle," Dino remarked. "I've tried in my own way to make it look good for you."

I smiled. "It is very nice. The roses are lovely. I must tell you, Dino, that I have come not for the purpose I know you have planned, but for another."

81

"Whatever the reason, you are here. I will show you the drawings for the development. As a Roman you can help me with your opinion on the Greek-Roman co-ordination I am attempting. Please tell me what you think; I respect your opinion."

I stood beside him, leaning over the table as he pointed out his plans for the façades of the temple on one side and the baths/library on the other side of a high arch leading into a long promenade under a series of Roman arches.

"The façades are Greek, with Corinthian columns. Corinthian is the current style in Greece, very popular, and appropriate for this work. Here are drawings for the triangle friezes in front of each building."

For the temple Dino had drawn a semi-nude Venus with a star over her shoulder, a bunch of grapes in one hand and a pomegranate in the other. Around the central figure were to be unclothed female figures cavorting. To match it on the baths and library building, Dino had designed a frieze with a central nude female, side view, one arm over her shoulder toward the back with a sponge in her hand. More maidens cavorted around her, some reading scrolls, others under simulated waterfalls.

"They are indeed beautiful," I said. "But a temple without purpose—without a true God—leaves something wanting; better it be the baths or the library, but not a place to worship."

"Forget the temple to worship; forget Venus as a symbol of worship. I am trying to glorify the female body—joyfully and sensually. Priscilla, you are the one who can do that. I want you to be the model of all women, of all beauty, of all worship, or what that creation is which a man looks for all his life! You must pose for the final drawings."

I stopped breathing for a moment. "Dino, don't say such things. They are wicked—they are wrong."

"Why?" he asked. He was very serious.

"I don't know why," I answered. "But you know it is impossible; you and I have two very different backgrounds. What you may see as right is wrong for me."

"Priscilla—" He picked up my hand, held it for a moment. "I do not mean to offend you. I respect what you believe, but we have been made a man and a woman with all the feelings and desires natural to us."

He kissed the back of my hand, then inside, between my fingers. I tried to take my hand away, but his arm went swiftly around my waist and pulled me close.

"Since that night I met you I have thought of no one else, seen no one else. It has never happened to me. I think all day, I dream all night of you. You have what I need. You have my life."

His face was over mine, his dark eyes close, his breath mingling with my own. For a moment I closed my eyes—*O God, give me strength*—His mouth came down on mine, I felt his tongue, his body pressed tight. His other arm encircled me, his hand on my back low down. All my senses suddenly went on fire.

For a moment I— but with all my strength I pushed back. His hold was too strong, I felt him the more. I turned my head.

"If only I were— but I'm not. I couldn't hate you but I would hate myself." I managed to gasp the words. "You can't possibly understand; it's agony. I would be miserable forever. Don't, don't let me have that misery, that guilt."

He released me partly, but the warmth of his body stayed close.

"I have never forced my love on a woman," he said. "I never had to. You are a strange one. I don't understand you now any more than I did the night I met you. I know you want me, but you deny the very beauty of love."

"This is not love, this is physical desire that would overrule our minds, our work, our reason for being here on earth. If you love me, let me be free from the guilt I already have."

Slowly he let me go.

"I have lost," he said. He looked at me closely. "Tell me, what was your purpose in coming here?"

I felt as if a cold wind had whipped across my body.

"Forgive me," I murmured. "I made an excuse to myself that by coming here I might make you see my way of life; I wanted to take you to hear Paul speak of God and Christ. I was wrong. Again I say try to forgive me. I, too, have lost."

Neither of us moved for a moment. There was a dreadful silence.

Then he told me, "I will go with you to hear Paul. When?"

"Perhaps, tomorrow?" I asked hesitantly. "At the house of Gaius, ten o'clock?"

I turned to go down the steps. Dino followed me to the narrow hallway below and opened the front door.

On the street I turned back once and looked over my shoulder. Dino was watching me. I waved.

On the evening of that same day, Aquila went to the workshop as usual. After washing the utensils of our evening meal, I returned to Paul.

"May I talk with you?" I asked him. "About myself. I have something to tell you of which I am not proud."

"Speak freely, my Prisca." He laughed, which he seldom did. "I can think of little about which you would have to confess."

"Don't laugh. You won't like what I have to say."

I told him the whole story of Dino, from our first meeting at Antonia's party, what Antonia told me later about his attraction for me, to what I did that afternoon. I forced myself to spare nothing in embarrassment about my feelings when Dino held me in his arms—how close I came to yielding.

I finished by telling him that Dino said he would come to hear him teach. Perhaps only to please me, but he might be there the next morning.

Paul waited a few moments before saying anything. He just looked at me intently.

"Why did you tell me these things?" he asked.

Such an unexpected question caught me unawares. My eyes grew wide.

"I— I— I guess I wanted to free myself of guilt; I went to Dino's house when I knew I should not. I thought—if I told you—"

"That I would forgive you? Who am I? Only a man. If you want to confess a guilt, go to one stronger than I am, go to Christ Jesus in your prayers. He will intercede for you directly to God. No man can do that. Only you yourself, through God's Holy Spirit within you."

I broke down completely. I cried, in reaction to all I had built up within myself.

Paul stood up from his seat, walked around the room, and stopped in front of me sitting on the couch.

"Prisca," he said, "I think I can tell you some things that will release you from confusion. You know how I can speak bluntly. If

84

you had yielded to the temptation of your body, I believe Christ would have forgiven you. He himself has lived as a human person on earth and knows all the temptations to which every man and woman are exposed. This is not to be taken as an excuse for giving in to temptation, no, never! But if any person falls to temptation in weakness despite his resolves, Christ will understand."

He reached out to touch the top of my head. I bowed low with my hands covering my face.

"I am glad for your experience," he said. "You have tested yourself with one of the greatest temptations a woman can feel, and you did not yield."

I looked up at him through tears. "Thank you, Paul."

I stood up, wiping my tears away.

"Now, Prisca, I have something more to say to you. Sit down again."

I did, as he walked around the room once more.

"I told you that I speak bluntly. I have noticed that for some time your husband has been in strange moods. I believe I guess the reason."

I was alarmed now. "Has Aquila talked with you today?"

"To me? No, Prisca, I assure you. You have been very busy lately, I know. So has he. Every wife has a duty to her husband, as also a husband has a duty to his wife. If a husband and wife do not have each other at suitable times, then one or the other, or both, will seek pleasures elsewhere. I say this as a warning."

I stared at him, speechless.

Paul continued. "Write this in your memory, my good Prisca: A wife's body belongs to her husband, and a husband's body belongs to his wife. Use your possessions well and often, dear ones, that neither of you will seek temptations in other places. Now good night, and I thank you in Christ's Name for all the help you are giving me in this work of ours."

After he had gone to his room I sat stunned. For Paul to say what he had. . . . Slowly I rose and went over to open the front door for a moment. Our part of the city was quiet at this hour. The fresh night air held the tang of the not-too-distant sea. I looked up at the bright shining stars, and thought of the wonder of God's world, of its greatness and infinity.

I thought of God's people, and how each person was intended

to relate to others. I recalled the events of the day—with Aquila, Antonia, Cornelia, Dino, now Paul. Yes, there was a wondrous greatness of God's world. How easily could one make it otherwise for oneself!

As I leaned against the frame of the doorway, I felt the joy of being alive—of being myself. I whispered aloud, "I thank Thee, my God, for what I am, and for what, with Thy help, I can be for others!"

I turned back into the house, closed and locked the door. Aquila was still working in the shop, cutting canvas.

Instead of calling, I went in to him. "Aquila, it's time to stop."

He nodded. "I've almost finished this piece. I'll be up at once. You go ahead."

I took one of the lighted lamps with me and climbed the stairs to our room. When Aquila came, I put my arms around his neck.

"Kiss me, Aquila. Tonight you have your wife again. I want my husband."

10

On the way to Gaius's house the following morning, I was exuberant. My spirits were high, the sun had not yet reached its heat, the sky was cloudless blue, the people passing on the street nodded and smiled in greeting. Children were out playing games.

I wanted to sing along with the little yellow bird in a cage hanging beside a doorway.

More than all else, I was happy about what had happened during the night. Aquila and I had found again the joy of our marriage. It had been one of our most wonderful nights.

Shortly before ten o'clock I arrived at the house of Gaius to find Cornelia and Antonia waiting for me. Cornelia was happy with anticipation of her baptism. Antonia was solemn in contrast.

"I told Cyrus last night I wanted to be baptized a Christian along with Cornelia," she said. "He will not allow it. He was very angry. He reminded me that the place of a wife was to obey her husband's commands, and no more. A wife must hold to the faith of her husband. That's Aphrodite! How can I believe in her when she takes my husband away? Priscilla, what should I do?"

"Antonia, be calm," I cautioned her. "If your husband feels this way you must obey him. That doesn't mean that you can't believe in Jesus for yourself, and pray to him."

A good number of people were gathering together that day, most of whom were women. I greeted those I knew, among them a Jewish woman from Rome named Phoebe. She had been a refugee from the Emperor Claudius' edict that drove us from Rome, but she had settled at Cenchreae, the eastern port town for Corinth. I heard that she had done a great deal of missionary work there among wayward girls in that town. Phoebe knew of Paul, had come up to hear him. Paul had told her that she could be of help in his ministry in the church.

Among the men I noticed Stephanas, who came often to the morning meetings. Gaius was welcoming newcomers at the door, showing them where to sit. Silas and Timothy both were there. Silas was to perform the baptism ceremony.

At precisely ten o'clock Dino arrived.

"I have come," he announced cheerfully.

"I'm glad," I told him. "I really am."

I took him over to Antonia and Cornelia, and we all sat together.

Paul announced Cornelia's baptism. She went hesitantly forward. Silas administered the sacrament. Cornelia knelt and received the gift of the Holy Spirit with the blessing in Christ's Name.

"Praise be to God," I heard her murmur.

She stood up and smiled at everyone with a confidence I had not expected from one so quiet—little though I knew her.

Paul had talked the day before about God's love. His subject on this morning had to do with the temptations in life, and God's response. Had he planned this after my confessions the night before? With Dino sitting beside me, I felt uneasy.

Since the world began, Paul explained, our invisible God made himself visible to all men through his creations of nature. His everlasting power and divinity were clearly to be seen. But mankind, though able to know God, thought itself wise and became foolish.

Men hid the Truth of God in wickedness. They changed the glory of an incorruptible God into the corruptible image of man. So God abandoned these people to their own dishonors, and they fell into ways of corruption, injustice, self-conceit, envy, cruelty, murder, with anti-God idol worship, defilements of their bodies, and all manner of wrong.

At a time long ago God did give to the Jewish people his Law, including the Ten Commandments, as definitions of sin. But Jesus Christ went further than the Law. Through Jesus we know the righteousness of God, and through righteousness alone we will be judged by Almighty God.

"What is righteousness?" Paul asked. I was glad that he answered his own question, for since childhood I had heard so much of the word that its meaning became lost to me. I had visualized a righteous person as one just too good to be true. Paul gave me the definition I needed.

"In my opinion," Paul told us, "it is an honest and open life, founded on love for God and respect for humanity. It is a life free of self-conceit, of malice, and of subterfuge, free of adultery, fornication, and unnatural defilement of the body. It must be a life for truth, honor, and peace, without judgment of errors against others for acts that we may be committing ourselves. This must be a life of good work, not alone for self-profit but for the profit of all. This life will stand well in the judgment of Almighty God.

"Yet this life will be beset by temptations on every side, and the choice between right and wrong will always be difficult," Paul went on. "Christ knows this, and he will be forgiving of transgressions, provided repentance is sincere and the transgression is involuntary, not planned for its own sake. But for those who give up righteousness for unrighteousness, who ignore our God in Heaven in pursuit of empty desires and conceits, who offer themselves to licentiousness and idolatry—of one form or another—these will suffer trouble, anguish, and death through the anger of God."

I had become so absorbed by Paul's explanations that I had forgotten Dino. Now I glanced at him as Paul announced the closing prayer. Dino looked at me, and drew a deep breath.

"I think I can understand you now," he whispered. "Your Paul is a powerful man."

"He speaks for a powerful God," I murmured in reply.

He nodded. "Yes, I believe it."

Following the prayer, I took Dino up to meet Paul.

"Master," Dino said, "thank you for permitting me to hear you. It has meant much to me. All my life I have believed in nothing except my work. I want only to create glorious works and buildings for use and inspiration for all people. You make me wonder if there is something even more than that."

Paul smiled and took Dino's hand. "By your works shall you be judged," he said cryptically. "I trust that you may find what you truly seek in the glory of Almighty God."

As Dino and I were leaving, Antonia and Cornelia were waiting for us at the door.

Timothy came running up to me. "The girl—Alcesta—from the Temple of Aphrodite," he cried urgently. "She is ill; please come quickly."

"Where is she?"

Timothy pointed to the far side of the atrium.

Antonia put her hand to her mouth. "The Temple—"

I hurried across the room, Dino followed with Timothy.

"Maybe I can help?" Dino asked.

We found the girl crumpled on a bench, dazed, crying. I knelt beside her, took her in my arms. "What is it?" I said to her. "Don't be afraid, tell me."

She seemed not to see me, but she kept talking incoherently. She seemed to be saying things in strange languages. Bewildered, I looked up at Timothy and Dino.

"How did she come here?" I asked Timothy.

"I saw her again in the Agora, listening to Paul. I told her to come today."

I tried to soothe the girl, in an effort to find out what was wrong. Her voice only rose higher with incomprehensible words. Her mind seemed far away.

Suddenly I realized what it was.

"She is talking in tongues!" I exclaimed. "It's a miracle. Quickly, bring Paul as fast as you can!"

Paul came while the girl was still lying in my arms, now calling out loudly in a language unknown to any of us. Her eyes rolled. Paul paused and listened for a moment. Then he leaned over and released her from my arms, took her hands, and pulled her to her feet.

"The Holy Spirit has come to you," he said gently. "God has received you. You are blessed beyond all others."

I told Paul in a low voice, "Her name is Alcesta, a slave girl from the Temple of Aphrodite."

Her mantle had fallen open, revealing the short tunica uniform of the priestess of the Temple. She came to her senses, stopped speaking. Her eyes focused on each of us in turn. Then she pulled back in fright.

Paul was more gentle than I had ever known him as he spoke again. "Alcesta, come with me to the Temple. God will protect you. He will set you free."

"I am afraid," she murmured, and shuddered.

Paul held her hand and led her away. The two disappeared together through the atrium door.

Antonia and Cornelia had gone already. Dino and I left the house of Gaius in silence. The hot sun and glare of the street brought us to some sense of reality.

"I must go to the market," I suddenly remembered.

"I'll walk with you and leave you at the corner leading to my house," he replied.

After we had gone a short way, I said, "I've never seen anything like that before—talking in strange tongues. I have only heard that it happens."

"It must have been a miracle. A priestess of the Temple! I never believed in such things as miracles. I thought, once, I knew everything of the world," Dino said. "I was wrong."

He left me at the corner of his street. I went on to the market.

During the afternoon Paul returned to the house. The girl Alcesta was with him.

I had been in the workshop with Aquila, sewing. I had already told him what had happened during the morning. Now, hearing Paul, I left my work and went into the atrium. I was startled to see the two together.

"It is done," Paul said. "I took her into the Temple of Aphrodite and told all the priests assembled that the girl belongs to the true Lord God in Heaven, no longer to them. I told them that if they did not let her go free, as she was possessed by the Holy Spirit, the Lord God would bring their Temple crashing down on their heads. So I took her away."

"Paul!" I gasped. "The Roman law! She is a slave who belongs to them."

"She is a slave of God, as we all are. That is enough."

Hearing Paul's voice rise, Aquila came in.

"Prisca," Paul said more softly. "I turn this child over to you, in your custody. Take care of her."

"The soldiers will come," I tried to tell him. "They will take her away."

"I will be responsible," Paul replied. "The Lord will protect her and you. Have no fear."

Aquila interrupted. "Of course we will keep her here, but there may have to be some settlement. The Law of God is from Heaven, but the law of the Romans is here in Corinth. This could be extremely serious."

Paul's reply was angry. "I told you that God will protect this child, and you. As you believe in God and Christ, believe what I say."

"But, Paul, you—" I begged him. "What will they do to you? I am afraid for you, not for Alcesta, Aquila, and me."

"They can do nothing more than they have done before." Paul rose into a rage. "They may beat me, throw me into prison, threaten me. All these things they have done in other places. There is only one thing they have not done—and if now I die in the service of Christ, I will follow him."

He stamped off into his room.

I glanced despairingly at Aquila.

"Paul doesn't realize what he has done," he said, his voice low. "The Roman authorities for one thing, the people of the city another. These priestesses are worshiped here."

I moved quickly to the terrified girl. "Alcesta, you will be safe with us," I told her. "Come, I will show you to the room that will be yours, and be at peace."

Aquila shook his head doubtfully, returned to his work. I took Alcesta upstairs to the sleeping room we had used only for storage. It contained a couch and other furniture, and she could be near us.

I told her to take off that temple tunica, and I brought her one of my own.

I noticed from her bare body that she was not long past puberty. But her small breasts were developed and firm, and her long black hair and wide dark eyes gave her an unusual beauty for her age. Yet her fear and the strangeness of her situation made her seem pathetic and lost. My heart felt for this young one who had experienced so much and so little.

My clothes, of course, were much too big for her. My smallest tunica fell loosely around her and reached nearly to her ankles. With the aid of a sash around her narrow waist, we were able to pull in the folds and lift the low hem up a bit.

All this time, since Paul brought her to me, she had not said a word. When she looked down at herself in my too large tunica, she suddenly laughed.

Then Alcesta looked up at me with her dark, somber eyes as if searching. I realized all at once that this young girl, this child, had never really known a woman. She had been brought up by the priests, instructed by them on how to serve the men who came to worship her—or, more truthfully and specifically, who were her clients for prostitution—and had known no women except her girl companions for Aphrodite.

"Alcesta," I said to her impulsively, "I want you to know that this is your home now. As Paul said this morning, you have the blessing of God upon you. The Lord Jesus stands at your side, always."

She nodded. "Yes, I love Jesus in Heaven."

Those were the first words she spoke in our house. I have never forgotten them.

During the evening meal, with the four of us at the table, she ate very little and said only polite phrases like "Thank you." For most of the time, she stared at Paul with awe. If she had any thoughts of her usual duties at this feast hour in the Temple, or what might happen to her if she returned there, she gave no evidence of it. She had complete trust.

Neither Paul, Aquila, nor I spoke of the events of the day, talking only of casual things. Aquila and I revealed nothing of our own dread of what could happen at any moment.

I put Alcesta to bed as soon as I could after our meal. She lay

92

contentedly on the couch as I pulled a blanket over her. I kissed her good night and received in return a spontaneous hug. I left a lamp burning low in her room in case she might be frightened.

When I returned downstairs I had mixed and emotional feelings, thinking of the daughter I could never have of my own.

Paul retired early that night to read letters he had received during the day. Aquila and I stayed awake in the atrium waiting for the feared knock on the door by a squad of soldiers wanting Paul and the girl. Aquila was too disturbed to go to his workshop.

A knock did come. Both of us jumped up in alarm. I motioned to Aquila to stay away from the door; they might seize him first. They would not a woman.

Cautiously I opened it. No soldiers were there; it was Stephanas. We more than welcomed him.

He looked around the room as he entered, a frown on his forehead.

"You two are alone?" he asked. "I came to tell you what happened this afternoon. Perhaps you know—is the girl here?"

"Yes," I answered. "She is asleep upstairs, in my charge."

"Sit down, please," Aquila said, pulling a couch around for him.

"Thank you." He took the seat. "This event is most serious. I was among the congregation this morning, Priscilla, as you know. I saw something of what occurred with the girl. I already believed in the power of God, and in what Paul said today. But I have never witnessed what came afterward. I do believe this slave girl has been blessed by God himself."

He drew a deep breath as we listened.

"But what Paul did this afternoon— the story is already all over Corinth. I heard at first hand that the priests of Aphrodite appealed to the authorities to punish a man who came into their Temple, threatening them with being killed by some strange God. Then he carried away by the strength of his arms one of the priestesses who belonged to them. Those girls are revered by Corinth."

Stephanas paused again before continuing.

"Whatever one's feelings and knowledge, Paul's action was in direct contradiction to Roman law. If I had not intervened with the authorities, Paul would have been taken at once. I explained to them that Paul was a Roman citizen and therefore had to have a fair trial. So I delayed the whole matter. After that I went to the Temple of Aphrodite, and as I do have some authority in this city, the priests listened to me. I told them that I myself held the belief that the God of Paul could indeed destroy their Temple and them if he was angered—that in Philippi in Macedonia, God had freed Paul from prison by causing an earthquake that broke down prison walls and opened locked doors. I told them to take this seriously, that they must not risk a confrontation with the God of Paul. They might find to their grief that Paul's God was indeed stronger than they were. Then I gave them full compensation, and double, for the loss of their slave girl. I have their receipt in writing."

"Oh, Stephanas!" I cried. "Then you have bought Alcesta from them? How wonderful you are!"

"We praise God for you," Aquila added with relief.

Stephanas raised his hand in protest. "No," he said, "I can do no more than be of assistance to Paul, to both of you, and all of your group who have shown me the Way to the living God. Tomorrow I will file the papers to give Alcesta freedom from the status of slavery. As she is under age, she will have to remain temporarily in the status of 'latin.' But she will be a free woman, no longer subject to the whims of Aphrodite's followers. You must care for her until she adjusts to the outside world. That will be difficult for her. In time I will see what I can do for her future education."

Aquila said quickly, "We will keep her here and do all we can for her." He hesitated. "You see—we have no child of our own—perhaps never. We will give Alcesta our love."

Precious and wonderful Aquila! How proud of him I was at that moment—and will never forget what he said that night.

I told Stephanas, "Paul told us that God would protect Alcesta. He was right, after our doubts. God must have sent you!"

"In the morning I will tell Paul what has been done." He stood up and smiled at us. "And I will also tell him that he must be more careful. God bless both of you, and good night."

When Paul appeared from his room in the morning, I told him
that Alcesta was safe.

"She is being made a free girl, out of the bonds of slavery.
Stephanas was here last night; he will tell you about it when he
sees you."

Paul was not surprised. "Didn't I tell you that God would protect her? You did not believe me."

He sat down to eat the piece of bread with a cupful of goat's
milk that I had put out for him.

"Paul," I asked, "how could you dare in the first place to go
into the Temple and do what you did, knowing the seriousness of
what might happen?"

"When I know that God is with me, why should I fear? I've told
you that I have been in many places of danger. I'll continue to do
so when the work of Christ calls me. Did Jesus fear when he went
into the Temple of Jerusalem and threw out the money-changers
who profaned it?"

I sighed.

As he ate his bread, Paul said to me, "I'll tell you this truly,
Prisca. One day, these temple walls will crash down and be buried
and forgotten under the sands. And the rulers of the government
will perish. These things I know, and the Word of God will endure
forever."

I left the house for the church meeting while Alcesta was still
asleep. Aquila promised to watch out for her when she awakened;
she would still be nervous.

The morning was as bright and cheerful as the day before, but
now I felt qualms of uneasiness. My feeling was not made less
when I met Antonia waiting for me at the door of Gaius's house.

"Priscilla," she told me in a low voice, "the story of your Paul
is being talked about by everyone in Corinth, how he attacked

Aphrodite's Temple yesterday and carried away one of the girls. There's another story, too, that she was the girl here yesterday morning who went out of her mind after hearing Paul talk. Some people heard her speaking in that unknown language. I heard as well. Is this true, Priscilla?"

"Antonia, it is all over now, the girl is safe. She was not out of her mind, I assure you."

"It's magic, some terrible magic." Antonia was very agitated. "More than that: my husband is in a fury that his Temple should be so desecrated. He swears revenge. . . . I'm afraid for you, Priscilla."

"Don't be afraid for us, nothing can happen. All is taken care of."

"Not with Cyrus, it isn't. Priscilla—this is hard for me to say— the girl's name was Alcesta, didn't I hear that? She was one— one of my husband's . . . favorites."

"Antonia!" I said sharply. "Don't tell me that. All of it is over; the girl is free! She has a new life, the old is forgotten forever!"

"But Cyrus—"

Suddenly Paul was standing beside us.

"I am glad to see you return," he greeted Antonia. "You are welcome here. I hope you will hear what I have to say this morning."

Antonia for a moment lost her voice to make a reply. She flushed with embarrassment.

I filled in quickly. "Antonia has come to hear more of the Way. She was just telling me that her husband is very angry. He belongs to the cult of Aphrodite."

Paul nodded. "So are many angry in Corinth. They are angry because they worship in vain a false and useless idol made by man. They have not yet heard the Word of the true God. Tell your husband to bring his anger to me."

"That would be dangerous," Antonia said. "You do not know my husband when he is angry."

Smiling, Paul replied, "Perhaps he is angry because he has forgotten his wife."

Paul turned away and disappeared into the house.

"Priscilla, you told him!" Antonia cried. "What I said was in confidence—"

"Wait, Antonia, I did not tell him. I respect your confidences. Remember, you told me about Alcesta just a moment ago. Paul must have known it for himself."

"Then this is magic. I'm leaving."

"What good will that do?" I asked. "Come, sit with me."

Antonia did, hesitantly. She heard Paul denounce the evil practice of idol worship. He condemned in harsh tones those who could let themselves be led into reverence of wanton lust and barbarian carnality. He decried the sponsors of such degradation of the human spirit, with all its consequences of misery and suffering.

Paul's anger was evident to all who heard, and I praised him silently within myself for it. He—Paul, apostle for Jesus—had personally invaded the sacred temple of the pagan goddess, whose priests took children into the slavery of men's depraved natures. Surely no one in the city of Corinth had ever dared to give in public the castigation of Aphrodite worshipers that Paul did that morning.

Then he tore into shreds the fables of Olympus. The men who believed such folly were only those who dared not face the Truth of the real God in Heaven. With blazing eyes and warning voice, Paul declared that he wished all in Corinth would come to hear him.

A number of Greeks were in the atrium of Gaius's house that morning, among them those who came out of curiosity to hear the man who challenged the priests of Aphrodite. There was silence through the room when he finished—and awe. We soon learned that his words were being repeated throughout the city. The rewards—and the penalties—were many.

Antonia was astounded. "How could your Paul have the courage to say these things here in Corinth? I fear for him, and you. I wish my husband could have heard— but it is better that he did not."

"Perhaps he will," I replied. "Paul's message is for the world to hear."

It was a long time before Antonia's husband did come to the Christian church. Antonia came as often as she could to hear Paul, in company with Cornelia, who had become one of the most devout in worship. Sometimes Lida was with them, half in belief and

97

half in wonder. The reading group of the four at the library fell apart, much to Druda's disgust as I was told.

Meanwhile Cyrus, Antonia's husband, continued to attend the feasts and to worship at Aphrodite's Temple. He must have heard frequently about the Christians, for after the slave-girl episode a number of the regular devotees of the goddess left pagan worship and were baptized into Christian belief. And other Gentiles, from the great Temple of Apollo, accepted faith in the Christian God.

Dino did not return to Gaius's house, but I did see him frequently at parties given by others of that Corinthian group. Aquila and I were increasingly invited into the social life around us, and usually we accepted. After all that had happened, we felt that it was right to go out and be seen, and not hide ourselves. But the parties were nothing like the orgiastic affair of Antonia's. Either in deference to us or to the influence of other Christians now among the guests, these dining parties were small and relatively restrained.

Through them we came to know many of the younger couples of Corinth. The city became more and more our own home.

In our social activities we did not neglect other friends. We invited the Jews who accepted Christ to our house a number of times, among them Chloe, my good friend, and Crispus, too. With them we had the Gentiles as well, as we believed that the company of Jesus meant full companionship of faith. In this way they had opportunity to meet Paul through a shared informal association.

One incident did trouble me, not for myself but for the church. I was surprised when I learned that Melas, the young man we had met at the games with Laodice, his stepmother, had joined the church. I did not like him and could not trust him. His conversion to Christ seemed to me an act with a motive. His rather insolent manner and dissolute appearance belied real faith in God. But, I argued with myself, I could have been too much repulsed by his insinuating attitude toward me. So, I thought, perhaps I was only prejudiced.

Yet, when he brought Laodice with him to church services, I shuddered. Laodice's husband, the old man, never appeared anywhere. Something indeed was odd. . . .

In our home Alcesta slowly adjusted to the normal world

around her. I bought for her suitable clothing, of course. For a long time she was afraid to go out of doors, always fearful that the soldiers or the priests would see her and take her. Her nightmares, however, became less frequent, and suddenly they stopped altogether. At mealtimes we talked casually of events of the Empire and the humorous things that happened during each day. She was intelligent and eager to know what had been previously forbidden to her. I taught her to sew the heavy pieces of canvas in the workshop, so that she was able to help make the sails, awnings, and tents.

Even from the beginning, Aquila said, "I love that child as I would my own daughter— Excuse me, Priscilla. I am afraid one day she must grow up and leave us."

I kissed him. "So do I, dear Aquila. I feel the joy that every mother must feel."

At last Alcesta was not afraid to appear on the street, and then she went with me each day to hear Paul's teaching. Afterward she helped me in the marketplace, a chore she undertook with enthusiasm. So she grew close to Aquila and to me.

Long before, Stephanas had given her the magistrate's papers proving evidence of her freed status. She was classed as "latin," not yet a full citizen of the Empire. But she was free—free from commands and ignoble tyranny.

One evening I was with Alcesta as usual, before she went to sleep. Each night I made a practice of kneeling with her beside the couch as we both said prayers of thanksgiving to the Lord God and to Jesus Christ. This time, as we stood up from our prayers, Alcesta said something deeply startling.

"One night, a while ago, I had a dream about Jesus," she confided. "Would you like to hear about it?"

"Yes, please, Alcesta, tell me."

She sat on the couch. I took the place beside her.

"I dreamt that he came to see me," she said. "At first I was frightened and wanted to call you, but then he spoke so gently I wasn't afraid any more." She pointed. "He stood over there somewhere, near the window."

"What did he say in your dream?"

"He told me about myself, mostly. He wants me to be a mother to many children, very many, not just my own. He wants me to take care of children who don't have mothers of *their* own—the way you take care of me, I suppose he meant. And I can learn how to take care of those who are sick, and lonely and hungry."

"That's a wonderful dream," I agreed. I felt awed as I listened to this beautiful child. "Did you say anything to Jesus?"

She thought for a moment. "I don't think so; I just listened. He said more: that I should teach all the children about him and his Father in Heaven, as you and Paul teach people. I should teach them so that they will remember, and teach their own children in turn. In that way I would help the Kingdom of God to grow."

She was silent again. Then she added, "I guess I woke up after that, because he wasn't there any more."

"Alcesta, I think something very wonderful has happened to you. You may know now what you will do when you are older. You may have been chosen by God to help him on earth."

Alcesta smiled. "I know it is what I am going to do, and I am happy all over." She threw her arms around my neck. "Thank you for showing me what having a mother means. I never really had one, you know, because my mother sold me to the priests of the Temple when I was just starting to grow up. She must never have loved me."

I tried to hide my shock; this was the first time since the girl had been in our care that she had mentioned her past. "We don't have to think of that any more, Alcesta. It's something to be forgotten."

"No," Alcesta replied, "how can I forget? I know it is over, I'm reborn, as Paul told me. Jesus has received me. If I do not remember the things of myself, how can I understand those children?"

I was left without an answer. I put my arm around her and hugged her. "You are wiser, my child, than I am."

"No, no, never, but I am different. You do not know what it is like not to have the love of a mother and father as a child. You are giving me so much, and Aquila, too. Stephanas has promised that I will be taught all the knowledge I must know. I am very happy."

"I am happy too, Alcesta." My throat tightened with emotion. "Now you are going to be like all the other girls your own age.

You will learn many things. Have fun and laughter, surrounded by those who love you. Now go to sleep, my little one. God will protect you and be with you."

I extinguished the light and left Alcesta curled up, ready for sleep.

12

First autumn and then winter—our third in Corinth—moved along uneventfully. We had the usual rains and cold winds from the north, but always interspersed with days of bright sunshine.

Our business continued to prosper, and with a more normal routine at the church I had more time to assist Aquila. Paul, too, had time to spare in the workshop, especially during periods of rain, when he did not attempt to find conversation in the open Agora. And we had Alcesta's help as well.

New members were coming to our Christian church, keeping Silas and Timothy busy with teaching the Way of Jesus as supplements to Paul's morning sessions. I continued with the women of the church, and in turn had their help.

One morning, Antonia came to me joyfully.

"Priscilla, guess! Cyrus has come back into my room, we are sleeping together! Oh, Priscilla, I hope so for our child!"

"Antonia, didn't the physician warn you, after three times, not to do it again?"

"I don't care; I'll die if I must. I want a child so much, and so does Cyrus. I'm sure he went to that Temple of Aphrodite because he was disgusted with me. He said the other day he wants nothing to do with religion; he doesn't believe in anything now."

"Perhaps that is the first step toward the Christian Church?"

Antonia smiled happily. "I'm hoping," she said. "At least I have him back."

Lida, too, finally accepted belief in Jesus, and persuaded her husband—his name was Pirros—to join her in baptism. Both of them had become disillusioned with worshiping unresponsive pieces of stone, Lida said.

To everyone's surprise, Antonia's other friend, Druda, the skeptical one, came to Gaius's house one day to say that she wanted to learn about the Way. She spoke to me first, and it was my turn to be skeptical of her. Very bluntly, I asked her if she had in mind replacing the former social library readings with social mornings at our church, and nothing more. With convincing sincerity she told me that she felt her life was empty. She hoped the church might fill it. I introduced her to Silas, that he might teach her the Way.

Then our relatively calm daily living suddenly came crashing down around us.

It happened on a normal morning, when Paul had left the house as usual and I remained behind with Alcesta to do household chores. Aquila was already in the shop.

A loud, desperate knocking resounded on our door. When I opened it, I found Timothy outside. His face was white.

"Paul—" Breathlessly he tried to speak. "The soldiers—they have taken him away--to prison."

"Timothy! Come inside. Aquila," I cried out, "come here."

Aquila, Alcesta, and I listened in horror as Timothy explained. When Paul arrived at the house of Gaius, a squad of soldiers was waiting for him in the street. The Roman centurion in charge immediately arrested him. Witnesses to identify Paul to the centurion were Sosthenes, now leader of the synagogue next door, and a group of the elders. They had also been waiting for Paul's arrival to denounce him.

"All of us were in the house, and knew nothing of it," Timothy exclaimed. "Apparently Paul demanded that we be told what was happening. The centurion allowed that, and a soldier knocked on the door and Bendis opened it."

Bendis screamed, he said. Timothy ran out into the street, along with Silas and Gaius. Luke happened to be in the house as well, and he followed. They found that the soldiers had already bound Paul with chains. Sosthenes and his group were standing nearby.

Gaius insisted that the centurion state the charges. He replied he did not know them; he thought that this had something to do with sedition against the Empire, he wasn't certain. His orders were to take Paul to prison on command of Gallio, the new pro-consul from Rome in Corinth.

Gallio's name was known to everyone. He had taken his post as Roman proconsul of Achaia on the previous first day of July. Already Gallio had a good reputation for fairness as governor representing Caesar to the whole province, including Corinth and Athens. His full name was Lucius Junius Gallio, and rumors said that his brother was the philosopher Seneca in Rome, tutor to the boy Nero, the stepson of Emperor Claudius. Therefore, gossip surmised, Gallio was close to the palace of Caesar himself.

"Gaius is trying to find out more information," Timothy reported. "Luke has gone to Stephanas, Silas is seeking Crispus, hoping that through his synagogue associations he can discover more of Sosthenes' intentions. I have come here to tell you—"

"What can we do?" I cried out in desperation.

"Nothing now," Timothy said. "I'll go back to Gaius's house, and as soon as something is known—"

Aquila intervened. "Wait! I think we should all go with you to Gaius's house. We can be together. . . ."

That was what we did. Aquila, Alcesta, and I went immediately with Timothy to the house of our church, finding there a number of the congregation who had come to hear Paul speak that morning. On learning the shocking news from Bendis, they waited to find out what was happening.

Among them were Antonia and Cornelia, both frightened.

All of us waited for what seemed an eternity. But we were not alone. The news seemed to be spreading all over the city, carried by those who may have seen Paul's arrest or his escort to the prison, and by word of mouth. A number of the Christian congregation—Jews and Gentiles alike—came to join us who were waiting. Many strangers asked what was happening, and even those whom we did not know expressed their sympathy. Paul apparently had great, unsuspected public support.

Meanwhile we noticed activity at the synagogue next door. Many people were coming and going. Our tension grew as the noon hour went by.

At last Gaius and Stephanas returned, with Luke. All three were weary. Yes, they had some information. Paul was to be brought before Gallio at the public judgment seat in the Agora that afternoon at four o'clock. His accusers were some of the elders of the synagogue, led by Sosthenes himself.

Gaius and Stephanas had found it impossible to see Paul in prison. He was closely guarded. And the imperial authorities in the city were not speaking to anyone, pending Paul's hearing before the proconsul.

Then Crispus and Silas came in, saying that Sosthenes, at the synagogue, had refused to talk to them. But Crispus, through friends, had learned what had led to the denunciation against Paul. He gave us a report:

The story went back to the Sabbath morning when Paul walked out of the synagogue following Sosthenes' accusations of heresy. The angry elders decided then to take no action, expecting that the heretical so-called Christian Church would collapse of itself. The wayward Jews would quickly recognize the falseness of Jesus' claims as a Messiah, and return in obedience to the Law of their fathers, the elders believed. And the sinful, uncircumcised Gentiles would not for long give up the licentious ways of their pagan world.

But, Crispus told us, Sosthenes and his group had far underestimated the power of Jesus through Paul. The Christian Church had not collapsed but instead grew in strength, absorbing even more of the Jewish congregation. Alarmed, Sosthenes had written to the Sanhedrin in Jerusalem, asking for advice. He learned in reply that the Christian faith was regrettably becoming strong in many areas of the Roman Empire, especially so in parts of Macedonia and Asia, across the Aegean Sea, where Paul had evangelized the people. The Sanhedrin was greatly concerned that the churches that Paul had founded at Philippi and Thessalonica, in Galatia, and in other places had not failed but seemed to stand firm in heresies. Sosthenes did discover that many Jews, especially among the Hellenist Asian party, were strongly opposed to Paul and wished for his destruction, Crispus said.

Sosthenes then decided that he would take the initiative in crushing Paul's blasphemous teaching once and for all, not only in Corinth but consequently elsewhere. It would be the basic blow to bring the whole Christian movement to a quick ending. Certain of the elders agreed to stand with him. Crispus knew who they were but he would not repeat their names.

104

The plan's purpose was to bring the mighty power of the Roman Empire against the elusive power of Paul. It would be done through means of the Roman law, very simply. The means were kept secret within the group.

The appointment of Gallio as the governing proconsul of the imperial Roman territory of Greece provided the right opportunity. Gallio was new to the post, free from Christian influence, supposed to be close to the Emperor Claudius, and certainly would be anxious to enhance his reputation by putting down a seditious religious cult unauthorized and unrecognized by law or the Emperor. So reasoned the group of Sosthenes' elders.

The list of accusations against Paul had been carefully drawn up and presented to Gallio. Paul's arrest had been the first result.

We who heard this report from Crispus were struck with foreboding. Until the four o'clock hearing before Gallio, we were helpless, and knelt in prayer vigils for the intervening hours. By this time the Christian group came to well over fifty.

If any one of us thought that by appearing together at the hearing in the Agora we would be risking our own safety, perhaps our lives, no one mentioned it. All of us were determined to stand together for Paul; not one person went away from the house of Gaius beforehand.

At about half past three all of us in the group walked to the Agora, not far from Gaius's house. I say "walked"—better, we marched, all together, fifty and more, in silence, our footsteps ringing on the cobblestones of the street. I walked with Aquila on my left and Alcesta on my right holding my hand. Beyond Aquila were Gaius and then Stephanas at the end of the line. Stephanas in his toga of rank walked grimly, eyes narrowed, jaw protruding in anger.

But on my right Antonia marched at the side of Alcesta, with a determined Cornelia at her end of our front line of approach.

It did not occur to me until much later, due to the preoccupation of the moment, that Alcesta and Antonia were together side by side. Alcesta probably had no idea of whom she was with, in her innocence. But Antonia certainly knew that the girl had once been her own husband's favorite paramour. Such is the power of Christ's forgiving nature passed on to his followers in times of fearful stress.

When we left the street before Gaius's house, the synagogue next door was locked and bolted. Sosthenes and his group were apparently ahead of us.

The early-spring day was bright with sunshine but cold and windy. As our large body of Christians approached the plaza of the Agora, we found it already crowded with the people of Corinth. The word of the public hearing had certainly spread over the city. That events pertaining to our church of Christ had reached so far gave Paul's hearing before Gallio a special importance. I must say that I was terribly frightened for the outcome.

As our crowd arrived, Paul was being brought in to stand at the left-hand side of the tribunal judgment seat, on the far end of the Agora. My friend—my master—I choked when I saw his wrists and arms, his ankles and legs bound with chains. Three soldiers walked on each side, swords drawn, their helmets and breast armor bright under the sun. In front of Paul strode the centurion, with plumed helmet. He held out his hand at the space reserved for the accused.

We came as close behind Paul as possible. But he did not turn his head to look. His head jutted forward, his shoulders were hunched, his hands clenched in a characteristic posture of deep anger. Had I been able to see his eyes, I knew I would have found them burning with that fiercely intent expression.

I almost cried out—"Paul, Paul, my Paul"—but I held back my emotion.

The people in the Agora by now must have numbered thousands, packed tightly together. Before the high judgment seat I noticed the bulky figure of Sosthenes with some of the synagogue elders. But through the crowd I saw a scattering of roughly dressed men carrying sticks, clubs, and even stones. I drew in my breath in terror. If the judgment went against Paul—I closed my eyes. . . .

It must have been exactly four o'clock when the proconsul, Gallio, appeared from a door of the government building behind the judgment seat called the Bema. I had often seen it empty on my way to the marketplace nearby. It was a high table of blue and white marble mounted on a marble platform of the same colors.

The crowd murmured as he appeared, and fell into silence.

Gallio stood looking over the mass of people on the plaza. Then he took his seat behind the table.

He was a smooth-shaven man of middle age, clad in the purple toga of Rome's highest authority. Every move he made was quick and definite. He picked up papers lying on the table.

"I have before me accusations brought by Sosthenes, leader of the Jewish synagogue in Corinth," he said. His voice was loud and clear enough to ring out over the whole plaza. "Is the said Sosthenes here?"

In front of the high tribunal Sosthenes raised his hand. "Yes, esteemed and honored governor, I am here."

"You have brought certain serious accusations against one Paul of Tarsus," Gallio said.

He glanced to his left, where Paul stood between the soldiers.

"I have read these accusations," Gallio said to Sosthenes. "You are accusing this Paul of Tarsus of a crime against the Empire of Rome, the Emperor himself, and the peace and welfare of this province of which I am governor. Are these facts true?"

"Yes, honorable governor, they are true."

Gallio frowned for a moment. "On what evidence do you base these truths?" he asked.

"This man has established a new religion, calling on a man named Jesus who was crucified by order of Roman authorities in Jerusalem under Roman law. The man Jesus called himself the Son of our God of the Jewish faith. He incited the people to believe in him. This Paul uses the name of Jesus for his so-called religion, which is practiced in this city without authorization by Roman law or imperial decree. It is seditious, stirring people to defy the authority of our great Caesar and his imperial rule. The evidence is plainly to be seen every day in our beloved city."

A voice from the crowd suddenly shouted, "Kill Paul!"

Other shouts joined: "Kill Paul! An imposter! Condemn him, master! Great is Caesar, down with traitors! Kill Paul! Crucify him!"

Gallio raised his hand for silence. Angrily he said, "This is a fair hearing for the accused. Any man interfering with justice in this case will be subject to immediate arrest and severest punishment. Is this understood?"

He raised his finger as a signal. Immediately soldiers appeared

107

on every side of the plaza, as if from nowhere. They stood waiting, watching, open swords pointed down at an angle. I noticed that the roughly dressed men among the people furtively dropped their stones, hid sticks and clubs in the folds of their robes.

Silence fell over the plaza crowd.

"I continue," Gallio said. "Sosthenes, leader of the Jewish synagogue in Corinth, you have charged this man Paul with a new religion not authorized by Rome. This is a serious offense. You charge also that Paul stirs people to defiance of Caesar, here in this city. What proof do you have that this is so?"

Sosthenes shook his fist high in anger. "Paul preaches that an imposter named Jesus is the Son of God, the Christ promised by the prophets. He stirs up the innocent people, Jews and Gentiles alike, by saying that this Jesus gives eternal life through this Christian Church. He gives promises to the public that even our great Caesar will not give, of eternal life. . . ." Sosthenes hesitated for a brief instant. "This man's teaching is against trust in our Emperor and the Empire of Rome!" he cried out.

Gallio looked over his papers again, while all listening waited in suspense. "You have not yet given evidence, in what you have said or in your written accusation, that this Paul has spoken against Caesar or the Empire," he said. "I ask you this: is the God of Jesus, and of Paul, the same God as the God of the Jews?"

I saw Sosthenes swallow hard.

"The same God in Heaven," he said. "But Jesus was an imposter—"

"How do you know he was an imposter?"

"By the Law of our fathers, the Law from God, according to Moses and the prophets—"

"Hold!" Gallio said sharply. "Is this man Paul also a Jew?"

"He claims to be," Sosthenes said in a state of desperation. "How should I know the truth from a blasphemer?"

"You speak of the Law of your fathers, from your God. This Law is not Roman law. Has the accused Paul broken any Roman law?"

"By establishing a church not approved by Caesar, a church and religion challenging Roman law—"

"Enough of this," he said. "You are a Jew bringing charges against another Jew over a difference of opinion within your faith. I find that what you call a new religion is not so, as all of you who are Jews believe in the same God. Worship of the God of the Jews has been authorized under imperial decrees and the laws of Rome for many, many years. If Gentiles in Corinth wish to accept this God, they break no Roman law."

Gallio picked up the papers from the table.

"If Roman law were involved," he continued, "I would follow this case through to its conclusion. If I had found anything of this purported sedition, it would be a case for my judgment. But I see no threat against Caesar or the Empire in your allegations. What you have brought to me is no more than an argument between you and the accused Paul on whether this Jesus was an imposter or the Son of your God."

Then Gallio stood up. He said distinctly, "This argument is not within my jurisdiction to settle."

He looked over at Paul.

"The case is dismissed," he said so that all could hear. "Centurion, free this man from his chains. He may go as he wills."

A roar swept over the people, some cheers and some angry cries. Were they turning against Paul? . . . No.

We rushed to him even as the chains were being removed. I threw my arms around his neck and kissed his cheek. All our church members gathered around him. . . .

Something else was happening. The crowd on the plaza turned against Sosthenes. The roughnecks with clubs and sticks rushed at him; others used fists, shouting, crying out. The leader of the synagogue was being beaten; he held his hands up to his head under a storm of imprecations, blows. . . .

Up on the tribunal platform Gallio looked down and saw what was happening. He turned away and disappeared through the door behind him. . . .

Some evenings later Paul called Aquila and me into his room, the gineceo. He was very solemn.

"I have something to say to both of you." He paced up and down across the floor. "Something of special importance."

I sat at the foot of the couch, suddenly nervous. Aquila went to the bench near the door.

Paul said as he walked, "I do not know whether you understand how important the decision of the proconsul, Gallio, has been—not because he released me, that is of little consequence—but for its effect on our carrying on of our work. Gallio as a Roman has an esteemed reputation in the Empire; his decisions will be respected. This means we are free to teach the Way of Jesus everywhere without harassment under the laws of Rome. We can move about without fear, for at least a reasonable time."

Paul paused, to emphasize his point.

"What— what would have happened if Gallio had decided the other way— against us?" Aquila asked with hesitation.

"Paul would have been put into prison. Our work here would have stopped," I cried.

"I would have willingly gone to prison, but our work here, I hope, is stronger than just one man. You, Prisca, and you, Aquila, and all the others would carry on the Way of Jesus as you are doing now. It would have been much more dangerous for you, and the work would have gone much more slowly. But faith in the Way of the Lord Jesus is far stronger than the need for any mortal man. Christ is more powerful than the laws of Rome."

Paul paced the floor again.

"I am pleased now with the founding of our church in Corinth, which is strong in spite of certain flaws." He stopped walking. "It is time now to move to Ephesus, the last great city of the East untouched."

I caught my breath. Somehow I had not thought this moment would come so soon.

"I have already told Silas and Timothy that I will send them first to make prior arrangements. Luke will follow when he can. I am asking others of the disciples to meet me there, for Ephesus is a large city and I will need much help."

Paul looked at me and then Aquila.

"Prisca and Aquila, I am asking you to come with me. I wish you both to be leaders of the first church for Christ in that city."

No thunderclap, no sudden earthquake could have shaken the two of us with so great a shock. For moments we were numb.

Paul waited.

At last Aquila managed to say, "Our— our business here, it is doing well. . . ."

Paul nodded. "I have thought of that, and have talked about it with Stephanas. He will care for it until you return here, whenever you wish. You will lose nothing."

"But—" I stammered, "we have our house here, our place. . . ."

"I have spoken of that to Gaius," Paul said. "He has a friend in Ephesus whose business is with houses and properties. A house adequate for our church will be available for you. You will make a place for our Lord Christ Jesus in that city."

"We would have to start a business there," Aquila stammered. "It was difficult enough here, as you know. . . ."

"Our friend Stephanas has business and many clients in Ephesus," Paul told him. "He himself travels there often. The city is a great seaport, with commerce from all the interior of Asia. You will have a good business there, and if possible I will help you with my own hands."

"No, no," Aquila answered quickly, "you have better work to do."

"We will do all our work together," Paul replied.

Then I had a terrible thought. "Alcesta," I said. "Alcesta will go with us, won't she?"

"Prisca," Paul replied gently, "I know your love for Alcesta, and the reason for it. And Aquila's love too, as for a daughter. I must tell you something. One day, Alcesta came to me and told me of a dream. She said she had told you, too, Prisca."

"Of Jesus speaking to her?"

"Perhaps it was not a dream. Perhaps it came from Jesus."

"A vision?" I was astounded.

"Perhaps; I do not know. What I say now may hurt both of you. Stephanas has offered to take Alcesta into his home with his family, and give her the education she needs along with his own children. Alcesta is interested in learning the care of children, the abandoned ones, the sick ones."

Paul chuckled. "And it so happens the eldest son, Tarsos, is very interested in medicine. I have seen the two of them lately talking about such things." Again he chuckled. "And maybe other things too. Who knows?"

So it seemed we were going to move again, to another unknown place. A city across the Aegean Sea.

I cannot describe my own turmoil of feelings. I will not try. . . .

111

II
EPHESUS

13

Weeks passed before we finally took ship from Cenchreae for Ephesus. We could not leave until spring fully arrived, with cessation of winter storms, so that ships could venture safely into the open sea. In the meantime there was much to do, and much happened before our departure from Corinth.

Gradually Stephanas took over our flourishing business into his own sailmaking shops. He accepted new orders for us in our name to preserve our identity until our return, and he guaranteed that workmanship by his people would not bring us discredit. Aquila taught the men in the sailmaking shops how to measure and sew tents and awnings, too. Stephanas assured us also that through his own channels of business we would have the work in Ephesus necessary for our living costs.

Already we recognized Stephanas as one of the kindest of men, an opinion of ours so greatly strengthened by the dramatic events to come.

The Corinthian church for Christ required many detailed matters for attention before Paul and his associates left it to continue on its own foundation. Paul made it very clear to all that his task as appointed apostle for the Lord God was only to teach the gospel of Jesus Christ to all people everywhere who would listen to him. His responsibility was not to remain with the churches he founded but to leave them in the hands of the faithful so that he could carry the gospel farther afield. Yet he always promised to return to each church after due intervals to help with problems arising and to renew the Word of the Lord God for every congregation. If he could not come at the best times, he would write letters to the congregations to answer questions and to urge adherence to his teachings on the Way.

He made these promises to his congregation at Corinth so that they would fully understand. He continued his morning teaching until the very last day in Corinth.

As soon as news spread that Aquila and I were leaving for an uncertain time, invitations came to us from the friends we had made—including Gentiles who had not yet accepted faith in our Lord God. We went to as many as we could at this busy interval, believing that in a very minor way we could be of some influence for the Church.

In fact, sometimes at the marketplace, girls of the hetaerae group, courtesans to the wealthy, met me and asked curiously about Jesus, of whom they had heard so much at some of the parties where they were invited. I welcomed their questions and asked them to come to our Sunday church services.

If I am to be criticized for this, let me be criticized. Paul had said: "Let any who come in faith in Christ Jesus remain in their present state or occupation; what matters is to keep God's commands. The slave who receives the call to be a Christian is a freedman to the Lord. The free man who receives that call is a slave in Christ's service. Let no one become in spirit a slave to man."

Before we left Corinth two things happened that gave me the greatest personal happiness:

Luke had gone a number of times to visit Cornelia's husband, crippled and unable to move from his bed. Through his knowledge of other cases, Luke was able to teach the unfortunate man certain muscle exercises that were slowly giving him ability to walk again.

Cornelia said to me with tears of joy, "The Lord has answered my prayers. God sent Luke to my husband, to our sons, and to me! Thanks be to God forever!"

And just before we sailed, Antonia told me that she thought she was pregnant.

"Cyrus has given permission for my baptism," she exclaimed. "I can do anything I want. If I can keep this child, my husband says he will believe in Jesus!"

One afternoon, we packed our belongings and tools into a wagon belonging to Stephanas. He loaned us his own personal

116

reda, a large carriage with comfortable seats and cushions for the three of us, on the drive to Cenchreae. We said our farewells to the friends who had grown so close to us, to our city of Corinth, and with almost unbearable pain of parting to our now beloved Alcesta—until we returned again. I had to be helped into the carriage, for the tears were blinding my eyes.

We spent the night with Phoebe, our Roman friend, in her house at Cenchreae, for our ship was to sail on the early-morning tide. Silas and Timothy had earlier gone over to Ephesus to make things ready, and Luke was to follow when he completed his medical obligations, as Paul had already told us. Aquila carried letters of introduction to a number of people in Ephesus, and other letters had preceded us.

On that evening with Phoebe, Paul asked for something unusual. He wanted Aquila to cut and trim his—Paul's—hair. I had noticed that for some time past he had let it grow until it was a shaggy mane down below his neck. I teased him once about it, but he had only shaken his head and put his finger to his lips without explaining. I had not pressed him beyond that.

Well before leaving Corinth, Paul had told us that he planned to continue on from Ephesus alone for a quick trip to Jerusalem, where he had not been for a long time. He hoped he could arrive before the Passover Feast and meet with other apostles of the faith. While Aquila was cutting his long locks, Paul gave us another reason for returning to Judea.

Some while before, at Corinth, he had taken a vow. It could be fulfilled only by making a sacrifice at the Temple of Jerusalem. In the meantime the vow required that he not cut his hair, until he was at least on his way to its fulfillment. What was his vow? I wanted to know.

"That is between God and me," he said solemnly.

And he never did tell us.

I wondered about it. I had heard of Nazirite vows from my father, and so had Aquila. They were of the oldest Jewish tradition, and not used often. I knew no more than that much. But that Paul —founder of Christian churches separate from the synagogues, bitterly opposed by traditionalist Jews for heresy, liberator for Gentile converts from Jewish laws—could still respect so deeply the faith of his father and ancestors seemed to be a contradiction. But

I realized that this was not so. Paul, farsighted, recognized that worship of the one Lord God Almighty bound Jews and Christians forever together in one supreme faith, however disparate their beliefs concerning Jesus as Messiah.

Yet it could never be that simple. Paul, through his own life and work, knew that too.

Stephanas and Gaius came down from the city with the dawn to see us off. Both of them kissed me good-by and shook hands with Paul and Aquila, saying that they knew we would be well cared for in our new surroundings. We boarded the vessel, one which belonged to the fleet of Stephanas. Sails were raised, lines cast off, and we were at sea again, with a widening space of water between us and the shore of Greece.

Our voyage was delightful, almost exactly due eastward from Corinth to Ephesus, passing through the famed Greek islands of legend. The breezes of spring pushed us onward under clearest skies. The boat was much smaller than the great ship that had brought us to Corinth from Italy, but it was more comfortable.

Yet Aquila and I still had mixed feelings as we approached each day nearer to our destination. Despite the assurance given us, Aquila worried about starting our business all over again. I was concerned with the responsibilities for the church that Paul was placing on us during his absence on further travels. Some nights, I prayed so long to Jesus for guidance and knowledge that I found myself asleep on the floor beside Aquila, who wakened me and took me up in his arms.

At the dock, all was confusion. Our vessel tied up in a line of other ships, longshoremen jumped aboard to unload the cargo, workmen loaded bales of goods onto other boats, horses and wagons roared past along the quay, the noise was deafening. Behind the quay were long warehouses marked with the name STEPHANAS in huge Latin letters. A man leaped across from the wharf to the deck where we stood.

"Master, you are Paul?" he shouted over the din. He looked at the piece of paper in his hand. "And Aquila? Mistress, you are Priscilla?"

We all nodded.

"Follow me."

A gangway had been thrown out from the wharf to the deck of the boat. He led us over it, and then, dodging racing wagons, carts, and every possible kind of conveyance he guided us across the quay to an office in one of the warehouses. Once we were inside with the door closed, the din in our ears subsided.

"We have been expecting you," the man said in Greek. "Forgive us, we could not know the exact time of your arrival. When we saw your ship, we sent at once to your friends. They will be here shortly. Please sit down to wait."

Even as he spoke, a servant appeared with cups of fruit juices for our refreshment. It was mixed nectar of many fruits. I drank mine gratefully.

We did not have to wait long. A sella with two bearers rushed up outside the door. Silas and Timothy came in, smiling cheerfully.

"Welcome!" Silas cried.

"You are here!" Timothy added, grinning as if he were surprised.

Silas asked Paul whether he still wished to go on to Jerusalem. Yes, he did, Paul replied. Silas told him he had found that a ship was sailing that evening direct to Caesarea, the port nearest Jerusalem. He had already reserved a place aboard it. But, meanwhile, certain of the elders of the synagogue in Ephesus were gathered together and wished to have Paul speak to them.

"They are very anxious to hear you," Silas said. "I told them you were leaving at once, but they persisted. You have six hours before sailing time—"

"I will go to them now," Paul agreed. "I can promise that I will return to Ephesus."

Then Timothy turned to Aquila and me. "And I am to take you to your house. All is arranged and ready for you."

Everything moved so quickly. Another sella, big enough for three, was waiting. Paul's traveling sack would be delivered safely to his ship, our baggage would follow us to the house.

Our farewell to Paul was brief—perhaps better so. I had a lump in my throat as he hugged me and shook Aquila's hand.

"God bless you both!" And he was gone with Silas.

My heart went out to him when he disappeared through the doorway. "Lord Jesus, bring him back in safety!" I murmured.

The man from the office took Aquila and me with Timothy out to our sella. Four tall slaves were bearers. Smiling happily, the office man bade us farewell, and we were on our way into the city of Ephesus.

At the first sight I saw, I cried out. "Aquila, look! Camels!"

The long line of camels plodded sedately along the quay, laden with bales of materials. They moved slowly, heedless of traffic rushing around them.

"They are carrying wool from the mountain districts," Timothy explained. "Probably it will be shipped to Rome."

Even besides camels, the scenes of Ephesus were very different from Corinth. The streets were wider, the houses different, built more on oriental lines. Our bearers took us up a wide avenue lined with trees and statues of heroes, one after another on both sides.

"This is the Arcadian Way," Timothy told us. "It's the city's main street, the center of the town. Everything seems to move out from here."

Other aspects of the city were also unlike Corinth. The people along the crowded pavements appeared to be more of a mixture of nationalities, with many tall Asians and Africans among them. Their dress was different, more colorful, and these men wore large turbans wrapped around their heads. Everywhere were trees and flowers; as a city, Ephesus seemed relaxed in its surroundings.

Timothy kept pointing out things of special interest as we proceeded up the avenue, explaining as much as he knew from his short time being here. He had a special pride in this city. He reminded us that he was an Asian himself, from the interior town of Lystra, in Galatia, beyond the great mountain ranges. He showed us the high walls of the Ephesus theater, a stadium with a capacity of twenty-five thousand people. Here and there between breaks in the rows of houses we had glimpses of an enormous white temple on the top of a hill.

"The Temple of Artemis," Timothy said. "For a thousand years she has been the protectress of Ephesus. Some people identify her with the Roman Diana, but here, this Artemis is more oriental in origin. She has a great number of breasts instead of just two, making her the Great Mother of all mankind. You must visit the Temple; it's supposed to be one of the Seven Wonders of the World.

What the other six are I don't know, but this one is said to be four times as large as the Parthenon in Athens."

Our bearers trotted with us up the avenue to the far side of the city, away from the sea. There they turned into a neighborhood of quiet streets, modest to wealthy houses mostly on one floor. Some of the houses, on large plots of land, were very old, perhaps four or five hundred years. Ephesus had not been destroyed, as Corinth had been two hundred years before. But generally the houses here were reasonably contemporary, having been a part of the city's development while the population grew over many decades.

Going up one street, we came to its end at the entrance to a long low house, with two other roads coming down and around its sides. Here the bearers stopped and gently put down the sella from their shoulders in front of a heavy wooden double door arched at the top.

"This is it," Timothy declared.

"Not—this?"

I stared at the door, its height, and at the sides of the house with long walls running back.

"There must be a mistake," Aquila protested. "This isn't the house for us."

"Oh, yes, it is." Timothy alighted from the sella. He went over to pound on the heavy bronze knocker. "Wait until you see it inside."

Confused and dismayed, Aquila and I stepped down from the sella. In a few moments one of the double doors opened after a rattling of chains. A white-haired man in gray tunic smiled at us and bowed low.

"This is Nambio," Timothy said. "Nambio, here are your master and mistress." Turning to us, he added, "Nambio is your steward and serviceman. Come in."

We walked through the doorway speechless. In front of us there was a blank wall—a shield to protect the inner house from view through the entrance. We followed Timothy around the wall to a hallway, and beyond to an opening into a large, sunny inner court —an atrium in the eastern style. It was wide open to the sky, and around the edges grew gardens of flowers and shrubs. The floor of the atrium was paved in geometric designs of blue and white mosaic tiles.

121

It was possible then to see that the house itself was triangular in shape, with two sides following the curves of the streets. The third side ran straight across the back, for the service units.

A buxom woman appeared, wiping her hands on an apron. Behind her a young black girl stared at us. Timothy took us over to meet them. He had forgotten their names, but they reminded him. The woman was Delia, who was to be our cook; she was an Asian from the north, near the Black Sea. The young girl who would serve as my personal maid was Nevia. Her grandfather had been a prince of Ethiopia slain in a battle with the Romans, and her grandmother had been captured as a slave.

Nambio stood behind us, and he was glad to tell us of himself. He was a descendant of tribes from Mesopotamia far east of the Roman Asian provinces, of Jewish origin.

Aquila motioned to Timothy.

"We must talk," he said as we drew off to one side. "Something is wrong, we could never afford all this. It's so far beyond us—"

"Wait." Timothy held up his hand. "Silas and I came here with your landlord when we first arrived, to be sure all was right. His name is Lucius Andronicus, a friend of Gaius. He owns properties all over Ephesus. I think you will find the rent is no more than you paid in Corinth. The three servants are slaves, and they come with the house. Once in a while they need a few coins for their own necessities, that's all."

"That is wonderful," I said, still doubtful, "but it means three more people to feed."

"They do not eat the same kind of food that you do," Timothy went on. "They're not used to that; they wouldn't even like it. And Silas and I have found already that costs of everything here are much less than in Corinth. Ephesus is so close to all supplies."

"But where do we do our work?" Aquila wanted to know. "Here in the court? What happens when it rains?"

Timothy laughed. "I doubt that it will rain here until next winter. But there is a large storage room in the back. It is empty, and there is a service entry from the rear alley. Lucius seems to have thought of everything, including the space you will need for your congregation."

"I suppose we can hold our meetings here in the court." I kept looking around. "We'll need benches when that time comes."

"Many people are used to sitting on cushions with legs crossed," Timothy said. "It's a custom from Arabia. Your landlord will help in any way he can. He is much interested in our work, although like most Ephesians he worships the goddess Artemis."

I glanced at Aquila. "I guess, then, everything is all right?"

Aquila nodded. "Thanks to you and Silas," he said to Timothy.

14

For our first dinner in our new home at Ephesus, Delia without a word to me prepared a feast. It was served at a table and divan brought into the atrium by Nambio and Nevia. We had fresh steamed mussels to start—Aquila had long since accepted the idea of shellfish—a vegetable soup, marinated beef with baked oranges, and a dessert of a kind of cake with dark wine sauce. Afterward, dried figs were placed on the table with goat cheese.

"I've never made anything like this for you." I bit into a juicy hot orange slice. "Just for the two of us."

"Ephesus isn't so terrible, after all." Aquila ate joyfully. "I thought we were coming to some primitive colony."

"We can't keep it up," I reminded him. "Somehow I will have to tell them we must watch expenses."

"Then we will go down in their estimation," Aquila replied.

Before dinner we had gone through the whole house with its numerous rooms. All were large and airy, with high ceilings for coolness. Most of the windows faced inside to the court, rather than onto the street, for protection and privacy. We selected for ourselves the largest corner one, furnished with a comfortable double couch, wardrobes, and dressing tables.

We retired for sleep early, as we were both tired. Then came Aquila's turn to be really startled. The girl Nevia appeared in our room to help me prepare for the night. Aquila abruptly stopped disrobing. Nevia was oblivious to his semi-naked body. I wanted to laugh at sight of my embarrassed husband.

"Thank you, Nevia. That will be all for the night," I said.

She was puzzled. "But, mistress, I must help you with your undressing, brush out your hair."

"Thank you, but I prefer doing that for myself," I told the bewildered slave girl. "There will be many things you can do for me. Good night."

Nevia bowed and left the room.

"Maybe I ought to call the man to help me undress. Then who would be embarrassed?" Aquila laughed.

When I turned off the lamp and we both slipped between the covers, Aquila took me in his arms. "Strange customs," he murmured as I nestled my head against his shoulder. "Where do we go from here?"

"Wherever our work leads us," I told him.

Then, in the morning, Nevia returned with a tray for the morning meal. "For my master and mistress," she said. "Your sleep has been good? Whatever you wish, I will bring. I will wait here so that I may serve you."

Aquila opened his eyes grumpily.

"Tell her, Priscilla, to leave whatever she brought and come back later. You know I'm not used to having anyone in our room."

He turned over on the couch and pulled the covers over his head.

I sat up. "Thank you, Nevia. Leave what you have so beautifully prepared on the table by the window. We will enjoy it. I'll call later."

The girl looked more confused than she had the night before. She was a plain girl with big eyes and black hair in braids down her back.

"Yes, mistress." Bowing, she disappeared.

Later that morning, I thanked Delia, the cook, for her good dinner. I talked with her about future marketing, endeavoring without much success to keep costs under control. I did learn that Timothy was right, that slaves—or servants, as I wished to think of them— never ate what their master and mistress were served, or any guests. They were content with boiling up fish heads, the stems of vegetables and skins of oranges or other fruits for a full meal.

They did like bowls of boiled screened wheat. For anything else, they would not want it.

I felt somewhat better in enjoying the delectable meals she served to Aquila and me.

Several days passed before I could convince my three servants that I enjoyed doing the marketing myself. Even so, Nambio and Nevia insisted on going with me, always walking a few steps behind in deference. They would not let me carry anything, and Nambio did the bargaining. I had to settle for that arrangement in this new life.

Soon after our arrival, our landlord, Lucius Andronicus, came to visit us. He was a tall, handsome man with a mass of black hair and a black beard on his chin. He was forceful, specific, and very kind to us. The rent he charged was even slightly less than for our small house in Corinth. When I told Lucius, as we came to call him, that his rent was too low for such luxury, he waved aside my protests.

"I am getting a fair return for this investment," he said. "I have heard about each one of you in Paul's group from my friend Gaius. He tells me that he has turned Christian. That is interesting. I have heard of the sect."

"Gaius has been wonderful to all of us," I said. "He loaned us his house for our church."

"I will do all I can for you here," he replied. He turned to Aquila. "I hear you are highly skilled at making tents and awnings."

"I cannot claim anything like that for myself. I can say that I have had much practice."

Lucius told him that he had just built a new house and needed awnings for it. He would send the specifications at once, together with names and addresses of several traders in canvas where Aquila could obtain materials. Then he looked around our atrium.

"This place needs awnings and umbrellas too," he said. "If you are entertaining many people here, you will want something against the hot summer sun. Why don't you make what you think is most suitable in your spare time? I will pay your bill."

So quickly we were in business again!

Lucius invited us to have an evening meal with himself and his wife at his house a few days later. Without stopping to remember that they were Gentiles and things were different now from what they had been in Corinth, we accepted at once. It did not occur to us that we should, for appearance sake, act once again under the strictness of Jewish Law.

We met with Silas and Timothy to confer on immediate plans. Lucius had rented a comfortable house to them also, on a small street in the city center near the amphitheater but not far from us. Their house was large enough to take care of Paul on his return to Ephesus, as well as others of his associates who might be coming, including Luke.

The four of us agreed, of course, that we should attend the Sabbath services at the synagogue and become part of the Jewish congregation. But we would not disguise the fact that we were followers of the Way of Jesus. Silas believed that the colony of Jews in Ephesus was quite large, and many of them were Asian Hellenists—the Jewish faction most inimical to belief in Christ as the Son of God. Silas had been with Paul when he met briefly with the group of synagogue elders on the first afternoon. Some of the group had been most interested in what Paul told them, and invited him to say more when he came back from his trip. But others had shown skepticism and outright resentment, among them one Alexander, who appeared to be a leader. So, between us four we agreed to be open about our faith but cautious so as not to cause too much trouble before Paul arrived.

Through it all, I missed very much the reassuring presence of Paul himself. I had become so used to having him near. . . .

The first several weeks passed uneventfully—more or less. The shipping office of Stephanas in Ephesus sent a man up to us with an order for a large ship's sail to replace one torn to shreds by the previous winter's storms. Ever since, the vessel had operated at sea with only its one spare, a dangerous practice in case of another storm.

In dimensions of canvas, the sail was the largest one-piece job that Aquila had ever faced. The ship office supplied us temporarily with an apprentice from their own shops to help with measuring and stretching. I know that I spent many hours sewing interminable lengths of hem binding as well as stitching into place at proper

126

angles the long wooden stays for sail support. I had little time left otherwise.

We did go to the synagogue each Sabbath. I returned to conventional behavior as a married woman and wore a shawl covering my head and knotting it under my chin despite the warm weather. I was careful to sit in the section at one side reserved for women, while Aquila used a bench with Silas and Timothy in the mid-section.

At our first Sabbath service, Silas took advantage of the time allotted to congregation members and strangers to speak. He stood up to read a portion of scriptures prophesying the coming of the Savior. At the close he added, "In the Name of the Lord Jesus Christ, Son of God. Amen."

It was a subtle opening for our evangelization. A quiet rustling spread over the people. Some may not have heard at all. But there was no subsequent comment.

Some of the congregation members warmly welcomed Aquila and me to Ephesus. They took our names and address, and we received later invitations from them. We did make a few lasting friends. Others, once they knew us as Christians, dropped us as they would a hot pan picked up by mistake from a stove.

Letters of introduction from Stephanas and Gaius took effect too. Knowing that Paul's work when he arrived in Ephesus would be among Gentiles as well as Jews, we accepted some invitations.

Ephesus was not much different from Corinth in the spread of gossip. We made no effort to hide our social activities. We not only had enjoyed becoming acquainted with Lucius Andronicus and his wife at their home but were entertained by leading citizens of the city—Gentiles. When some of our Jewish friends heard of this, they became sharply critical.

Gentiles not only served unclean food but also they were worshipers of idols and participated in pagan rites. Their hospitality was forbidden to Jews, they said.

When I reminded them—these were usually women—that through Jesus Christ Jews and Gentiles were equally welcome to faith in the Lord God and that all mankind would be judged together not just by the Law but by the righteousness of their lives, they turned their backs on me.

A whispering campaign against us started among the Jews of

Ephesus. Not by all, but by many. People looked at us oddly as we entered the synagogue. They did not speak to us as we left after services. This was the time when some whom we had thought of as friends refused to associate with us.

Aquila became more and more uncomfortable about it. I could see this growing.

Then, one day, it burst into a real quarrel.

After we reached home one Sabbath following the synagogue services, Aquila said to me, "Priscilla, I do not want you to accept any more Gentile invitations."

"Aquila! What do you mean?"

"I feel like a dog every time I go into the synagogue. I am ashamed, even among our own people. We know what we are doing—trying to break up their congregation with our own beliefs. We're like enemies in their camp!"

"Aquila, what are you trying to say?"

"That I don't like this situation. We ought to be all Jew or all Gentile—and I won't be a Gentile! We go into the synagogue pretending we are Jews, and at the same time break the Law of the Jews and go to the Gentiles pretending we are like them, eating their food—"

"I'm not pretending anything; I'm a Christian and so are you!" I shouted. "That's more important than being either Jew or Gentile. Pretending! I don't pretend to anyone; I have hidden nothing!"

He raised his voice too. "I was born a Jew and grew up to worship God in accordance with the Laws God gave the Jews. Now I sneak in with Jews at their worship as if I believed the way they do. I don't belong to them any more. I don't belong anywhere. I can't take this further—"

"I don't sneak in, those people know how I feel! I tell them every time I get the chance that we belong to Christ!"

"And they sneer at you for it. I'm sure they're saying you ought to stay home and keep from disturbing their own faith. That's what we are doing. I didn't realize it until now."

"You've forgotten everything that Paul has told us. How can you say these things—"

"Suppose Paul is wrong?" he shouted at me now. "Maybe we're displeasing God with what we're doing!"

"Aquila!" I gasped. "You frighten me!"

"There is nothing to be frightened about if we obey our own Jewish Law. We can't go wrong no matter what we believe."

We were standing in the atrium during this. I saw Nambio and Nevia peering out at us with curiosity. "That would be false to Jesus Christ," I said. "Didn't Christ tell Paul to go to the Gentiles? That's the same as Christ telling us, if we believe Paul at all."

Aquila glanced toward the door and saw both Nambio and Nevia.

I whispered to him, "They have been watching us."

He turned and walked toward his workshop without another word.

For a long time neither of us spoke about our argument. Then, one night before going to sleep, we both admitted while in each other's embrace we were overwrought. We were in a situation we had not yet learned to handle.

During the following week, a coincidence occurred. A visitor came to our house and Nambio brought her to me.

The moment I met her I was certain that I had seen her before.

Her name was Flavia, she told me, and she lived in a small house nearby. Through our respective cooks she had heard about the awnings. She needed a small one for a corner of her own atrium. Of course, I told her, my husband would be glad to take the measurements.

She kept looking at me oddly. One of us had to say it.

"Haven't we met somewhere?"

"You couldn't—possibly—be from Rome?"

There it was. We had never met, but we had passed each other at meetings, seen each other in groups, probably greeted each other. This, briefly, was the story:

Flavia and her husband, Actius, a Jewish couple, were expelled from Rome by the Emperor Claudius at the same time we were, along with other Jews. They came to Ephesus; we went to Corinth. As we did, they left most of their possessions in Rome. But they, too, in Rome, had heard the unknown apostle in the synagogue they attended, had accepted Jesus as the Messiah, and become baptized as Jewish Christians. She and I must have attended later meetings of those in the Way, and remembered each other only by casual sight.

Their life in Ephesus as Christians had been hard. Flavia and Actius first attended the synagogue as usual until they told others of their Christian baptisms. They were dropped socially and finally were ordered by the elders to come no longer to the Sabbath services unless they repented. Otherwise they would be profaning a holy place of God. Since then they had stealthily crept into the synagogue only when no one else was there, to make their prayers to Jesus Christ and God himself. As Jews, they had continued to conform to the Law and had no association with Gentiles. So they had no friends, no associates, and were very lonely people in a strange city; yet they could not forsake their staunch conviction and love for Jesus Christ.

I invited them immediately to come for our evening meal. They did, and the four of us became good friends at once. We have remained so ever since.

Flavia is small and plump, with a cheerful disposition and lively nature. Her husband is quieter, with good humor. Actius and Aquila were congenial immediately.

It was that evening as we talked late into the night that we decided we would start our first service on Sunday in the Christian Way. Silas and Timothy would attend, which would make our number six.

Little did I realize then that we would have a seventh, a most unusual guest.

15

A letter came from Paul, a very brief one in his own handwriting. He had been at Jerusalem, all was well, and at time of writing he was in Antioch, Syria, the headquarters of the Asian Christian Church. From there he planned to retrace his earlier travels to churches he had founded in the Asian provinces beyond the northern mountains. Then he would come to Ephesus.

This meant that he would be delayed in coming back to us. My heart did sink at this news. I was chafing now at our indefinite situation, after the outburst between Aquila and me. Even though we had smoothed out our differences, I had to admit to myself that Aquila had a point in not liking to worship at the synagogue under apparently false pretenses. I had tried to be honest about it in my conversations with other Jews there, but I kept thinking, Are we really being fair? But how else could we tell the Jews of Jesus Christ if we did not mix with them?

On the next Sabbath morning I almost decided I would plead a headache to Aquila and stay away from the synagogue service. I banished such an excuse as cowardly, and that I hope never to be. I only wished that I were a man and had the right to stand up to the congregation and say to them I am a Jew and a Christian, a believer in Christ, the Son of God. As a woman, I could not speak.

But Aquila and I went together as usual, not mentioning our separate opinions.

Our entrance was greeted as before with stares and whispers. Aquila's face turned grim as he left me to go to his seat beside Silas and Timothy. I remembered what Flavia had told me, that she and her husband had been expelled from the synagogue for their heretical beliefs in Jesus. How soon would this happen to us? How much would that hurt Paul's plan to start his teaching in the synagogue here, as he had in each city new to him?

On this particular Sabbath, Silas had planned what he would say to the congregation at the right moment, nothing to warrant extreme action from the elders. To the amazement of us all, when the time came a complete stranger stood up ahead of Silas.

He was a young man, clean-shaven, with rounded face, bright eyes, and intense enthusiasm. Instead of standing by his bench, he walked up rapidly to the front and turned to face the people.

"My name is Apollos, a Jew like yourselves. I am from Alexandria. I am here in Ephesus to bring to you the best news for all Jews everywhere. In accordance with the scriptures from the Lord God given to us through the prophets, the Messiah has come to us! His name is Jesus Christ, the Son of God sent to us to redeem our lives and teach the way of righteousness. If you have not heard of him already, then receive him now, for Jesus is our Savior for life eternal, as the scriptures have said. . . ."

Who was this man who spoke so strongly? Apollos, of Alexandria, in Egypt? Paul had never mentioned him; did Paul know him? I glanced toward Aquila, found him turned to look with a question toward me in my women's section. I noticed that Silas and Timothy seemed puzzled too.

The stranger went on to tell of the life of Jesus and his teaching. He spoke confidently like one well informed. In their way, I think the congregation were as surprised as I was. Apollos quoted the scriptures that told of the coming of the Savior for the people of Israel, bringing every proof to bear on the fact the Savior was indeed Jesus of Nazareth. He spoke persuasively, with strength and smoothness.

Then his voice broke, with a catch in it.

"Through a terrible misunderstanding, the elders in Jerusalem and the authorities of our government did not realize that they were fulfilling the prophecies of the scriptures. They did not stop to think that they were tools to make these prophecies come true. So they crucified our Jesus Christ, our Messiah. They hanged him on a cross until he was dead, there in Jerusalem."

Apollos fell to his knees and bowed his head.

"They who crucified him did not know what they had done. Even as he hung on the cross, Jesus called out to Heaven, 'Forgive them, Father, for they know not what they do.' We, too, gathered here together, must ask God to forgive those who did not know what they did. They crucified the Son of God!"

He paused. Not one sound could be heard throughout the synagogue.

He jumped to his feet and held out an arm.

"But they couldn't kill the Son of God," he cried. "He lives! He rose from his tomb after three days, and appeared alone to his apostles and to others! They believed! Jesus was the Son of God, our Messiah for all Jews! Our Savior for eternity. . . ."

Again he paused.

"My friends here in Ephesus," he continued, "this is the news I bring you. Jesus, the Messiah promised to all of us, has lived among us on earth and now resides in Heaven with the Father. We know these things through the pronouncements of John, the last great prophet to announce the Coming One, John who baptized thousands of people along the River Jordan to cleanse them of their sins, that they might be ready for the Messiah. The life of Jesus, his death, and his Resurrection fulfilled the prophecies of

John and the prophets of old. Let us not repeat, my friends, the tragedy of Jerusalem and crucify Jesus again. Believe in him, Jesus the Christ. Amen."

Slowly Apollos walked back to his bench and sat down. The congregation stirred uneasily.

The stranger's teaching was dramatic, compelling. But he had only spoken of baptisms by John the Baptist, not the essential sacrament of baptism in the Name of Jesus. Didn't the stranger know?

I had difficulty in following the rest of the service.

At the end, Apollos was surrounded by members of the congregation asking questions. Aquila, Silas, and Timothy waited for me.

"Who is he?" I asked.

Silas shook his head. "Paul never mentioned him to us; probably he does not know of him. This man spoke only of John's baptisms."

"He said nothing of the Holy Spirit," I observed.

Silas suggested that we take him back to our house and talk with him. As soon as the people around him dispersed, Aquila and I asked Apollos to share a meal with us at our home. We told him who we were and why we were in Ephesus. He had heard of Paul but did not know him. He gladly accepted our invitation.

We had a long conversation with Apollos all through our meal and the rest of the afternoon. It began when he said that he stopped off in Ephesus briefly on his way to Corinth, to evangelize there. When we told him that a Corinthian church for Christ was already established in that city, he was astonished. All that Apollos knew of Jesus and the great spreading of the Way came through travelers to Alexandria, Egypt's main seaport, mostly from Galilee, where John the Baptist had baptized so many. Apollos had never been in Jerusalem or talked with any of Christ's apostles. He had long been a scholar of Jewish scripture, including the prophecies, and had become convinced through what he had heard that Jesus was in truth the Messiah. He dedicated his life to giving this message to Jews wherever he found them throughout the world.

When we explained that the Holy Spirit of God came only through baptism in the Name of Jesus, not through John, he did not understand.

"I do not know of the Holy Spirit," he said.

Aquila and I took care to explain that the Holy Spirit was fundamental to faith in the Way of Jesus. The Spirit, which had first come upon the apostles after the Resurrection, freed Jews and Gentiles alike from the strictness of the Law and circumcision, and made all people equal in the sight of God. As Christ through his crucifixion freed all men from sin, so through the Holy Spirit every person could find the life of righteousness before the judgment of God.

Apollos was astonished.

"I thought I had found the path to Jesus," he said. "Now I see the broad road to the infinity of God's Heaven."

We instructed him in many more things previously not clear to him.

As he left us that night to return to his lodgings, I invited him to come the following day, Sunday, to the first service of the new Ephesus church. Yes, he would come. He had one request to make: could he be baptized in Christ's name?

I am sure that Sunday, the next day, will always be one of the happiest days of my life. At five o'clock on that afternoon we held in our atrium the first service of worship of the Christian church in Ephesus. The heat of the day was gone, and long, cooling shadows fell across the court.

The sounds of the city itself seemed far away. We had no fanfare, no outward signs of the importance of the event in the long march forward of the Church of Christ. It was the simplest of ceremonies, with the few of us present. But I felt the peace of God enter into our home.

There were seven, with Flavia and Actius, Silas, Timothy and our guest, Apollos. The three servants watched from across the atrium.

I missed Paul so much, with a longing in my heart that he could have been with us. I missed his gruff voice, his appearance in his brown robe, which would have meant so much to all present.

Before we began the service, Silas baptized Apollos into the full faith of the Way. For the first time, the Alexandrian knew the awesome power of the Holy Spirit.

During the service, Silas dedicated the house and each one of us present to the service of Almighty God. We prayed for Paul and his return in safety to our midst. We prayed also for our church in Corinth, and asked God's blessing on the work Apollos would do there when he arrived. Then, at the end, we celebrated the sacrament of the Lord's Supper as we gathered together around the table in the atrium.

Apollos asked if he might speak the final blessing. As we knelt, he thanked the Lord for bringing him to us, so that he might gain the knowledge he had not had. He prayed that he would use it well. He thanked God also for the gift of the Holy Spirit, and he asked that the grace of the Lord in Christ's Name would be upon our new church in this city.

And so our church was established.

I had arranged with Delia for a refreshment supper to be placed at the end of the atrium, close to a flower bed. A soft flow of water circulated around the plants, bringing with it a sound of coolness and tranquillity.

We had a wonderful, sociable evening, talking long into the night with Apollos, telling him much about the church in Corinth for his benefit.

Flavia and Actius told us how much this day meant to them. After a long time, they were able at last to be with Christians. Flavia offered to help me with the work of our church as it grew. Neither of us could foresee what the nature of that help would finally be.

Several days later, Apollos continued on his way to Corinth. All of us gave him letters of introduction, especially to Gaius, Stephanas, and to Luke if he had not already left.

I took that opportunity to send a letter to Antonia, telling her about Apollos and describing our life in Ephesus. I even took a woman's satisfaction in saying that our atrium was just as large as hers in her Corinth house.

Not long afterward, another letter came from Paul. He was somewhere up in the northern province of Galatia, working his way down toward Ephesus. He hoped to be arriving soon, bringing with him Aristarchus and Epaphras, both of them long-time disciples and associates of Paul. Silas and Timothy knew them well.

I was overjoyed. From then on my impatience had no limits.

16

On a hot afternoon a sudden banging rang out on our front-door brass knocker. The rhythm seemed oddly familiar. I happened to be in the atrium examining our flower beds after finishing the hem of an awning in the shop. I waited while Nambio hurried from the service quarters to answer the knocking.

I heard the door open. Then shouts, laughter, greetings for Nambio. Startled, I stood up from the flowers. Around the corner of the wall shielding the atrium, a bearded man appeared—in a brown robe. He held out his arms.

"Paul!"

I rushed to him, threw myself at him. He clasped me in his arms with a chuckle of laughter. I could not speak.

"Prisca, my girl!" he rumbled joyfully.

With him were Silas and Timothy, and two strangers—and Luke.

All were laughing happily.

At last I stood back and looked at him. All I could say was, "Paul, your robe! You need a new one!" Then I shouted for Aquila to come.

The reunion was indeed exuberant. The older stranger was Aristarchus of Thessalonica, a fully bearded man of about the same age as Silas, with mischievous eyes that gleamed out through his mat of hair. The younger one, Epaphras, even younger than Timothy, came originally from Colossae, only several days' journey inland from Ephesus. For an Asian he was fair-skinned, with dark curly hair and smooth face. In a few minutes we were all close friends—Paul and his seven assistants including Aquila and me.

We sat on divans in the atrium in the shade of the first awning that Aquila had made in accordance with our landlord's order. Without being told, Nevia appeared with a tray of cups and a jug of fruit juices. The girl smiled cheerfully at each of the guests.

Everyone tried to talk at once. Some sense finally came through. Luke had arrived unexpectedly the night before. Paul and his two companions had come at noontime. The six of them had eaten some light food in the house where Silas and Timothy were staying, and where all of them would now be living. Then they had walked up to see us.

I went quickly back to Delia, told her there would be eight all together for an evening dinner. She sent Nambio out immediately for supplies. Even though the market was closed at this hour in the afternoon, he knew where to find shops that were open. Nevia stayed behind to set up the dining table for us.

Our conversation quieted to a more reasonable pitch. We told Paul about Apollos; he was much interested, somewhat concerned. Luke had met the man from Alexandria in Corinth briefly, heard him preach once in the synagogue. Luke thought he was very effective in reaching the Jews because of his knowledge of the scriptures. What success he might have with the Gentiles in the church he did not know. (Luke told me later that he was disturbed now by the numbers of Corinthian Gentiles abandoning paganism and joining the church. It seemed to be a social thing-to-do, with what sincerity or true faith was unclear. He did not want to disturb Paul with this news just as he had arrived from his travels—later, yes.)

Paul gave us the latest news from Jerusalem of the whole Church, as well as from Antioch. In Jerusalem he had seen only James, who remained at headquarters while the other apostles, including Peter, were out on ministries. In Antioch and in all the inland churches of Asia he had visited, he found only steadfastness in the Way.

Aquila turned to me to report on our new church in Ephesus. We had held services each Sunday since our beginning, small though our number. Four members of the synagogue had now been baptized: one couple who had been good friends of ours from our first arrival, and another couple who were the first to criticize us for straying from the Jewish faith until they heard Apollos speak that one Sabbath.

Silas and Timothy were teaching at least five Gentiles, who came to their house three mornings each week to receive more instruction. They were potential converts.

137

None of us had more news to add for Paul.

Paul said he would speak in the synagogue the next Sabbath day, and afterward teach there each morning. I watched Paul as he talked. He was tired from his journeys. No one else would notice it —perhaps Luke might. I wished to myself that he would rest before starting work, but I knew enough to keep from saying so. I couldn't make him angry on his first night back with us.

His cheeriness did not suggest weariness. Delia gave us an evening dinner of fish soup, then boiled chicken with a spiced sauce, a special delicacy. My guests ate hungrily, especially Paul. For dessert we had all the summer fruits of Asia: grapes red and juicy, ripe figs with purple-red centers, sweetened oranges, and pomegranates. With the fruit, Delia made sweet cakes of flour, whites of egg, and paste of crushed almonds, quickly baked. Nambio served white wine, and Nevia carried away empty dishes.

Before the meal, Aquila as host had asked God's grace on our coming together. At the end, Paul bowed his head to say, "We give thanks to Thee, Almighty God, in the Name of Christ Jesus, Thy Son, in gratitude for Thy Holy Spirit, which has blessed us all. Amen."

I felt that my cup of happiness was running over. I pinched my arm to be sure that all was real.

Yet, over the next weeks nothing seemed to happen. It was as if a wall in Ephesus surrounded us, keeping us from contact with people. We gained three or four Gentiles for our congregation, and one more Jewish man. But with such a small number for church services, without apparent change, a sense of inspiration and lift was lacking. I worried that our converts might drop away.

Paul, in his Sabbath talks and daily teaching, achieved little. On some days two or three might come to hear him, on other days no one at all. The large Jewish colony of Ephesus ignored him.

All the work by Paul's associates in street conversations, house-to-house calls, talks to groups of Gentile businessmen, follow-ups of leads, achieved only minor response. The goddess Artemis in her temple reigned supreme.

I made a practice of going down to Paul's house every second afternoon to find out if I could be of help in any direction. I wrote out many of his letters for him as he dictated. He had a great deal

138

of correspondence to carry on following his trip: thanking people for their kindnesses, reminding others of their promises concerning their faith, and to church congregations on their spiritual problems.

But each time I went I felt more keenly the despondence from each of his associates for their failure to arouse the people.

Paul never showed it—except once.

The house that Lucius Andronicus had rented to Silas and Timothy for use of Paul and his friends was, like ours, on one floor. The atrium was smaller, roofed over. The rooms and service quarters were, as for us, built around the sides. One room furnished as a gineceo, or study, Paul had taken over for his work. This was where I wrote out his letters for him.

Lucius had given to the group for their housekeeping a married couple from his own staff of slaves. The woman did the cooking, laundry, and general cleaning, while the man acted as steward to serve, keep the floors washed, and handle the shopping.

One afternoon after my knock on the door, the steward opened it as usual. This time he seemed troubled.

"The master is in the gineceo," he said. "He has taken no food today."

I glanced at him askance. "Then bring us a pitcher of fruit juice, please."

Very lightly I tapped on the study door and opened it part way. Paul was on his knees before the window that looked out into the street, in prayer. His face was turned toward the sky, his lips moving. I stood quietly by the door, leaving it partly ajar so I could take in the fruit juice without disturbing him.

Paul was fasting, something I had never known him to do. As I stayed by the door I added a brief silent prayer of my own for him. I knew Paul so well: He was a man of moods—fiery, strong, aggressive when occasion called for him to be so. His other public side could be just as gentle, compassionate. But behind these façades he was a man with doubts of his worth, fearful of failure, nervous of his ministry if it did not go well. I always thought it might have something to do with the "thorn in his side," as he called it. He had never explained it to me, often as I had asked

139

him to tell me. He tried not to show it, except that at times when I was alone with him he dropped all pretenses.

The steward brought the pitcher of juice and two cups. I took them from him, nodded my thanks, and entered, closing the door quietly behind me. I put the refreshment on a table.

"Prisca," Paul said without moving from his knees.

"Yes, Paul, I am here. I did not want to disturb you."

"I am glad you have come."

Slowly he stood up. I noticed that he winced as he stretched his legs.

"You have eaten nothing all day," I said. "I have a cup of fruit juice for you."

"I am fasting. I have been praying."

"You have no right to fast. Do you think God wants you to lose your strength just now?"

He looked at me; I thought he was going to be angry. But he said wearily, "I have no strength."

"Nonsense. Take this and drink it."

He took the cup, hesitating. He looked down into the golden juice.

"Drink it," I commanded.

He did, to the last drop.

"Now you'll feel better," I said. "You are tired, that's all. I wished you would rest for a time after your travels, but I dared not to say it to you. Of course, you did not."

"The Lord gave me this work to do for him. I have failed in it."

"Not yet, there has not been time. Of course, we are worried, but the break will come. This is a city strange to all of us. We have to find our way slowly."

He shook his head. I wanted to see that fiery light in his eyes, but it was not there.

"Again today no one came to the synagogue to hear me," he said. "Even those elders who made me promise to return on that first day in Ephesus before I sailed for Jerusalem have not responded. No, Prisca, you cannot deny that this is failure. I have prayed, I have prayed—the Lord himself has not responded."

"Paul!" I broke in suddenly. "Haven't you said again and again that God sent you to talk to the Gentiles?"

"That is so, but—"

"Then, why are you talking to the Jews in the synagogue?"

Paul stared at me. He was silent for a moment. He started to speak, stopped. Then he asked, "What would you have me do?"

"Leave the Jews alone for now. They will follow us eventually as they did in Corinth and other places where you have been. Now find a place to teach where the Gentiles can come; that will give Silas and Aristarchus and the others something definite to offer the Gentiles."

He smiled. "Prisca, my dear—"

Rashly I added, "No wonder God didn't listen to your prayers. You were not doing what he asked you to do."

Paul poured for himself another cup of juice. "Where do we find such a place?" he asked.

"Go to Lucius Andronicus, he will find one. Silas and Timothy know him. He said he would help us with anything we needed."

Paul lifted his head high, his jaw came forward, the intensity in his eyes glowed again. "I will go to Lucius Andronicus immediately."

As I left him to return home, I announced happily, "I am asking your cook to give you a special dinner this evening. I am telling her you are hungry."

"Good!" he responded enthusiastically.

Each time I walked between our house and Paul's, I used the wide avenue, the Arcadian Way. The distance was not great, for the avenue led quickly into the heart of the city.

Almost always, I passed an elderly beggar woman sitting on a stool in the shade of a mimosa tree near to a sculptured bust of some Ephesian patriot. The beggar woman always looked at me pathetically, even when on a return trip from Paul's I found myself giving her a second coin on the same afternoon.

I asked her several times about herself. She said that she had been crippled for most of her life after she fell from a wagon as a child. She could not walk, as one leg was shriveled. Once, she pulled up her long tunica to the knee to show me, and it was true. For many years, she had been brought by a kind man in his small carriage to the same place, where she begged. Her only money came from the alms she received. Everyone in Ephesus was so kind to her, she said.

141

"May Artemis bless you with many children," she always repeated as I dropped a coin into her basket.

At times I smiled sadly to myself. God had not chosen me to bear children. I was barren. Perhaps that was why God had chosen me to help to establish his churches in the name of his Son, Jesus.

I mention the beggar woman only because, soon after that special afternoon, she was a great influence on our lives.

In fact, a series of events began to happen immediately after I made my suggestion to Paul.

The first came about the very next day. Timothy came up to our house in the evening to tell us that our church congregation for the next Sunday would probably be doubled. He wanted us to know so that we could be prepared.

He told us what had happened. It seemed that a small colony of Jewish Christians lived in Ephesus, their businesses being in various trades. Originally they had come from Galilee, and all of them had received baptism from John the Baptist. In many ways their story resembled that of Apollos. These Christians kept closely to themselves in their faith, for they feared the possible wrath of the Roman authorities.

During the afternoon, a group of these men, about twelve, came to the house to see Paul. They had heard he was teaching the Way of Jesus. They wished to know more about Christ, for their knowledge was small.

Paul asked them, "Since you believe, have you received the Holy Spirit?"

The twelve were confused. "If there is a Holy Spirit we have not heard of it," they answered.

Then Paul asked, "By whom were you baptized?"

By John the Baptist, in Galilee by the Jordan River, they said. Paul explained that John's baptism was one of repentance in preparation for Jesus, the Son of God in whom they should believe. Seeing that these men did believe, Paul baptized each one in the name of Christ Jesus. When they felt the Holy Spirit coming upon them, they burst into ecstasies of joy, spoke together in tongues, and tried to tell one another what Jesus meant to them.

As they quieted, Paul suggested they attend the Christian service in our house on the following Sunday, bringing their wives with them and other believers who would want to be baptized.

So our congregation might increase all at once by some twenty or thirty persons.

In the morning Aquila hastily began to make benches from hewn timbers, and I bought rugs and cushions for the atrium. Our landlord sent to the house a number of spare divans, so that when we finished preparations we could have provided for many, many people.

On that morning I was so busy with the church planning that I sent Nambio out alone to the marketplace, keeping Nevia with me. When he returned he was breathless.

"Mistress Priscilla," he gasped, "your friend who comes, whom you call Paul. He speaks to all of you of a God of whom we do not know. I saw this morning—after the market—I saw what happened!"

"What was it?" I asked, alarmed.

"With my own eyes I saw!" Nambio managed to say through his excitement. "You know the old woman who is so crippled she cannot walk? She begs for alms on the Arcadian Way, she has done so for years—"

"Yes, yes, what happened?"

"Coming from the market with my basket—" he pointed at it—"I saw the one whom you call Paul. He passed by this woman, then turned back and gave her a piece of money. I watched because—because I knew him. He said to her"—Nambio spoke slowly—"He said, 'Woman, believe in the only God. . . .' I could not hear the rest, mistress, but he said, 'If you believe, stand up and walk!'"

Nambio paused, still trying to catch his breath. His eyes were wide.

"Go on, tell me," I urged.

"She said after a few moments, while Paul leaned over her, 'I will believe.' And, mistress, I could not believe even my eyes. She did stand up and walk, she did! It is impossible, after so many years!"

"Nambio, you saw this?"

"I did. I watched it happen; she walked; she threw away the

stick she carried. She walked down the pavement and back again. Then she screamed, 'I walk! I walk!' "

"Where was Paul?"

"He watched; he was with another one who comes here often. The woman came to him, took his hand, and kissed it. But your friend, he put his hand on her head and said something to her again. Then the master, Paul, went on, the two of them did. But the woman ran—ran, I tell you—to the people standing there. She screamed and laughed and hugged them all."

Nambio demonstrated by throwing his arms around himself.

I was too stunned. Nevia stood by me open-mouthed, looking from Nambio to me and back again.

"Mistress," Nambio said, "now I know. Your friend who comes here, whom I serve, is indeed a god. What he did, a miracle, only a god can do. I understand now what I have heard—pardon me, mistress, I have heard only by chance what those of your guests have said—"

"Nambio," I interrupted him, "I have not talked with you of these things, or with Delia, or with Nevia here, because the time was not ready. Now I can do so, and later we will start, with the three of you. But I will say to you now, our friend Paul is not a god himself. But there is a God whom you cannot see but who has given Paul the power to do this thing. He is not a god of stone or carvings, but a living God in whom we believe. We will talk more of this when you and I, and Delia and Nevia are together."

Nambio was more awed than ever.

"Thank you, mistress Priscilla, we will listen. It is to our honor that we serve you and your guests here."

I hurried to tell Aquila this news. He laid down his cutting knife.

"Do you suppose it's true?" he asked. "Perhaps the old woman was only a faker all along."

"No," I said, "she showed me her shriveled leg. Something has happened. Paul has received the gift of healing which Jesus had! The breakthrough that Paul needs in Ephesus has come, as God meant it to be!"

On the Sabbath, Paul spoke to the congregation of the synagogue with words that burned like fires.

"You are Jews. You have heard me speak to you concerning Jesus, the Son of God, and you do not hear. You know that I come here daily to tell how the coming of Christ Jesus has fulfilled the scriptures of your ancestors. Yet you stay away. Do you wish to shut your eyes as though blind, that you would not see? Do you hold your ears tight, that you do not hear? Are you closing your minds to what I say, for fear that you might believe me? Are you afraid to decide for yourselves the truth of what I say? Or do you cringe to the censure of your elders, who point their fingers at you as if *they* were your judges, not the Lord?

"Oh, you Jews, who deny the will of your own God! Are you not hypocrites who refuse to hear reason? Through your own consciences, you are free to reach your own decisions, whether I lie or speak the truth. But you forbid yourselves that freedom, you bow only to those who condemn you through false authority, as if they were God himself."

He paused, then said gently, "I have told you that once I was the worst of these. I, who studied every word of the scriptures and should have understood the prophecies. I was the most fierce of those who condemned those of the Way of Jesus. I, as a rabbi myself, stood in judgment against God."

Paul's voice rose again. "But I say to you, how many of you have heard the voice of Jesus say, 'Why do you persecute me?' Ask of your elders who command you, 'How many have heard the voice of God?' You unbelievers! I will say no more; this is in the hands of Almighty God! Let those who wish find me; I speak no more to you here."

With that, Paul turned and walked away.

But the synagogue leader, the one called Alexander, leaped to his feet from a bench. Behind Paul's back he shouted, "This man speaks evil! Pay no attention; he has the voice of Satan; he pretends like an evil spirit to heal the crippled beggars. . . ."

His voice was lost in the synagogue's turmoil.

Aquila and I joined Paul's other disciples, and we left through the door in a body after Paul. In a few moments we were joined, to our amazement, by others from the Jewish congregation: three of the synagogue elders who had listened to Paul on that first day after our arrival in Ephesus, several more who had been our

145

friends in Ephesus from the beginning, and some who were strangers.

Paul looked at the group. He held out his arms.

"Blessed be the Name of the Lord Jesus Christ," he shouted.

Someone said, "Amen." Others repeated it, "Amen, Amen." The word was picked up by all in a spontaneous chant: "Amen, Amen, Amen. Blessed be the Name of the Lord Jesus Christ. Amen, Amen, Amen. . . ."

The synagogue door slammed shut from inside to keep out the sound.

We walked as a group together down the street, chanting. Slowly we dispersed, with smiles and handshakes, going our separate ways.

17

Our church service on the following day, Sunday, was overwhelming. Ahead of time, I sent Nambio to bring back Flavia and Actius to help greet the newcomers. Delia busied herself all afternoon making pitchers of fruit juices and biscuits. Nevia set out cups on the table near the flower bed for a later, social togetherness.

The atrium was swept clean, the benches, divans, pillows, and rugs arranged well before our congregation arrived. They came before our five o'clock time, and I could not believe the number. Aquila kept count, and we had forty-five persons.

Silas and Aristarchus were busy to the last minute baptizing new believers in the Way of Jesus. We had the Christians from Galilee, Jews from the synagogue, including the three elders, their wives, and some children, in addition to those who had been coming previously.

Paul led the service with simplicity and feeling. Along with prayers, scripture reading, psalms and blessings, he spoke briefly about the great gift the Lord had sent to the world of Jews and Gentiles, his own Son, to redeem mankind from sin and give the promise of eternal life to those who followed his Way. At the end, all present joined in the sacrament of Christ's Communion, an especially moving occasion for those who celebrated the Lord's Supper for the first time.

Everyone stayed for the refreshments afterward, and some remained until late in the evening, making friends with each other and discussing what had happened to bring them here. Flavia and Actius were our cohosts, making sure that no one was left alone. Delia kept pressing more fruit for juice; Nambio and Nevia refilled cups. It was a joyful, happy evening.

Shortly after the service itself, a distraught man came to our door asking for Luke. He was the father of a boy whom Luke had tended during the afternoon—a young boy who had been taken with a sudden fever. Before he left his patient, Luke had given word where he could be found if the child turned worse during the evening.

The father believed his son was near death. Desperately he begged Luke to come.

Luke went at once to Paul. "Give me your handkerchief?" he asked.

Without a word Paul reached into a pocket of his robe and drew it out. He handed it to Luke, who carried it off as he followed the boy's father to their home.

Several hours later Luke returned, while our gathering was still lively. I saw him come into the atrium smiling.

"How is the boy?" I asked anxiously.

"He is recovered," Luke reported. "I gave him Paul's handkerchief to hold. His fever broke; he left his bed to play with his toys. Priscilla, God has allowed to Paul the special gift of healing."

Ephesus is a city strange in itself. As a place with a seaport outlet for trade from the inland provinces of Asia and as a point of transit for travelers from every section of the world, Ephesus contains many extraordinary people. Unexpected events happen in this city.

One of the most unusual concerned a band of traveling Jewish exorcists who stopped for a time.

Paul had arranged, through Lucius, with a schoolmaster for use of his hall for teaching the Way. The teacher's name was

Tyrannus; he taught more prosaic subjects in the cool of the morning and toward sundown. The hall was available through the heat of the day from eleven to four, and Paul took it for its roomy facilities.

Meanwhile, the news of his miraculous healing of the beggar woman on the Arcadian Way and the curing of the boy dying of fever with the touch of only his handkerchief spread all over the city. Appeals from the ill began pouring into the house where Paul lived. The blind came; the crippled, the ones possessed of evil spirits arrived at Paul's door if only to touch his robe. Mothers wanted a piece of his clothing to take back to sick children. Paul was nearly besieged in his house. Epaphras and Timothy had to walk with him to his teaching at the hall of Tyrannus to make way through the people. Paul fulfilled all hopes, his name was heard everywhere.

"What manner of man is this?" the people asked.

The exorcist band heard of Paul's power in the name of Jesus. They were seven sons of one Sceva, known as a Jewish chief priest. A man possessed by an evil spirit came to them, and the band decided they could use Paul's method. So they called on the evil spirit by saying, "I exorcise you by Jesus, whom Paul proclaims." The evil spirit answered, "Jesus indeed I know, and Paul I understand. But who are you?" And the man possessed by the spirit leaped on them, tore their clothing, and overpowered them so that the exorcists fled from the house naked and battered.

This story was told to us many times over, as it quickly went to both Jews and Gentiles living in Ephesus. It could have been an event to laugh about, but it was not. For fear and awe spread over the people. The name of the Lord Jesus was no longer ignored, but came to be held in highest respect.

The effect on the lives of all of us with Paul was tremendous. The hall of Tyrannus was filled each day by believers who came to hear Paul speak of the Way. Silas and Aristarchus were occupied with baptisms from morning until evening. Luke had little time to sleep between calls from the sick. We added a second day for services for the church, and expected soon to have a third. Silas, Aristarchus, and Paul took turns in leading the worship. Sometimes our congregation numbered over one hundred.

Between assisting Paul down at his house, now every afternoon, and the increased responsibilities of our church, I had to give up much of my assistance to Aquila in the shop. We engaged full time the apprentice from the sail yard of Stephanas, as too many orders were coming in for us to handle. Somehow I managed in midnight hours to keep up with the accounts.

In this situation I called on Flavia's help. In the time she gave each day, she responded all the way. I took on the added duty of paying special attention to women converts, as I had done in Corinth. In this work Flavia not only assisted but did much on her own. We explained to the women the real meaning of the Way of Jesus in their own lives.

Finally we decided on daily morning meetings for women in our atrium, informal so that they could ask questions and more deeply establish their faith.

One more episode in Ephesus gave even greater emphasis to all our work in Christ.

The city, being filled with unusual people as I have said, contained a number of resident magicians, sorcerers, and the like. They made a great business of selling writing on these subjects, locally called "Ephesian Letters," telling fortunes, and prophesying. Ephesus had a reputation for such secret practices. Many of these men gathered together to acknowledge the greater power of the gospel of Jesus over their own abilities. They brought all their writings, books, and scrolls to a pile at a crossroads in the Arcadian Way, and burned them before the population. Reports circulated through the city that the works consumed in the spectacular fire came to a total value of fifty thousand pieces of silver.

Travelers to and from Ephesus heard all these things and carried the news back into the far reaches of Asia and other parts of the Empire.

So the Word of God grew in strength everywhere.

Yet, a dark cloud began to take form from the west, over Corinth. First I received a joyful letter from Antonia telling me that she had given birth normally to a healthy son, now growing into a strong baby boy. Her happiness was more than she could describe. She gave thankful prayers to Jesus every morning. Antonia said that she attended church every Sunday in company with

Lida and Cornelia. Cornelia's husband had resumed almost normal life by using the exercises prescribed by Luke, and her happiness paralleled Antonia's own.

And news about my beloved Alcesta: The girl was soon to be married to Tarsos, the eldest son of Stephanas. After their marriage, the couple planned to establish an infirmary for young waifs and children of the poor. Tarsos would be the physician, Alcesta the nurse. Both were studying intensely to gain their own qualifications. Alcesta sent her dearest love to Aquila and to me, and hoped we would soon be back in Corinth to take part in her joy.

The rest of Antonia's letter was different, as she probably intended it to be without unduly alarming me. After the birth of her son, her husband, Cyrus, kept his promise of becoming a convert to Christianity. He attended church on Sundays with her, having cut all his ties to the Temple of Aphrodite. But, to celebrate his conversion, he had given a huge party at their house for all his friends, some Christian but most not. Antonia intimated indirectly that it was much the same kind of party that Aquila and I had gone to so long before. They held a church service, and the guests drank a great deal of the wine and ate cakes instead of plain bread to celebrate the Supper of Christ. Antonia wrote:

I told Cyrus I did not think this was quite the way Jesus meant it to be, but he assured me it was all right. Most of the guests openly played their sexual games on the divans as they used to do, but I did not want to see, so I hid in my own room with my son and prayed. My husband says that if Jesus died to make men free of sin, then nothing is sinful. We are free to do as we please, he thinks. I know this is not true.

Then I received a letter from Chloe in Corinth, my Jewish friend turned Christian. I had continued a correspondence with her, and this letter was in reply to one of mine describing our church in Ephesus. She wrote in part:

I wish I could tell you that our church in Corinth does as well as yours. Here we are sinking deeper into contention and division. Since Apollos left us, some time ago, we have had no leaders to hold our congregation together. Each man seems to desire to lead the rest, but none will follow any but himself. So the Word of God is divided into different ways by men, and the Way of Jesus into all manner of interpretations. I am ashamed to say that some of the women are no better than the men. Each one seeks to be more privileged than the other for her own gain. I do not mean to distress you. . . .

Distress is scarcely the word to describe my feelings when I read this. I showed the letter to Aquila.

"What will you do?" he asked.

"I don't know," I answered. "Paul has so much on his mind already. . . ."

But Paul received a letter from Gaius, whose house had been overflowing with numbers of the congregation. He gave it to me to read.

Gaius feared that the Corinthian church would split into divisions, each going its own way. He wrote:

You have taught us that our church is a whole in one body, through faith in Jesus. You have also taught us that each church of Jesus is in one whole body of a united Church of Christ through the Word. With us in Corinth these things are not so. . . .

He added in his letter that our friend Stephanas would soon be making his long-deferred business trip to Ephesus. He would bring with him more details, together with a recommendation from them both that Paul send an emissary to Corinth to help put matters together again.

"Whom can you spare?" I asked Paul.

"I do not know yet," Paul replied. "I have sent for Titus to come quickly from Antioch to help us here. Perhaps when he arrives we could send Timothy to Corinth; he is well known to them all."

Titus, as I had been told, had been a disciple with Paul from the earliest days. Paul put great trust in him. I was glad to hear that he would join us.

Then an event occurred in Ephesus that temporarily put everything else out of our minds.

I had often noticed in the shops in Corinth silver replicas of the goddess Artemis, with her many breasts. Once, on a statue of her I counted twenty-two breasts, complete with nipples. Almost every Gentile household of the unconverted contained one or more of these silver replicas, usually finely done. I saw them in those houses where we had been.

Travelers through Ephesus bought the statuettes to take with them, especially those from the east, where Artemis—often confused with the Roman Diana—was greatly revered as a fertility goddess. Until the episode I now tell of, it never occurred to me how great a business the Artemis replicas must be to Ephesian silversmiths.

Early one afternoon as I walked down the Arcadian Way to Paul's house, I heard a tumult, off to one side, coming from somewhere near the amphitheater. As I approached, the sound grew louder, sustained, as a roar from thousands of voices. The Arcadian Way seemed unusually deserted. My first thought was of some sort of game being played in the stadium; the sound must be spectators cheering.

Three or four men ran past me, carrying sticks. Their faces looked ugly. As they met a lone man passer-by, they shouted at him and pointed toward the noise.

"Artemis . . . Artemis . . . saving Artemis!" was all that I could hear of their words. They raced on, the passer-by with them.

Now the roar did not resemble cheering; it was angry. A feeling of something was in the air. I hurried, keeping my head turned down. No other women were in sight. Even the avenue itself was clear of wagons and carriages.

Two more men ran by, glancing at me as they went. Did I imagine they hesitated? I kept walking fast. A man came out of a building doorway, called out to the men: "What is it? What is happening?"

I heard part of their answer. "The theater, for Artemis . . . silver . . . that Paul . . . Christian. Hurry!"

The two ran on.

I felt dizzy, sick. Paul had often spoken of violence against him. I had never tried to imagine what it was like. The roar reaching me was clear now. I put my hand to my mouth—agonized. Did they have Paul there?

I walked faster, not daring to run and attract attention to where I was going. Other men passed me. One stopped to look at me. He said something I didn't understand. I went on, paying no heed. I reached the narrow street of Paul's house, turned into it. It was quiet there, but I kept close to the house walls. The roar from the amphitheater rose and fell in waves.

As I reached the door of the house, I found Lucius Andronicus hurrying up from the other direction.

"Where is Paul?" he demanded without ceremony.

"I don't know."

I pounded on the door frantically. So did Lucius.

"Did you come down the avenue? Thank God, they didn't see you," he said.

"Who is it?" a voice called from inside the house.

"Me, Priscilla," I called back.

The door was hastily unbolted and opened. Epaphras was there.

"Priscilla, what are you—? Lucius, come in quickly."

We did even as I echoed Lucius. "Where is Paul?"

"Here in the gineceo, resting. We had a warning at noontime at the Tyrannus hall. We made Paul come back here. He is safe so far. What is happening?"

"The silversmiths are demonstrating. It's a nasty affair," Lucius said. He added, "I hear they have caught two of your men, I don't know which."

"Oh, no!" Epaphras gasped. "Silas is here, and Timothy—Aristarchus! It could be him, and Gaius—Gaius arrived only this morning from Macedonia. Tychicus sent him down from there. We didn't know until then he was coming. Aristarchus went to meet him at the docks—"

"Gaius?" I asked faintly.

"Not Gaius from Corinth; another, who assisted Paul in the north. Don't mention this to Paul yet—"

"Don't mention what?"

The three of us jumped at the roaring voice behind us. Paul stood there like an angry bull.

Epaphras stammered. "Lucius thinks they may have caught Aristarchus and Gaius—"

"Where?" Paul demanded.

"The silversmiths are demonstrating against you in the amphitheater," Lucius said. "You cannot go out there—"

153

Paul strode toward the door. Lucius Andronicus was a big man, and strong. Paul pushed him aside like a piece of straw. He pulled up the wooden beam that secured the door.

"Silas, Timothy, quick!" Epaphras shouted.

As one, Epaphras, Lucius and I clutched at Paul as he threw the door open. He was out on the street, brushing us off as he might flies. He started toward the amphitheater.

"Paul!" I cried. "Don't! Don't, for the sake of God! They'll kill you! You are just one against a mad mob!"

He strode away, head forward. Epaphras and Lucius ran after him; Silas and Timothy tore out of the house to block him from the front. I could not help, my poor strength was as nothing against the power of an angry Paul. The four men tried to hold those long arms, did their best to lift him up off the ground, grunting as they did so.

Paul kept plowing ahead, dragging them.

I ran beside him.

"Paul!" I shouted into his ear. "You're not doing this for Christ, you're doing it for your own sake!"

He gave up, stopped struggling. Instantly the four men lifted him, their holds secure. They rushed Paul back through the door of the house, slammed it shut and put the heavy beam across it again.

Everyone was out of breath. We stared at each other. Epaphras sat on a bench in relief.

"Paul," Lucius said, "there are twenty-five thousand men in that place. You can't fight that many. They would kill you and the other two as well. Be reasonable."

Paul hesitated. Then he turned abruptly and went back into his gineceo.

"Leave him alone; he wants time to think," I said.

"Don't let him go," Lucius ordered. "I'll try to find out what I can do. Wait here, all of you."

We opened the door for Lucius, and he disappeared. But during the moment it was open I could hear a thundering chant in unison. The words were clear: "Great is Artemis of the Ephesians! Great is—"

The door closed.

We waited together in the small atrium, each trying to ease the

154

tension of the others—Silas, Timothy, Epaphras, and I. None of us disturbed Paul, behind his closed gineceo door.

Then, late in the afternoon, a knock came from outside. We all leaped up. Epaphras asked who was there.

Lucius had returned at last. Aristarchus and Gaius were with him. Both of them were in dreadful condition, exhausted, pale, clothing torn, dirty. But they were not physically harmed.

I slipped away from the others, went into Paul's gineceo without knocking. I found him praying, as I suppose all of us waiting had known he would be doing through those hours.

"Paul," I said quietly, "they are home. They are all right."

He looked up at me from the side of the divan, where he was kneeling.

"Prisca," he said, "kneel with me. With me, give thanks to our God for saving them."

I knelt beside him. We prayed together in silence. I thanked the Lord God not only for the safety of the two in danger but even more—I confess—for the safety of Paul, so narrowly diverted from almost certain death.

It took some little time for us to hear the full story. The leader of the silversmiths in Ephesus was a man named Demetrius. He called the demonstration to protest the great loss of business all silversmiths were experiencing because Paul preached not only in Ephesus but throughout Asia against the worship of idols made by men. The craft was in danger of disappearing. Not only that, Demetrius told the assembled crowd, but the Temple of the great goddess Artemis was being despised, and her greatness diminished, she whom all Asia and the inhabited earth worshiped. Those who heard cried out in their anger, "Great is Artemis of the Ephesians." The throng grew from all over the city, most of the men not knowing what the uproar was about. Aristarchus and Gaius had been seized on the way from the docks and dragged into the amphitheater filled with people who had caught the contagion of wrath. The Jews of the synagogue heard of the riot. They came down with Alexander, their leader, and pushed him onto the speaker's platform so that he could say to all that the Jews were not responsible for this. But the moment the huge assembly heard that he was a Jew, they shouted him down, for they knew that

Jews also were against their goddess. For some two hours they chanted together, "Great is Artemis of the Ephesians!"

At length the town clerk was able to make himself heard from the platform. He said that everyone knew the city of the Ephesians was warden of the Temple of Artemis, and this being undeniable they should quit. The two men brought in had not blasphemed against the goddess, and if Demetrius had a claim let him bring lawful charges in lawful assembly. For indeed, the town clerk said, all of them were in danger of being charged by the Roman authorities with insurrection, and there would be no excuse. He told them to go home. That was the end of it.

"But," Lucius Andronicus warned all of us, "do not think that the silversmith Demetrius is satisfied. Be on your guard!"

Epaphras was about to walk home with me through the gathering darkness. Aquila came running to the door, banged on it.

When he saw me he cried, "Thank God! You are safe." He was out of breath. "Nambio just now heard about the riot, and told me. You were not home yet—"

At home later, I had a reaction from the tension. It had been the first time I experienced the terror of mad violence. I had never known what it could be. I had no appetite for Delia's evening meal. Neither did Aquila.

18

The situation in Ephesus seemed quieter after the riot, for a time at least. Paul continued teaching at the hall of Tyrannus to full audiences, from which we gained many converts. Some were Jews, finally convinced by their friends already turned Christian that Jesus was the promised Savior. Most converts were Gentiles who confessed that they had been idol-worshipers of Artemis. After listening to Paul they saw the falseness of revering a carved stone, even though the legend had it that the sculptured goddess had fallen miraculously from the sky, as some said, a thousand years before.

Increasing numbers of the church congregation now made it necessary to increase our services to three each week. After talking with Paul, Flavia and I decided we would hold two on Sundays, one at the hour of eleven in the morning and the other, as before, at five in the afternoon. The third service was the extra one we had already started, at the hour of seven on Monday evenings. Flavia took over many of the responsibilities and, as matters shortly turned out, soon had to assume most of them.

During the mornings, both of us held daily question-and-answer meetings for the women of the church.

According to my promise to Nambio, I had long since talked with my three servants about religious beliefs. I explained to them together what our church services meant, without trying to proselytize them. I felt I had the advantage; they would believe anything I said and would accept Jesus as a command from their mistress, slaves as they were. To my surprise, nothing of the sort happened. Nambio knew about the God of the Jews, his ancestral heritage. As a young man he had read the scriptures, but through a succession of Gentile owners he had dropped any religious beliefs at all. He wanted nothing to do with idols. Delia's owners, on the contrary, had forced her to pray to the replicas of Artemis in their houses, believing that one more prayer might sway the goddess in their favor. Religion to her had become as nothing, worthless. Nevia had not learned anything at all about any religion. She had been taught only about her duties as a servant. As she was quick to follow instructions, she had been promised by Lucius that when she was older he would have her taught in a trade. These three lived their lives as they were told by masters and mistresses, and to be loyal to them even if they were sold from one to another. Life was a breathing spell of existence, and when it finished all was gone in death.

I told them that belief in Jesus brought promise of eternal life in Heaven, where slaves and masters were equal. They smiled at me, all three, and Nambio expressed their feelings:

"As slaves, we have no plans, no worries. We are fed, and we do the best work we can for you, mistress. When we no longer exist, well—we no longer exist."

Each afternoon that was possible for me, I walked down to

157

Paul's house to find out what I could do to help. The place was usually in confusion, with so many demands pressing down. Silas and Aristarchus had lists of baptisms to be recorded. I found myself taking care of this. Timothy had names of women to be seen in every part of the city by either Flavia or me, and Epaphras, who guarded the house now for possible trouble, was always confronted at the door by sick and maimed persons waiting for Paul's cures. Luke had become so busy we seldom saw him. When Paul returned after his teaching, usually late, Gaius, the new associate, walked with him as a safeguard.

Paul had increasing correspondence, for which he wanted my help. Some letters now I could do on my own, such as acknowledgments of contributions coming in from other churches and individuals. Letters of advice to church groups, Paul dictated to me. And a hundred other details crowded in on him.

This appeared to be a brief interval of waiting—for what? The arrival of Titus from Antioch for one, but also of Stephanas from Corinth. I had told Paul something of the letters to me from Antonia and from Chloe, although I did soften the reports. We had not mentioned Corinth again, but the worry was hanging over him. The strain of these things drained his enormous strength. I could see it. If the others did, they said nothing to me. But now we were all under strain.

Much worse was to come.

Titus and Stephanas arrived in Ephesus within twenty-four hours of each other. I was glad to meet Titus, of whom I had heard so much. As for my good friend and rescuer, Stephanas, I was overjoyed. He came to Paul's house late one afternoon while I was looking over letters Paul had not yet read.

When I heard Stephanas' voice out in the hallway, I rushed out of the gineceo to greet him. He gave me a big hug and a kiss on the cheek.

"Priscilla, as beautiful as always!" he exclaimed, holding me away while he looked at me. "Ephesus has been good to you."

"Yes," I replied, "we are doing what we came for and I'm happy."

"I think we need you back in Corinth. I have much to say about that. Is Paul here?"

"He's not yet back from teaching, but he should be here at any moment. How are your family—and Alcesta?"

"The family is fine. My wife sends her love to you." Then he grinned. "As for Alcesta—she is the happiest girl in the world. You knew she will be my daughter-in-law? She and Tarsos will be married as soon as their studies are completed."

"Antonia told me. I'm so happy about it, Stephanas."

"So am I, and Dorice, too. So many good things have come through the church for all of us—most of us."

"About that," I said, "Paul has been looking for you. He is very concerned."

Stephanas nodded. "I regret that I must tell him—"

Someone's knock at the door interrupted. Epaphras opened it carefully, then let in a woman in a black shawl and mantle. She held a little girl in her arms.

"Master," she cried out, "my grandchild—she's very ill. I seek the master Paul, I fear she may die. Is he here?"

"Not yet, but very soon. Please sit here and wait." Epaphras led her to a bench in the hall.

Stephanas glanced at me. "What is this? You have an infirmary?"

I smiled. "This happens all day and some nights. Paul has a power from God to heal. Everyone in Ephesus knows it. Epaphras, did you meet our friend from Corinth, Stephanas?"

"At the door when he came in. So glad to meet you, and welcome to our midst."

I had already told Paul that Aquila and I would like to have Stephanas come with him to our home for dinner on the first night of his arrival, if that was proper. We would ask Silas and Timothy, too, as a reunion, and we would hear Stephanas tell of the Corinth troubles without interruption from outside callers. Paul agreed readily.

So as soon as Paul came in, I slipped out of the house to tell Delia. But as I left I watched Paul place his hand on the sick little girl's head. He spoke a few words over her. The young one suddenly looked up at her grandmother.

"Let me down," she demanded. "I want to walk home. . . ."

That evening in our atrium, Stephanas told us the whole story of what had happened in Corinth. Paul, Silas, and Timothy listened, and so did Aquila and I.

After Apollos left the city, Stephanas said, the church congregation divided itself.

"Forgive me, Paul. I must speak very frankly, so you will understand. One group likes Apollos better than they do you. The other group favors you over Apollos. Even though you and Apollos taught the same things, perhaps in different wording, your personalities differed and, most unreasonably, became a cause for each group. Beyond that, the apostle Peter, called Cephas, visited Corinth only briefly but long enough to speak to the church members a few times—"

"Cephas!" Paul exclaimed. "I did not know."

"Some of his teaching was at variance, but only in detail, from what the people had learned through you and Apollos. Many were impressed, and a third group formed itself. Wait—there has come into existence a fourth division. These are Greek intellectuals, who claim that you, Paul, and Apollos and Cephas are all Jews and what you three say about Jesus is based on your own background of Jewish Law. In other words, all of you are too strict. They say they believe in Christ, but their belief must be from the viewpoint of Greek philosophy. They interpret the Way of Jesus as one pointing to 'self-realization,' they call it. This group thinks that as Christ forgave sins—which you have said, Paul—then Christians are free to do what they wish to 'realize' themselves. There is no such thing as sin, they claim, and they act as they wish."

Paul leaned over on the divan where he was sitting, and held his head between his hands.

"I must tell you, Priscilla," Stephanas continued, "that the leader of this last group is Cyrus, husband of your friend Antonia, a very loyal church member herself."

Antonia's letter! That's what she had been trying to tell me.

I could only say, "Poor Antonia!"

Stephanas summed it up by saying that the Corinthian church was divided into four sections, or "parties," as he called them: the Paul party; the Apollos party; the Cephas, or Peter, party; and the Christ party, the last being the Greek intellectuals.

The dangers were not only in division of church unity, Stephanas believed, but especially that the supreme Word of God was being forgotten and was being replaced by the words of men—the church members themselves.

They argue at meetings of the congregation, and even interrupt church services, he went on. Wives have become involved, he said, and speak out in contradiction of their husbands. They seem to have lost respect for reasonable order and decorum. One woman, a widow by name of Druda, insists on having meetings in her house, Stephanas reported. This causes jealousy and friction among others.

"Druda!" I cried in distress. "I am responsible for her."

"No," Silas interrupted. "You turned her over to me, and I baptized her."

Immorality was growing through many of those calling themselves Christians, Stephanas said. Did we remember the name of Melas, and his father's wife, Laodice? They were openly sleeping together, to the approval of the intellectuals, the "Christ party."

This news was further shock, but I was not surprised at all. Paul jumped up and paced across the atrium before returning to his seat.

"I must make this point," Stephanas declared. "What I have told you reflects only a part of the church you founded, Paul. The rest of us remember the Holy Spirit, which resides in us. I have brought a letter with me signed by many, asking from you answers to reasonable questions concerning their actions and their ways of life. They need your help."

Stephanas said that two of his associates had come with him on this business trip, by name Fortunatus and Achaicus, whom none of us knew, as they had become faithful Christians after we left. They, too, could give information to Paul similar to what he had reported.

But, he finished, the dissidents causing trouble—a great many of whom had been recent converts, if that was the word—had brought the Christian church to a state of crisis in Corinth.

Paul rose again from the divan and strode across the atrium. I saw his shoulders pushed forward, his jaw jutting out, the gleam in his eyes from the lamplight in the night's darkness. Paul was very, very angry.

We kept silent.

Then Paul stopped in front of Timothy.

"It is my wish, Timothy, that you go at once to Corinth. You will remind these people that it is not Paul, or Apollos, or Cephas who will judge them, but only Christ Jesus and Almighty God himself. I will write a full letter to them—" he swung around to me "—but in your handwriting, Prisca. This will be my letter to the Corinthians. . . ."

We began the letter the following afternoon, in Paul's ginceo. He had cut short his afternoon teaching and returned to the house early. He told Epaphras we were not to be disturbed.

I say "we" referring to the letter only because it was in my handwriting. It was a long letter, taking a number of days to complete. I cannot remember the words he dictated, and will not attempt to report on the letter, as it speaks for itself—and for Paul. It must still be in the hands of the church elders in Corinth.

But certain statements made by Paul I do remember, as they seemed pertinent not only to the Corinth church but to the whole Church of Christ throughout our world. Also, I did take the liberty he gave me of asking him the meaning of some sentences he dictated which puzzled me.

These few things which I remember are probably not in order as dictated but, rather, as they come to my mind.

After his opening greeting, Paul severely condemned the divisions and disruptions of the Corinth church.

Each member was saying, he had heard, "I belong to Paul" or "I belong to Apollos" or "to Cephas" or "Christ." "Has Christ become so divided?" Paul asked. "Was I crucified on your behalf?" Paul had planted the seed, Apollos watered it, but God caused the plant to grow. Let no man glory in his own nature, he told them. All things belonged to them, whether Paul or Apollos or Cephas, or the world, or life and death, things present or things to come—all were theirs. But they themselves belonged to Christ, and Christ belonged to God.

When he returned to Corinth, Paul demanded, What did they want him to bring, a rod, or to come with love and gentle spirit?

Paul was harsh on the case of Melas and Laodice. Even as he dictated, his voice rose in anger. In brief, he told the church that for one of them to lie in fornication with his father's wife was far worse than the fornication commonplace among pagan Gentiles. Still worse, some among them approved of such a thing. Paul said that although he was not with them in person, he was there in spirit. Already he had judged in the Name of the Lord Jesus that this man, in full assembly of all members, should be delivered to Satan. Put him away from yourselves, Paul commanded.

Their approval of such acts was wicked, Paul lashed out. He used a metaphor as an example. Didn't they know that a little leaven leavens the pan of dough? Throw out the old leaven of malice and sin, he told them, and keep faith in Christ with new bread of sinlessness and truth.

Paul warned the Corinthians against their transgressions. He told them that a man's body as well as his spirit is a member of Christ. Should he, then, join his body with that of a prostitute? No! he exclaimed in his letter. Jesus said two in joining one to another became one flesh. (This was direct rebuttal of the Greek intellectuals' claim that body gratification with a prostitute was not sin. But sin it was, because one became as a prostitute oneself. This was my unspoken comment.)

Not all of Paul's letter was criticism. He included a section of the most beautiful poetic philosophy on the meaning of love—a meaning in its broadest sense of charity and fraternity. I was amazed, as well as I knew him, that my gruff, outspoken friend with the single-minded purpose of life could write with such perception of words and feelings. It is a section that deserves to go down through the ages. I wish I could include all of it, but it begins with the words: *Though I speak with the tongues of men and of angels, and have not love, I have become as sounding brass or a tinkling cymbal. . . .* It ends with: *But now remains faith, hope, love, these three; and the greatest of these is love.*

We reached the afternoon when Paul had before him the questioning letter that Stephanas had brought from the Corinthian congregation.

His first phrase startled me: *Now, about the things of which you wrote to me, it is good for a man not to touch a woman*—although his next words clarified what he meant for the wayward Corinthians—*but because of the temptations existing let every man have for himself a wife, and each woman have her own husband. Let*

163

each husband give to his wife what she needs, and also the wife give to the husband what he needs. Let not one hold back on the other, except by consent for a time for a retreat in prayer, then come together again so Satan will not tempt your lack of self-control.

He started to dictate another thought, but I interrupted him gently.

"Paul, before you go on—do you remember what you told me, one night, in our house in Corinth?"

He looked at me with irritation, for I had broken into his concentration. "What? What was that? In Corinth?"

I was sorry I had said anything, and felt foolish. "You will remember, Paul," I said, embarrassed. "It meant so much to Aquila and to me—perhaps it will also to others. . . ."

Paul was puzzled. Then, suddenly, he smiled.

"Yes, Prisca, now I do remember. You are right; I had forgotten."

Most of the time while he dictated, Paul stood and paced the floor despite his pain. Now he walked toward me. I looked up at him from my seat at the writing table. For the briefest instant our glances met. I turned my head away. Abruptly Paul swung around, his back to me.

"Insert this in the proper place, Prisca. Where? Two sentences ago?" He stood for a moment, then said slowly, *A wife's body does not belong to her but to her husband. Likewise, a husband's body belongs not to him but to his wife. Use your possessions well and often, dear ones.*

Paul sat down. I did not write the last sentence into the letter.

On another afternoon, we reached the next part of Paul's letter, still having to do with relations between men and women. He gave advice to unmarried men and widows that they remain as they were, celibate as he was himself. But if self-control was impossible they should marry. It was better to marry than to suffer from their own emotions.

I never asked Paul about his preference, expressed a number of times in his letter, for states of chastity rather than marriage. I had no right to do so, and also I felt that he had some vision of the impermanence of present world conditions, either for the Roman

164

Empire or through a suspicion that God's Day of Judgment was near. I had heard him stress a number of times that Christians be content in their present states, as the span of earthly life was so brief in relation to eternity with God in Heaven.

But, one day, Paul and I did have our first argument. During that afternoon, he had dictated on the relationship of men and women to God and to Christ, followed by a strong comment that women should have their heads covered while at prayer in church. In still another section he made it clear that wives should not speak out in church. If they had questions, they should ask their husbands about them at home.

I waited until our work for the afternoon was finished. Then I did ask Paul about what seemed to be discrepancies in his teaching.

"You wrote today that Christ is the head of every man, and man is the head of the woman, and God is the head of Christ. Then you said that a man is the image and glory of God, but a woman is the glory of the man. This had to do with head coverings at prayer. These things seem to make women lesser creatures than men. I suppose in some ways they are, but I have heard you so often say that in the sight of God men and women are equal."

"That is true, and I will say it again, Prisca. Yet, have you ever heard me say women were equal in the sight of men?"

"No," I had to admit.

"Prisca, you have been brought up under the Jewish Law, which requires that a married woman must never go out in public without a covering over her head that fastens under her chin. Now that you are no longer under the Law, I notice that you use only a light scarf tied in back of your neck. Why do you do even that much?"

I laughed. "You are too observant, Paul. I use it because it is customary, and I would look odd if I didn't have any scarf."

"So it is custom that makes the inequality, not God?"

"All right," I said. "You win your point. I understand."

"No," he said, "let me say more. In accordance with our belief, God created Adam in his image. But, from the side of Adam, God created woman. So man was not created because of the woman, but woman because of the man, at the beginning. If you will read again what I also said today in the letter, *'Nevertheless, neither is*

165

woman without the man, nor man without the woman. For as woman is from the man, so is man through the woman, but all things are from God.'"

"Then, why are wives not allowed to speak out in church?"

"Prisca!" Paul's eyebrows seemed to bristle, but he smiled. "You think you will catch me. Yes, there is a custom of men, and of women, too, and of God—the custom that worship is to be in peace and decorum. I have said enough to men in my letter about unity in the church. Should I say nothing to women? You yourself told me of the women in Corinth from Chloe's letter, and you heard the report from Stephanas concerning those like the one called Druda. How else do we keep such women quiet?"

"Paul, my master, forgive me for my silly questions. You are too patient with an impatient woman."

I stood up from the table where I had been writing, but he motioned me to wait.

"Prisca," he said, "I think we should add one sentence to the part where women should wear head coverings at prayer according to the custom of our time. Please write: *But if anyone wants to be contentious about this matter, we do not have such a custom, nor do the churches of Christ.*"

19

Even before our letter to the Corinthians was finished, a disturbing rumor reached us through several of the Jewish colony in Ephesus who had been baptized in the Way. The rumor, unconfirmed, raised suspicions that Alexander, leader of the synagogue, had allied himself with Demetrius of the silversmiths to denounce Paul to the Roman authorities for causing the riot in the amphitheater.

It was most improbable, of course, as the Jews of Ephesus were just as much against the worship of silver replicas of the goddess Artemis as Paul. But Alexander was losing synagogue members through Paul's conversions, as Demetrius' business was decreasing because so many Gentiles became Christians. Demetrius had failed in his purpose with the great demonstration against Paul. It was possible, and paradoxical, that the two opposites could join together in common hatred of the Christian apostle. And if Alexander had heard of the unsuccessful attempt of the synagogue in Corinth to get rid of Paul, he might have felt he needed the ready-made political and economical support of Demetrius in confronting the Roman authorities in Ephesus.

We of Paul's group heard only the rumors. So a new cloud of worry descended over all of us.

Paul and I worked longer hours to complete the Corinthian letter to his satisfaction, especially as Fortunatus and Achaicus were about to return to Corinth and had agreed to carry the letter with them. Stephanas, with business still to do, planned to stay in Ephesus a few days longer.

Timothy, on Paul's orders, had long since gone to Corinth, but no word had yet come from him regarding his reception there.

Otherwise, affairs continued at an accelerated level. Our church grew steadily in membership and strength. The energetic Flavia seemed to be everywhere at once, in our house arranging for the church services, assisting with the morning women's sessions, visiting other women in their houses to follow the work of Silas and Aristarchus. The lives of Flavia and her husband had changed so much; they were accepted now by Gentiles as well as Christianized Jews who had formerly rejected them. And, in our business, Aquila and his apprentice kept up with the steady flow of orders for tents, awnings, and sails for boats. Our financial assets continued to increase.

Such comparative steadiness did not last long.

Early one morning while Aquila and I were still asleep, Nevia quietly came into our room to wake me.

"Mistress Priscilla," she whispered. "Master Epaphras is here. He wishes to speak with you. I— I think he has something bad to tell you."

Paul, I thought. I jumped from my couch. Nevia quickly took one of my mantles from its hook and held it for me while I slipped into it.

"He is waiting by the atrium entrance," Nevia said.

I hurried from the room with Nevia following. Aquila had not awakened.

167

Epaphras put out his hands toward me as I ran to him. "I am sorry to wake you."

"Paul! Is it Paul?"

He nodded. "Last night, late, he was put under arrest. The soldiers came, and took him away. He said he had been expecting them soon."

I put my hands to my face and cried. Sobs shook me. "Paul, oh, Paul—"

Nevia's comforting arm went around my shoulder.

"Priscilla," Epaphras said, trying to ease the shock, "I am sure it will be all right. Paul has been in prison before. It is part of our work for the gospel."

"I know, I know," I managed to say through my tears. "It's on account of that terrible man Alexander."

"Paul does not say he is terrible, only misguided," Epaphras reminded me. "I was allowed to follow the soldiers, and the centurion in charge let me go into the prison with Paul. He is very strong, our Paul."

"What did they do to him there? Will he be tortured?"

"No, I am sure he will not be. The head of the prison had orders to whip him, as usual for those arrested. But Paul told them he was a Roman citizen, and they refrained from that. The rank of citizen protects him from harm."

"They put him in chains!" I imagined him with wrists and hands bound, and the heavy weights around his legs. "They did it in Corinth."

"That is required for all prisoners. Priscilla, Paul gave me a message for you. He wanted me to tell you that he finished in his own hand the final salutation to the Corinthian letter, before the soldiers came. He added greetings from you and Aquila and your church. Silas is taking it to Fortunatus and Achaicus this morning, as they leave today. Paul also told me . . . that you should not be distressed. He said . . . he is glad for this . . . for Christ's sake—"

Epaphras' voice broke now. Tears were in his own eyes. He reached for my hand, and his closed on mine with a tight grip.

"Is it possible that I can see him in the prison?"

"No, they would not permit that. But I did arrange with the captain of the prison that I can go there once each day, for a short time, and I believe Silas can come with me. They would not allow a woman."

All of us tried to keep up the daily routines as best we could without him. Silas, Aristarchus, and Titus, among them, took care of the daily instruction groups at the hall of Tyrannus, as we did in our house. We made house calls, and continued to spread the gospel of Jesus through Ephesus. But, everywhere I went, in my mind I kept seeing Paul.

Every day Delia prepared special breads, cakes, and fruits, which Epaphras could carry into the prison. Paul sent word back that he asked God's blessings on her and Flavia for the work they were carrying on in his absence.

The moment Stephanas heard the news, he canceled indefinitely his return to Corinth. He thought he could be of use at the trial. He did, in fact, manage to see the Roman proconsul of these Asian provinces who had ordered Paul's arrest. Through that visit, Paul's trial was scheduled within ten days instead of being delayed for a long period.

The name of Stephanas was perhaps even more powerful in Ephesus than it was in Corinth, due to the numbers of his ships with their home port here. Much of the city's commerce was handled through Stephanas.

The trial itself was a private one, not in public. Aquila and I were told not to come, as only special witnesses would be permitted inside the judgment room. The accusers were indeed Alexander, some of his group from the synagogue, and, we heard, probably Demetrius.

On that day, needless to report, all of us were tense with anxiety. The hour was to be late in the afternoon. We heard what happened from Epaphras, who came to us immediately after it was over. Epaphras had found a guard who let him sit unnoticed at the very back of the courtroom, where he could overhear everything.

Only Silas and Aristarchus of our group were permitted to be present, as witnesses if necessary. Alexander appeared with two of his associates. Stephanas was on hand, and Lucius Andronicus.

Demetrius came with two of his silversmiths flanking him. His presence at the trial confirmed the rumors we had heard.

To everyone's surprise, the town clerk who had quieted the riotous assembly in the amphitheater had also been called as a primary witness.

The proconsul of this Asian part of the Roman Empire carefully read the charges against Paul as brought by the Jews, and asked their leaders to offer their proofs. Alexander was spokesman. He claimed that this disgraceful riot in Ephesus would never have happened if Paul had not been in the city upsetting the balance between the religions as determined by Roman law. The peaceful Jews residing here could not be responsible for the acts of this crazed preacher who disturbed the minds of both Jews and Gentiles by his mad talk—

The proconsul stopped him by raising his hand. "Are these your opinions?" he asked Alexander.

"They are my considered opinions, for the sake of preserving the peace of Ephesus—"

"I do not want opinions, I want facts," the proconsul snapped. "You have given me no facts, either verbally or written in the charges."

He turned to Demetrius and asked for proofs of the charges he had brought against Paul and the Christians.

The silversmith leader burst out with a diatribe against Paul, who had injured the business of his tradesmen by speaking against Artemis, great goddess of Ephesus, revered by Ephesians, visitors, and those throughout the world as the mother goddess of all. His fellow workers and silversmiths had been reduced to penury by the Christian slanders—

Once again the proconsul raised his hand, and demanded that Demetrius state exactly what Paul had said against Artemis.

"He speaks of some unknown god of the Jews who should be more revered than Artemis of Ephesus. He offers nothing to replace our silver replicas of the most wondrous Artemis—"

"Enough." The proconsul halted him.

The town clerk was next called as witness. He testified that the amphitheater riot had been incited by Demetrius as a protest against loss of business. The Christians had nothing to do with it, he declared, nor to his knowledge had ever caused disturbance or spoken against Artemis. Lucius Andronicus added that the Christians were people of peace, and had never in Ephesus spoken against the Empire or Artemis but only in favor of their own God, the same God as that of the Jews. Then Stephanas told of what had happened in Corinth and how the proconsul Gallio there had declared the dispute was between Jews over a matter of interpretation, and did not involve any violation of the laws of Rome. He reported that Gallio had dismissed the case brought by certain Jews.

Hearing this, the proconsul of Asia immediately found in favor of Paul, and severely reprimanded Alexander's group for bringing unprovable accusations and wasting his time and that of the city authorities. He warned them against making further trouble. As for Demetrius, he condemned him for bringing charges against a Roman citizen who had done no more than speak to the people of his own Jewish religious beliefs, which were protected by the laws of Rome. If the silversmiths had suffered economic losses for their failure to meet natural competition, that was a matter for civil judges to investigate; it had nothing to do with criminal charges against this man Paul. He cautioned Demetrius, however, that he could see no possibility of redress for any loss of business that came about through voluntary changes of persons' beliefs, for every subject under Roman law had the right of freedom of worship.

Then he instructed Demetrius to bring no more incitement against the Christians or undertake violence, or face the severest penalties that he, as proconsul, could order.

He dismissed the case against Paul as unjust.

We were overjoyed and thankful, as an understatement. Paul had gone to his house, Epaphras said. He was very tired and needed rest. For the first time in many days I could smile and laugh, with a prayer in my heart of thanksgiving.

But, long after midnight, all in our house were awakened by a loud and urgent knocking on our door. Nambio opened it as Aquila hurried to find out who was there.

Gaius brought dreadful news. Paul had been taken suddenly very ill during the night, and Luke was extremely alarmed. Paul started with chills and fever, which grew steadily worse and brought on delirium.

"Luke wants him brought immediately to you," Gaius reported

breathlessly. "You can care for him better here than where he is. Luke will stay with you to watch over him."

"Yes, of course," I agreed. "How can he be brought here?"

"Epaphras went to find a litter," Gaius answered. "Paul will be wrapped in blankets. He must have taken something in that prison. It was very damp."

"He has been too tired for too long. Nothing matters now; hurry back to Luke. A room will be ready."

Nevia and I quickly prepared the couch in a room off the hallway, on the far side of the atrium, between our corner room and the service area. Nambio lit enough lamps so that everyone could see.

We then waited by the front door. I was too upset to stand still. Remarkably quickly the litter with Paul arrived, and the bearers carried him across the atrium to the room I had selected. Luke stayed at his side; Silas and Titus followed. Epaphras and the others remained in a far corner of the atrium. Aquila came into the room to help lift the nearly unconscious Paul from the litter onto the couch, while Silas paid off the litter bearers.

Lying on the couch, Paul opened his eyes, looked up at me as I leaned over him, and murmured one word: "Prisca."

He closed his eyes again. I felt his forehead, almost too hot to touch. I cannot describe how I felt when I looked down at my Paul, eyes already sunken, mouth half open, breathing hard, face red with fever, sweat all over his face—perhaps other women will understand if they have had such an experience.

I turned to Luke.

"Should we use blankets soaked with cold water for the fever?" I asked.

"We can try," Luke replied.

Quickly Nevia slipped out of the room, returned with two blankets that Delia had soaked in cold water from the supply lines. Carefully we wrapped Paul in the blankets.

Then I drew Luke off to one side. "What do you think?" I asked.

"I do not know," he replied. "I have given him the medicine that I have used before for high fevers. Would that we knew more about these things! It came so suddenly, after the evening meal."

"Might he die?" I tried to keep my voice from shaking.

"It is for Almighty God to say, not me. If it were only me, I would say he might. But the Lord is greater in knowledge than I am."

Paul seemed to lapse into deeper unconsciousness. His fever heightened. We changed the cold, wet blankets from time to time as Delia made them ready and Nevia brought them to us. Luke administered other medicine, and listened to Paul's heart.

Then Luke whispered, "He is failing."

Luke and I stayed beside Paul through the rest of the night, each of us in prayer. Nevia knelt beside the couch with a cloth wiping the sweat from his brow. Once, Aquila tiptoed in and asked me to let him take the vigilance with Luke so I might rest. I only shook my head. Aquila dropped to his knees and prayed silently with us.

Outside, across the atrium, the others of Paul's group waited: Silas, Aristarchus, Titus, Epaphras, Gaius. Timothy was still in Corinth. Delia and Nambio stood outside the room for any orders that might be given. Toward dawn these two brought to all of us steaming-hot broth to sustain our strength.

When daylight came, Paul was still alive, his fever somewhat lowered. He opened his eyes slightly, saw Luke standing above him. "Will I die?" Paul asked in a hoarse whisper.

"The Lord must not let it be so," Luke said.

"I am under sentence of death," Paul murmured. "I have failed Jesus in so many ways. . . ." His voice trailed off into unconsciousness again.

Luke listened again to his heartbeat, took his pulse as he had been doing all through the night. "So far, he is a little better," he told me. "That does not mean too much, because he could slip back again so quickly."

I walked out into the dawn coming over the open atrium. "My God, my God, all merciful in the abundance of your love for all people—" I burst into tears. Aquila came to me and held me in his arms until I subsided.

With daybreak Luke sent Nambio for two other physicians he knew in Ephesus. They came at once and felt Paul's heartbeat and the heat of his forehead.

173

One of them said, "He has healed others through the strength of his God; now he must heal himself."

The other physician looked with disapproval at the cold, wet blankets. "They may congest his lungs. I have no other suggestion to offer except to continue, because the fever will kill him anyway if it is not lowered."

The physicians left. Watching them go, I saw them both shaking their heads.

I went over to the far corner of the atrium alone and knelt on the paving. "Almighty God," I murmured aloud, "preserve the life of your servant Paul, who serves you with all of himself. Preserve him, O God and our Lord Jesus Christ, for us and for all to whom he means so much on earth. Grant in Jesus' Name this may be your Will."

When I rose to my feet I found Aquila standing behind me. His head was bowed, his lips moving. I kissed him gently and returned to the room where Paul lay.

All at once he turned worse. His fever grew to where it seemed his body would burst. Sweat rolled over his reddened face while Nevia stood over him wiping away the steaming drops. While I rubbed Paul's feet and legs to keep up the circulation, Luke held one hand on his pulse and with the other massaged a rhythmic tempo over his heart.

Luke turned to me and his lips moved silently with the words, "He is going. . . ."

But all at once, miraculously it seemed, the fever broke. Paul's breathing became more normal; the redness of his face subsided. His heart grew stronger.

Luke could say, "Our prayers may be answered. Thanks be to God."

Paul fell into a deep but regular sleep. I straightened up and pulled the blankets over his feet. I glanced at Luke. "Thanks be to God," I repeated.

I told Nevia, "You have not slept all night. Go now to get some rest. There will be much for us to do later."

The girl took the cloth and wiped her own eyes. "I, too, thank God that he is saved." She fled.

Still, Paul was far from recovery. His fever returned in the afternoon. He was too weak to speak. Delia made a broth of five

174

different kinds of fish heads boiled with a pinch of salt, prescribed by Luke.

I held his head on my arm, putting the cup of warm soup to his lips but being careful that he could swallow it. "Please, Paul, try to take one more sip," I urged.

Delia stood by and mumbled under her breath either Christian or pagan pleas that Paul might drink of the soup and become better. Luke watched and waited. . . .

From then on, Paul very slowly improved and gained strength.

20

One day, startling news came from Rome.

Quite early in the morning, I was dressing for our regular meeting of instruction for the women of the church. I already had seen that Nevia had given Paul his usual breakfast of bread and goat's milk, and that Nambio had helped him to bathe. The routine now was that Paul worked in his room until after Flavia and I held our women session, as I called it. Then Nambio would help him come out into the empty atrium for fresh air and sunshine.

On this morning I heard the town crier passing by on the street outside. Usually I did not bother to listen to him, either on his morning or evening rounds, shouting the news of Ephesus. But this time his voice was louder and more urgent. I paused to hear. The words, first in Greek, then in Latin, were hard to distinguish, but I finally pieced them together.

"Caesar is dead! The Emperor Claudius is dead! Nero is Emperor in Rome! Hail to Caesar Nero! Hail to Nero, Emperor of Rome! Hail to imperial Rome! Claudius Caesar is dead. . . ."

The crier passed around the corner to the next street, his voice echoing. I heard doors opening and shutting, footsteps running.

I stood thoughtfully in our room. Claudius, Emperor, dead in Rome. I could not feel grieved about it. He was the Caesar who had issued the edict driving us and all Jews out of Rome, breaking up families including our own, disrupting friendships, homes. His ruling had forced us to flee to Corinth, leaving our beautiful house, our possessions, our mothers and fathers. So he was dead.

I knew very little about Nero, stepson of Claudius, except that he was a young man well liked in Rome. I hoped that this was for the better, for one word from Caesar was enough to build a man or break a nation.

After finishing my dressing, I went back to the workshop to tell Aquila this news. I was sure he would be interested. I did not expect the reaction.

He dropped his sewing, rushed to me, grasped my shoulders.

"Claudius dead!" he shouted. "Claudius, Caesar, dead! Priscilla, do you realize what this means? We can return to Rome! To Rome, our home! We are free to go! Oh, Priscilla, how we have waited for this day!"

I felt the shock through my body. I had not thought of that. "How do we know it?" I gasped.

He grabbed me in his arms, exuberant. "Caesar is dead! His edict dies with him! Rome is free, free to all of us who are Jews! Oh, for so long, to return to Rome—"

"Aquila!" I stepped back. "Are you sure we want to go? We have made new lives here, at least temporarily, and we have a home in Corinth with our friends there. Our business has been good in both places—"

He looked at me incredulously. "Rome is our home, our birthplace," he burst out. "We are Romans. Of course we go back—"

"Wait, Aquila; we have our work here for Paul."

Aquila's mouth was tight. "Paul has many associates," he said grimly. "He has established the churches here and in Corinth. He will move on again to other places. He does this work by command of God. God has not commanded us."

He turned back to his work. In his sewing he missed some stitches. I returned to the atrium; it was time for the women to come. Flavia had already arrived.

"Did you hear the news?" she asked brightly. "Claudius is dead. But Actius and I will never go back to Rome. We have made our lives here, for Jesus Christ. . . ."

Late that night I sat again in the open atrium, alone. I thought everyone in the house was asleep. I was too restless, and had crept from our couch to think. I knew Paul was all right in his room; his recovery was progressing. Nevia was always wakeful in case he wanted something.

A hot wind blew over the rooftops. Another thunderstorm was coming our way. Everyone said there were so many more storms this season than ordinarily—but that was the usual comment about any kind of weather. Lightning reflections covered the clouds in the sky, rumbling of thunder in the distance seemed nearly continuous.

I was still too stunned by the imminent change in our lives. To return to Rome. . . . Yes, it would be good to see my mother and father again. I had missed them so much more than mere letters between us could balance. Both parents still stayed at the family villa down the coast on the Tyrrhenian Sea. In Rome we would have to find a house to live in. Our business would have to be built up again, without the help of people like Stephanas. Our former Jewish friends were scattered around the Empire. Many, like Flavia and Actius, would not return. And—this was a strange thought —we had never had Gentile friends in Rome. All our earlier lives had been under the Law, which, of course, forbade social meetings with non-Jews.

I had to admit to myself that the most painful hurt in my heart was the prospect of leaving Paul. My association with him had been so close over these years, I could not imagine living without his being near. I truly loved Paul—

That admission in my deepest thoughts caught me by surprise. Yes, I did love Paul, not in a wrong way, but in a very right way. Love comes in so many ways and with so many meanings. My love for Aquila was all these things, capped with the sexual feelings known to husband and wife. I loved my Jesus, my God, an all-consuming love. But the love I had for Paul was simply for what he himself was—a strength—a wisdom—an opening into wide spaces of life I had not known existed.

Rome, my home, my birthright, my— without Paul . . . I dared not think. . . .

Someone interrupted my thoughts by knocking at the door. Who, at this hour? I was startled, but I waited when I saw, through a window across the atrium, Nambio lighting a lamp. I watched him come from his room carrying the light, cross through the shadows of the atrium, and disappear toward the door.

A streak of lightning overhead and a near crash of thunder showed that the storm was approaching.

I stood up from the bench where I had been sitting to follow Nambio. Who could be knocking so late? I moved from the atrium around the wall between it and the front door.

Several more knockings followed the first, each more insistent. I saw Nambio at the door, lamp in hand.

"Who is it?" Nambio called. "What do you want?"

A muffled answer came: "Open, open, it is important. We seek the one named Paul."

Hearing this, I walked quickly to the door as Nambio called back: "By what name are you?"

A slight pause. The voice that replied was different from the first one. "We are citizens of Ephesus. We have a man here who is very ill. We seek the magician Paul who cures those who may die. Go find your master that he may let us in!"

I glanced doubtfully at Nambio. He answered the voice outside.

"By whose authority do you come, that I may tell the master?"

"In the name of mercy, open the door," the voice replied. "A storm is upon us. Would you have the man die on your doorstep? Bring this Paul to us."

This time I made the gravest error. I myself called back, "Paul is not available. Have you gone to a doctor?"

There was a long pause, interrupted by a crash of thunder.

"Mistress, it is too late for a doctor. Have mercy, open the door!"

"Wait," I answered.

I remembered that I had helped Paul back onto his couch during the afternoon, and he had put his arm around my shoulder to steady himself. I wore then the same mantle I had on now. His hand and his arm had been over it. I took the chance that it had the healing quality. I took off the mantle, handing it to Nambio.

"Pass it through the door," I said. "Tell them to let the collar and the arms touch the sick man."

Nambio shook his head skeptically but did as he was told. He held the lamp and mantle in one hand, and undid the bolts of the door.

178

I stood back a little, that they would not see me in my under tunica.

Another crash of thunder shook the house. The rain outside fell like a flood.

The moment the door was free, someone kicked it from outside. It swung open, knocking Nambio away. Two men leaped through the open entrance with drawn swords. One of them lifted the point of his blade to my chest, between my breasts.

"Where is Paul?" he demanded.

I screamed. The sword point went through to my skin, I felt the prick.

A third man, from behind, stepped up to the door.

"Now," he said grimly, "take us to Paul. Where is he? Quickly, or you lie here while we find him ourselves."

"Demetrius!" I heard Nambio gasp.

The second man with a sword turned on him, but Nambio pushed the lamp in his face so he could not see beyond, and stepped aside.

Instantly I knew what this was: Demetrius the silversmith—the riot against Paul, Lucius' warning that he was not satisfied. . . . They meant to kill Paul.

"Hold!" I screamed again, feeling the sword point on my breastbone. "You can take me. I will satisfy your revenge. That is enough, take away your sword, I will come with you—"

"No, you Christians!"

I will never forget the snarling face of Demetrius as he stood inside the door, hair dripping from the rain.

"I know you, too—" he cried out. He could not finish for a fearful crash of thunder. "Best you die as well," he finished when he could be heard.

At that moment, Aquila appeared out of the inside darkness, a raging shape with a huge iron bar poised over his head—a heavy bar that we used as a weight in stretching canvas.

"You beasts, ruffians, murderers!" Aquila shouted in a voice I had never heard before. "Get out before I crush your skulls! Get back, I order you!"

He swung the bar toward the one pointing the sword into me. All three jumped back.

179

The storm reached a peak of violence. Lightning flashed, thunder shook the very air.

"The Lord God will strike you dead!" Aquila shouted against the storm. "Out!"

But Demetrius pointed at Aquila.

"Get that one!" he screamed at his men.

A flash of lightning blinded me, with an instant thunder crash so violent the whole world seemed to fall apart. The air was full of fire. I was dazed. I blinked my eyes, saw the sword lying at my feet, another beside it. The two men were gone. Aquila lunged forward at Demetrius, swinging the iron bar down toward his head. The man dodged, and ran. At that moment, the tree across from our door fell to the street from the lightning bolt that had split it apart.

The storm itself paused. In the silence we heard footsteps of marching men approaching. A rain-soaked Nevia ran up to me.

"Thank our God!" she cried, out of breath. "We were in time!"

Nevia, hearing the noise at the door, had run out through the back entry and found the night watch on their rounds nearby, a squad of soldiers under a centurion. She had led them to our house at a double run.

"What happened here?" the centurion asked, looking at me, Aquila, and Nambio, the swords on the floor, and the split tree on the street.

We let Nambio explain in an Asian language we did not know. Neither Aquila nor I had voices to say anything. His explanation came out in excited bursts. The centurion was astonished.

"This God of yours is miraculous," he said to us in Greek. "I would like to know more about him. That Demetrius makes trouble for you the last time, I assure you. We know him well. Lock your door, two of my men will stand guard for the night."

One of the soldiers picked up the swords.

The centurion smiled farewell before he marched off with his squad of men. "I will report the fallen tree," he said. "By morning it will be cleared away."

After Nambio secured the door shut and locked it, I asked rather hysterically, "What happened to the storm?"

The night air was quiet.

I took Nevia into my arms and hugged her, and held out my hand to Nambio. I looked at Aquila, still holding his iron bar.

Nevia screamed, pointing to my breast. "Mistress Priscilla, you are hurt!"

A stain of blood showed through my under tunica.

"O God, our thanks be to Thee!" I cried out. "We are alive, and so is Paul."

I think Aquila carried me to my room. I suppose I must have fainted.

When we awakened in the morning, Aquila was still holding me tightly. All through the night my dreams had kept me from sleeping for more than a few minutes at a time. The faces. The sword. . . . In one dream I had seen a sword sunk deep into Paul's chest as he lay on his couch. I screamed aloud.

Aquila asked me now how I felt. He told me that Nevia had washed the wound from the sword. For a moment I had forgotten. Then, on moving my arm, I felt the soreness.

"It will be all right," I answered. "I don't think it is deep."

"How did you get to the door last night?" he asked.

"I had gone into the atrium, thinking about Rome. I was confused, I suppose. I will not be any more, and I love you very much."

"And I do you. Why did Nambio open the door?"

"I ordered him to. They kept saying they had a sick man out there, dying. I gave my mantle to Nambio to pass out to them, for Paul had touched it earlier. They tricked me."

"God's miracle saved us," Aquila said, his voice cracking.

"The lightning might have struck the tree anyway. It was a terrible storm."

"The Lord sent the storm. The lightning came into those swords, that's why the men dropped them. I felt the power in my iron bar, it was hot in my hands. I will never again doubt the power of God."

"Have you ever, Aquila?"

"Yes. To be truthful, yes. All these months I have often wondered why we were—you were—doing so much for the Lord Jesus when no one could be that certain about him. God forgive me."

"You never told me."

181

"No. How could I? And then, I didn't always doubt, only every once in a while." He sat up on the couch. "Priscilla, last night I heard you offer your life for Paul's. Just as I came to you. I thought about it all night. We don't have to go back to Rome. We can stay here to help him with his work, or go anywhere he wants us to go. Your work for Christ comes first."

I sat up beside him, put my arms around his neck. "Thank you for saying that. I'm glad you did. No, Aquila, we are Romans, and I will be happy to be home. We can work for Christ there, can't we? There are many who have not heard of Jesus Christ."

"Even the new Caesar. Why don't we start a church in our house?"

We put our arms around each other in a new kind of joy.

Nevia, bringing the breakfast tray, found us in our embrace. She laughed. "It is a beautiful morning for my master and mistress."

When I had finished the morning meal and dressed, I found Paul already sitting on a divan in the atrium. He chuckled at my expression of astonishment.

"You see, Prisca, I am well and strong again, thanks be to you, my dear, and to Aquila and to those faithful three of your household. And thanks be to our Lord Jesus and our God, who kept me with you. Your prayers were heard. These are things that will never be forgotten."

"You may be feeling better right now, but, Paul, you don't realize how ill you really were. You will have to take things slowly."

"Prisca, sit here beside me. I have much to say."

His expression turned serious as I sat on the divan. "Nambio told me what happened during the night. I wish this had not been brought on you, but I thank Almighty God for your life and your safety, and Aquila's too."

"Nambio told you? I hoped he wouldn't."

"You and Aquila risked your necks for me. I know all. You, dear Prisca, offered yourself for my life. No man can deserve such sacrifice as that. I do not have words to tell of my feelings. . . ." Paul stopped talking, and looked away.

"I was frightened for you. They came to kill you."

"Better I were dead a thousand times than have one like you

come to harm, Prisca my dearest. You were wounded, Nevia told me."

"It was nothing; just a slight cut."

Paul looked at me then, and what he did not say was far more than any words could have expressed.

It was my turn to be at a loss to speak.

"You know that I once told you about the dangers of a life for Christ," Paul said, very slowly. "The way ahead for those who hold to the faith will be long and terrible until the peace of God can come for all people. Remember this: Whatever one day I may say to you will also be heard by Almighty God. The time may come when you must remember what I am telling you now."

"I will remember, Paul."

The strangest feeling came over me, surrounded me, as if I were all at once somewhere else, with nothing but space around me, all reality vanished, even Paul. I tried to speak but I had no voice. I tried to move an arm but I had no strength. The space lighted up to brilliance. I was breathless; time stopped. I felt—dare I say it?— as though I was in the Presence of God.

The brilliance of light grew and grew, so bright I could see nothing— suddenly someone stood beside me. I could not turn to look, I knew only that someone was there. I felt no fear, no excitement, only a sensation of peace. The space around me, under me, deepened, and I was floating in that great space of light with the One standing close by me.

I thought I heard a voice. The voice spoke one word: "Priscilla."

Did I feel someone touch the top of my head? I do not know. But a great surge of joy swept over me, lifted me, carried me upward. I was exalted; I wanted to cry out but could not. I knew— I knew— the One beside me was Jesus Christ!

The Lord Jesus had spoken to me, I was certain—to me! "Priscilla," he had said. In the Presence of God, in the Light of Heaven, Jesus had spoken my name!

Slowly the light faded. Gently I came out of it. I was in my atrium; the sun shone above me; I sat on the divan beside Paul. I heard Delia in the kitchen, children shouting on the street outside, the twitter of a swallow overhead.

183

But I knew I had been somewhere else.

For an instant—for an eternity. . . .

Paul gazed at me without stirring. I returned to the world around me, and stared back at him. I felt so much within myself, but I could not speak of it. I am sure that the expression in my wide eyes must have told him. For then he smiled at me. He knew. He said nothing to me about it, nor did I to him.

He stood up, walked away and back again, as he habitually did.

I have told no one what happened to me on that morning in Ephesus, not until now, at this time of writing.

Paul sat again on the divan, and talked in a matter-of-fact way. "While recovering these past few days, I have made my plans. In a little while my work in Ephesus will be finished. Then I will leave here, with Silas, Aristarchus, Luke, and perhaps several others. I will go north to Troas, on the Aegean Sea, and across to Macedonia again to visit the churches there. Afterward I will return to Corinth for a time, and finally take a ship to Jerusalem. This will bring to an end my work for the gospel in this part of the world; I will have done all that I can do. From Jerusalem I will go to Rome, where I have never been."

"To Rome!"

"Only for a short time. If God so wills, then I will go to the West, to Spain."

"Spain!"

"It is a new area for the Way of Jesus. I hope to take his gospel to the Gentiles there."

"But you will come to Rome first?"

"Yes. I will meet you there."

"How—how do you know?"

"Because I heard the town crier yesterday say that Caesar is dead. There is a new Caesar. This means that you and Aquila will return to your home in Rome. Aquila wanted this for a long time. You must do what your husband wishes."

I nodded. "This morning Aquila and I planned that we would have a church in our home in Rome."

"I hoped this would be." Paul took my hand and squeezed it, with the greatest understanding a man could have.

How abruptly events can change one's life! That same afternoon a message came from Timothy in Corinth, sent jointly with Stephanas, who had returned to his home after the trial and Paul's first recovery. The message urged Paul to come immediately for a brief emergency visit to save the Corinthian church. The letter sent from Ephesus had only made matters worse, dividing the Christians even more. One faction threatened to break away from the congregation and form a church of their own, with their own interpretation of the Way of Jesus. Their leader was Cyrus, Antonia's husband.

Paul decided to leave for Corinth at once. He would stay only a few days, then return to Ephesus to finish his work before carrying out the plans he had described to me.

But Paul asked us to go with him to Corinth, as a stopover on our way to Rome.

III
CORINTH, AND ROME

21

In all my life I had never been so rushed. We had three days before the next ship sailed to Corinth. First, after talking with Paul,
Aquila and I asked Flavia and Actius if they would take over our
house and be responsible for continuing the services of the church
in Ephesus. They were awed by this responsibility, but agreed.
Flavia by now was well qualified, and those of Paul's group said
they would help them in every way they could. Lucius Andronicus
said they could have the same agreement that we had, including
the house and the three servants, Delia, Nevia, and Nambio. In
fact, I suspected that Lucius and his wife might soon become
Christians also.

I worked with Aquila far into the night, completing work on orders already begun. The remainder we handed over to the apprentice who had been helping us. He returned to the sail yard of
Stephanas, now a fully qualified artisan.

We packed our belongings and on the last evening had a party
to open the way for Flavia and Actius. We invited all those whom
we had come to know so well, and I tried in vain to control my
sentimental self. The next morning, when we said farewell, Delia
and Nevia broke down in tears as I kissed them both, and Nambio
kept blinking his eyes. To leave a place with such memories is a
terribly emotional experience.

So we were again on a ship at sea, sails straining overhead—
Paul, Aquila, and I. The shoreline of Asia faded, with the city of
Ephesus disappearing in the afternoon haze.

No one met us at Cenchreae, port of Corinth, as there had not
been time to send word of our arrival. We hired a carriage to take

us to the city center, and a wagon to follow with our own baggage. Paul had only his one sack.

We went directly to the house of Gaius, as we had done on that first arrival so long since. We were greeted by Gaius and Timothy with the greatest joy and surprise. No one had expected us to be with Paul.

"Welcome home!" Gaius cried, hugging me. "I have kept the house ready, not knowing when you would return. I'll send Bendis right down with you to settle in."

Neither Aquila nor I had the heart to say just then that we were on our way to Rome.

Paul stayed with Gaius to be close to the church meeting place in Gaius's atrium. We went on to our house, Bendis carrying enough food for the evening and the next-morning meals.

How like our first arrival! Our small house was neat and clean, Bendis cooking in the kitchen—it might have been all the years before over again. Knowing it would be for the shortest time, already I felt homesick for Corinth.

News traveled fast. As we were about to sit at our table, we heard light, running footsteps on the street, an impatient tapping at the door—

Alcesta! Oh, the tears of joy! Our girl, our Alcesta! How she had grown, a young woman now, taller, hair long, eyes shining. She took her usual place at the table, while a smiling Bendis brought another plate.

"Bendis, wait." Aquila restrained her. "The four of us will say our thanksgiving together."

We joined hands in the fellowship of Christ.

"Our God, we give Thee thanks for bringing us together in safety and health. We thank Thee also for bringing us to those in this city who worship Thee in the Name of Christ, that we may be united with one Spirit, for the sake of the Lord Jesus. Amen."

I noticed the peculiar expressions on the faces of both girls when the prayer was over. I told them why we had come at Paul's request, that we might be of help in what we had heard was a crisis in Corinth. I was certain, I said, that Paul would set matters straight. Alcesta and Bendis glanced at each other skeptically, but said nothing.

Alcesta turned the conversation to her news: she would be married soon; she loved Tarsos so much, he was a wonderful man! "I have studied so hard, and learned so many things," she declared. "But there is always more."

I had to tell her about Rome.

She grew very quiet, with tears in her eyes. We would not be here for her wedding, then, nor for the opening of their infirmary.

We talked long that evening about many things, but not of the church. Alcesta spent the night on her old couch in her former room. I went in to pray with her and kiss her good night, as I had used to do. We hugged each other and cried with happiness—and sadness at a new parting.

In the morning Alcesta ran off to her studies, while Aquila and I walked to the house of Gaius on the streets so familiar. Traffic rolled over the cobblestones, children played on the pavements as always. I noticed the little yellow bird still singing in its cage outside one of the houses—or maybe it was another one by now. Everything seemed so much like home to me.

Aquila felt it, too.

"Perhaps we are making a mistake," he said. "I mean, in returning to Rome."

"No, Aquila, you know that Rome calls us."

We found Paul with Gaius, Stephanas, and Timothy. Paul was insisting on holding a church meeting at noontime. He would start with a very short period of worship; then he would talk. He would not hear of delaying what he came for.

"Paul, they will shout you down," Stephanas warned. "It would be very unpleasant for you."

"This is true," Timothy agreed. "I have heard them; they fight with each other even without you."

I, too, wanted to urge him not to speak, but I knew Paul too well. When he made up his mind, he was adamant.

So Gaius reluctantly arranged to have message bearers run to the houses of all congregation members, calling them to the meeting. Paul was here to speak to them.

Aquila and I learned more of the church troubles. Among other things, it appeared that one group of Greek converts completely rejected Paul's letter from Ephesus to the Corinthians. They called themselves the *illuminati,* the "enlightened ones," who were convinced that the teaching of Christ's Resurrection was false, based only on a Jewish delusion that there could be a Messiah rising from death. They believed in immortality—but in accordance with an ancient Greek philosophy that one's spirit became immortal without reference to the body. This group welcomed faith in a Christ who died to end sin. So, when a body died, its sin was ended and the spirit continued to exist. "All things are lawful for me," group members declared.

This group was led by Cyrus, who threatened to establish a separate church in his own house.

Certain of the women were still another source of dissatisfaction with the Christian church.

"Paul, some of them want to think that the freedom you taught them meant release from subservience to men. Now they resent the things you said in your letter as contrary to your teaching," Stephanas explained. "They say so in this church—loudly."

"Then, let them talk elsewhere," Paul retorted, "not before God."

It seemed the whole congregation had received the morning message, and came to Gaius's house. When Antonia, Lida, and Cornelia arrived together and saw me, they burst out with surprise and excitement. Their enthusiasm made me feel so—well, happy inside myself. Chloe, too, was warm in her welcome. Aquila and I were kept busy greeting friends. I saw Cyrus come in. He did not speak to us. Druda appeared alone, did not see us.

I noticed that many of the congregation were tense, fearful. Others clearly anticipated with pleasure the opportunity to cause trouble. People filled the atrium, some standing at the rear.

I was terribly nervous, I admit.

Paul led a brief service of worship: an opening prayer of thanks to God for the presence of so many here in the Way of Jesus, recital of a psalm, a prayer for Christian churches throughout the world that they would always remain united for Christ Jesus, and a final blessing.

Then Paul stood before them all, spreading his arms wide. He was an impressive figure in his brown robe, matted hair and beard, head thrust forward, jaw out, eyes aflame. His appearance was enough to quell any normal revolt. Never will I forget that picture of Paul, ready to do battle for his Lord.

He spoke gently at first. Feeling the tension of the very air, my heart sank with foreboding.

"My friends of the church of Corinth," Paul began, "I come to you with gratitude at seeing so many who have faith for Christ. I thank God for you." He paused. "But I have heard again that there is division among some of you. Let us remember the Lord Jesus, his body on the cross for your sake. He died for each one of you that you might receive in baptism the Holy Spirit of God. If you had been standing at the foot of that cross, would you have thought to tear apart Christ's body? A limb for one, a limb for another, as the soldiers drew lots for his clothing? God forbid! Why, then, would you tear apart the body of Christ in this church? Why should you destroy the unity of the whole into separate parts? Do you not understand that Christ Jesus is a whole for all of you, as the body of the church?"

He paused again, and no one stirred.

"I preached to you over many months of the Resurrection of Jesus from death. I hear that some of you believe there was no Resurrection. If there was no Resurrection of Christ, how could I say there was Resurrection for all mankind? And if there were no Resurrection for all of you who believe in Christ, then Jesus himself would be an imposter, a villain above villains, and I would be even worse for telling you that Jesus came to me after his death and I heard his voice. Would I lie to you? If I have lied, take pity on yourselves, for there would be nothing left for all of you but death."

A voice came from the congregation—Cyrus. He rose from the bench where he had been sitting.

"Master, we understand that you have no desire to lie to us. We do not accuse you of that. You are sincere in your own belief. But we cannot accept what you are saying. It is foolish nonsense to us. There was no Resurrection of Christ. A man does not rise from his grave. That is impossible. Immortality of the spirit: yes, we can believe that, as our philosophers have told us for a far longer time than your Christ lived."

Paul smiled. He did not raise his voice yet. "Has the Holy Spirit of God, which you received in baptism, told you this?"

Someone in the congregation laughed.

"Holy Spirit?" Cyrus replied. "Our own knowledge tells us what is true, and what we should believe."

Paul pointed a finger at him. This time his voice roared. "So you will say that your knowledge is greater than the Holy Spirit of Almighty God? May God help you!"

Cyrus shrank back, but only for a moment. "We believe in Jesus Christ, the Son of God!" he shouted. "He died to release us from sin! We believe what we have been taught, not by you but by others in this city! Your smooth words will not deter us from our beliefs."

Shouts burst out from all over the congregation. Men and women stood up, crying out imprecations, insults against Paul. They waved their arms, stood up on the benches, screaming. I was aghast at the scene.

Paul's enormous voice rose above the uproar, drowning out the shouts and cries as if they were nothing. "You defy your God? You use the Holy Name of Jesus to excuse your vile wickedness, your fornications, your slanders, your pride, your evil ways?" Paul's fierce gaze turned to the center of the room. "I see here in this assembly the one whom I commanded you to throw out, the one whose wickedness excels all limits, he who sleeps with his father's wife. You still associate with the worst of the earth, you glory in this offspring of Satan, this one who blackens the Name of Jesus by sitting in the midst of these faithful people! I will say to him what you have not said: get out!"

Paul's finger pointed now at the man Melas! I had not noticed him. His face turned white, then violent red. He stood, shook his fist at Paul, and stalked out in the dead silence that fell.

Paul's final sentence followed him. "May the pity of Christ be with you on Judgment Day, if you do not repent!"

I, who had been nervous for Paul, was nervous no more. I wanted to shout "Hail!" to him.

The people appeared stunned at Paul's act, and the suddenness of it. There was no more shouting. Those who stood on the benches sat down.

Cyrus pointed his own finger at Paul. "You condemn us for what you call sins. You have no more right to judge us than we have to judge ourselves!"

194

"I do not judge you," Paul answered. "Only Jesus Christ and Almighty God can do that."

"We have heard enough!" Cyrus cried. "We leave you and your church; we will have our own church in accordance with our beliefs in the liberty of Christ." Cyrus turned and walked through the people toward the door.

"Christ gave you liberty but not license." Paul's voice had a cutting edge. "Let God judge the difference." He folded his arms and waited. Even from where I sat I could see that fire of anger in his eyes.

A number of men jumped to their feet as Cyrus called them, perhaps twenty, and some women, too. They started to follow, then hesitated, glanced from one to another. Some sat again at once. Slowly others turned back to their seats with heads lowered. The women gave up first, except Druda. I saw her standing; she opened her mouth to shout, changed her mind, sat down.

Cyrus turned angrily. "Antonia, come with me!"

She was on her knees, praying. Her head jerked up at her husband's command. A dead silence fell over the congregation. "I cannot." Her voice was loud and clear.

A buzz of excited talk burst out through the room as Cyrus strode out of the house of Gaius, alone.

Paul waited patiently. Then he raised both arms high, lifted his head, and stood still before them. "God, our Father Almighty in Heaven, give Thy blessing to this church of the Lord Jesus Christ, that it may remain forever united as one whole body, and take its rightful place beside those other churches in union throughout this world. Eternal God, bless Thy people here present in the Holy Spirit, in the Name of Jesus, Thy Son. Amen."

Paul's voice rolled over the lowered heads. With him, the people joined in chorus: "Amen."

The meeting was over.

On their way out, Lida and Cornelia stopped to talk to me. Antonia was with them, but she turned her head in shame for her husband.

"Priscilla," Cornelia said, "I wish Paul had spoken to the women; I'm sure they are not satisfied."

"Some of them will still make trouble," Lida added.

I had an inspiration. "Can you all meet at my house tomorrow morning? Just so we can talk among ourselves?"

Both agreed at once.

Antonia looked at me with red eyes. "Are you sure?"

"Yes, everyone will have a chance to talk. Can you get them to come?"

Cornelia was positive. "Every woman can tell two others. They will come."

Later, Paul admitted that he had been too harsh on the man Melas. "When I saw him my anger was too much for me."

I reminded him of what he had once said. "Some will stand, some will fall!"

"Put out thy hand to the fallen," he acknowledged.

The next morning, I received more women than I expected. Alcesta was with me, and Bendis made cakes and fruit juice for us to serve. Aquila discreetly disappeared.

Antonia came early, in her litter, excited and glowing. "Priscilla, you will never believe what I have to tell you! Yesterday, when I did not follow my husband's order to leave the meeting with him, I felt that my world had fallen apart. But when I arrived home, dreading every bit of it, I found Cyrus in the nursery with our son. He came to me and told me how much he regretted his actions. He hoped that Paul would forgive him. Yes, he explained, he was confused and trying to excuse himself for a lot of things I wouldn't understand. Of course I understood, but I said that I was sorry too. We almost cried in each other's arms. Then he said that he wanted our son to grow up being a Christian! Oh, Priscilla, what more can I say? Jesus has blessed us. . . ."

The women guests arrived, filling the small room in the house to the doors. I sat on the floor beside Lida. Many of them were strangers to me, more than those whom I had known. This may have been a clue to what had happened in the church, that so many had become Christians without understanding it. To some, the Christian Church had been a social attraction, terrible though that sounds. They quieted down and expectantly watched me, a few as if they would like to bite.

I should have been nervous, but I wasn't. "I'm happy you could come," I said for an opening. "We have some things to talk about, just among ourselves. Nothing formal, just conversation. No men are around—" I looked this way and that—"so we can talk on any subject at all; we don't have to be reticent. Where shall we start?"

The women looked at each other.

Cornelia initiated the discussion. "Priscilla, I think most of us here feel that Paul is being unfair to women. In that letter, he sounded so forbidding it worried us."

I was grateful to Cornelia for giving me just the opening I needed. "I think you misunderstand him," I explained. "Some of you here do not really know him—"

"Not the way you do, after being away with him all this time." That came from Druda, at the back of the room, my friend, up to her old tricks.

I flushed. My lips were tight in anger, but I controlled myself.

"My husband and I consider it a great privilege to have had the opportunity to know Paul and have him teach us how we, all of us, can teach others of our Jesus, our Messiah."

An older woman, standing against the back wall, grunted aloud. "Paul told us that men should not marry. Where does that leave us? We cannot have husbands, or have men touch us. What kind of life is that?"

A din of voices broke out in the room, everyone talking at once.

I held up my hand. "Let's talk clearly. First, shall we start with Paul? Being a man, he may not find it easy to understand the inner feelings of women, although I believe he does. Considering the responsibility he had from Christ to carry his Name to the Gentiles of the world as well as to Jews, can we wonder that he keeps himself celibate? His work is for God, not for himself. If you will read his letter to you again, you will see that he has never spoken against marriage. He does understand the nature and needs of men and women. If it were not for marriage, its place would be taken by fornication, use of prostitutes, and things forbidden by Christ."

I chose my next words carefully. "Paul does think that, considering these times of troubles and uncertainties, some men and women are better off by remaining unmarried. But if any two people truly love and desire each other, then they should marry, with the blessing of God upon them."

Another woman spoke up. "You said we should be open with each other this morning. We all know that many husbands go to women other than their wives for pleasure. What should a wife do about it?"

I smiled at that question. "How many wives do we know who have gone to other men for the same reason? There is something wrong between husband and wife when these things happen."

A titter went around the room.

I decided I would say it whether they liked it or not: "Paul wrote in his letter something very personal to all of us. He said that a wife's body does not belong to her, it belongs to her husband. At the same time, a husband's body does not belong to him, it belongs to his wife. This is Paul's opinion, not a command from God. May I add, in my own opinion, if such an understanding were followed, would adultery and prostitutes be necessary?"

The women were startled; they looked at each other. Some nodded agreement, others frowned. Even Lida, beside me, seemed surprised.

Chloe had been silent all this time. Now she brought up a subject. "Paul wrote that women should not speak or ask questions in church. I think some here resent such a comment from him."

I was glad that question was asked. "I think Paul's comment fits those women who worry about it," I answered. "Church is a place of worship before God. It is only right for men and women to respect the prayers and meditation of others. Do you suppose some women are more likely than men to forget this?"

Most of them laughed. My arrow had hit home. Except Druda; she drew herself up and glared. Other women involuntarily glanced at her.

I quickly changed the drift. "This is an informal gathering. We have cakes and fruit juices. Alcesta, dear, do you mind passing them? We can keep on talking if there is anything else. . . ."

The women seemed to be satisfied. They all lapsed into general conversation, and there seemed to be congeniality not present before. I was talking with Lida about herself—

Suddenly there was a loud exclamation and a harsh voice: "Do you expect me to take food and drink from one who has been a prostitute in a pagan temple?"

The instant silence was of shock; all heads turned. Alcesta stood frozen in front of Druda.

"Alcesta, my daughter, you haven't served me—or the others." I reacted as calmly as my rage would allow.

The girl continued around the room. The women tried to talk together again as if nothing had happened. Each one made a point of taking a cup of juice and a cake from her. No one spoke to Druda. Every woman there knew the story of Alcesta, of her closeness to me, and how she was being accepted into the family of Stephanas, the most esteemed in Corinth.

When she came to me, I took the last cup of juice and the cake. "Thank you, Alcesta. Go into the kitchen and see if Bendis has more cakes."

The moment she disappeared, I said in a tone that all could hear, "Druda, this is a Christian gathering, for love of Jesus. Did you ever hear what Jesus once said of the prostitute: 'Let the one without guilt throw the first stone'?"

The woman's face turned purple, her expression as nasty as I have ever seen on anyone. "You accuse me— Insult! Double insults! You—" Druda sputtered the words, couldn't think of what to say. She looked at the women around her, found nothing but cold stares. Pulling her mantle around herself, she pushed her way to the door, practically spitting, "I'll have no more of this!" She left, slamming the door.

Poor Druda. In a way, I felt sorry for her. Probably she could not help the nature she had cultivated. I learned later that her friends dropped her after that episode, and finally she moved from Corinth to Athens.

Our gathering ended quietly. Every one of those women came to me separately to thank me for the explanations; all seemed now to be satisfied. I was glad that this final part of the church difficulties had been settled.

As she left, Antonia said that she would have a dinner party for me and Aquila, with our mutually close friends. It would be for us a welcome back to Corinth—but also a farewell before we went to Rome.

When all our guests were gone, Alcesta and Bendis picked up the empty cups. I put my arm around Alcesta. "This should not have happened. I am sorry." I felt so inadequate in saying anything to this bright, young, and happy girl.

She smiled. "It did not hurt me. I was more concerned with

what you felt. Paul told me long ago I was reborn. God has given happiness to Tarsos and me. Who can hurt me? I have your love, and the blessing of the Lord Jesus. What more can I have?"

During that afternoon, I learned that the men of the church had met again at noontime in the house of Gaius, this time without Paul's presence. They agreed on a settlement of their differences so that the church could become reunited with single-mindedness in faith in Christ. To insure their unity, they asked Gaius and Stephanas to form a group of elders from themselves, as a symbol of authority to keep order. These two immediately called on, among others, Crispus, former leader of the Jewish synagogue, Fortunatus and Achaicus, and, surprisingly—Cyrus. This much accomplished, they requested Paul to join them to hear the report and to ask the blessing of Jesus Christ on this, his church in Corinth.

The crisis of Corinth was over, the church future assured.

Antonia held her party the following night. She had Lida and her husband, as well as Cornelia and her husband, who was now healthy and strong. Chloe, the Jewess turned Christian, as I am too, was there, along with many others, such as Stephanas and Dorice, whom I had not seen for so long, and Gaius. Timothy came; as did Crispus. It was a wonderful party, with good food, the girls serving, and entertainment. But it was different. The previous accent was gone. The musicians were of the best; dancers performed traditional Greek steps. There was joy and laughter, and congeniality—and that was it.

To Aquila's and my astonishment, Paul came. Cyrus asked him to give a blessing before the meal. He enjoyed himself thoroughly through the evening.

Dino, of course, was there. At first opportunity he came to me with hands outstretched. "Priscilla," he began, "I am sorry you have come back to Corinth."

"Dino! That's not nice to say."

"I say it because you have lingered with me for so long as a dream, a dream I have tried to forget. Now that I see you, I must try over again, for my dream is leaving for Rome!"

"Dino," I laughed, "I think I know you too well to think that you have lived with a dream."

He laughed too. "I admit it is hard to stay faithful to a dream. I only wish mine had come true."

"You will find a better dream, Dino. One that will come true."

"Never. For I have learned that the perfect dream is unattainable."

As much as for anything else, we enjoyed the party by seeing Antonia and Cyrus finding the truth of happiness.

When we reached our home that night, we discovered Bendis still awake to give us a message from the dockside office of Stephanas: A ship was to sail for Italy the next afternoon. Space was reserved for us, if we wished to take it.

22

Oh, times of worries, anxieties, terrors, and final frightful tragedies! How long has it been since I last wrote on these sheets of paper? Too many years.

When Aquila and I left Paul in Corinth, he assured us that he would see us in Rome within two years, on his way to a new ministry in Spain. But will the evil of mankind ever be deterred? Five years and more passed before we met again. The circumstances were far different from what we could have imagined.

A large group of Rome's Christian colony met before dawn one morning at the Porta Pia, the gate in the walls of Rome leading to the Appian Way, the coastal highway southward. All of us started out together, in wagons, carriages, horseback, with a great goal to achieve.

For we had learned that Paul had finally arrived in Italy, at the port of Puteoli, far down the coast. Members of the church in our house, as well as representatives of congregations from the many Christian churches all over Rome, had decided to give Paul a welcoming reception of support by meeting him part way on his journey north to face trial before the Emperor.

With Aquila and me, in a wagon with a driver we had hired,

were our old friends Timothy and Epaphras, who had come from Asia months before in anticipation of Paul's being brought to Rome.

Our group moved briskly as the dawn threw light over the tall pines along the highway and was reflected from the tombs of illustrious families of Rome. We confronted heavy traffic both to and from the Imperial City: huge, four-horse wagons thundering over the cobblestones, racing chariots, farmers' carts filled with produce. Of all our crowd, I was surely the most anxious. How I wished our horses would hurry!

Aquila finally protested. "You are so restless, Priscilla."

"I am impatient," I exclaimed. "It has been so long. . . ."

The cool of the morning gave way to the searing heat of the sun. Still no one faltered, and we traveled on. I could not count how many people we were, several hundred or more.

After noontime we reached the place on the Via Appia known as the Three Taverns. Here, according to plan, some of the group waited. After resting the horses, others of us went farther, to Apii Forum, a small town nearly half way to Puteoli, where we spent the night.

In the early morning, our cavalcade was on the road again. After what seemed an interminable time we saw, far down the highway under a cloud of dust, a large contingent coming from the opposite direction. Some were on horseback, most others on foot. Sunlight flashed on the armor and helmets of soldiers. Steadily they approached.

"It's Paul!" some of us cried out.

We left our vehicles and ran down the road to meet them. There, on the Via Appia, between open fields, we came together, the familiar figure in the brown robe looking down at us.

"Paul!"

"Prisca!" He dismounted and threw his reins to a soldier. He took me in his arms. I could not see him, for the tears of joy in my eyes.

"It has been so long!" I cried.

"Too long," he said.

My face was against his rough shoulder, I heard that deep rumble in his chest as he spoke. He shook hands with Aquila. Timothy and Epaphras and others greeted him. As Paul looked over the

202

numbers of people who had come, tears appeared in his own eyes.

"God bless you all," he shouted, and raised his arm high above them.

Luke and Aristarchus dismounted from their horses. The two had been with Paul on the whole long, long journey and through the terrible events that had occurred. The centurion in charge, named Julius, stayed up on his horse but laughed with good humor at the joyous occasion. He had been in charge of Paul since the disastrous voyage began, from Caesarea, port of Jerusalem. Even the foot soldiers who formed the guard smiled at seeing their prisoner's reception.

Finally Paul and the others remounted, and the two groups as one began to move on the long way back to Rome. . . .

There is no reason for me to explain in these memories here what happened to Paul during those years, five and more, since we had seen him in Corinth. I knew his plans at that time: to return to Ephesus for a short stay, to go through Asia to Macedonia, and back to Corinth before returning to Jerusalem for a final visit prior to Rome and Spain. On this third Corinth visit, he spent the winter with Gaius, and it was from there that Paul wrote his long, beautiful letter to the Roman Christians describing his teachings for the Lord Jesus. At the end of the letter, we were happy to find, he added his greetings to "Prisca and Aquila, my fellow workers in Christ Jesus, who risked their necks for my life, to whom not only I but also all the Christian churches give thanks." He included greetings to the church we had established in our Rome house, which our members appreciated very much.

I say there is no reason to repeat what happened later. Luke himself, through letters to us and other churches, gave us eyewitness reports of Paul's journey back to Caesarea and Jerusalem and of the dreadful things that happened there, how Paul was so nearly killed time and again, and how he was saved by his arrest and transfer to the governor's palace in Caesarea, where he was held in "open" imprisonment in the palace for two years by Felix, the Roman governor of Judea.

Luke's more recent letters recounted how Paul in Caesarea had made an appeal to Caesar, "as the right of a Roman citizen," for a trial in Rome instead of being sent back to Jerusalem, where certain death awaited him. Every report from Luke could only reassure us that Paul was still alive at that time of writing. We had lived in dread for the next letter, which might tell us different and terrible news—such had been the constant danger around our beloved Paul. I cannot describe our anxieties and torments of mind.

In Rome, Paul was allowed to remain under "house arrest" in a residence of his own under surveillance by one Praetorian Guard. He could have his associates live with him, have visitors, and teach the Word of Jesus Christ as he wished. No restriction was placed on his writing letters. But he was not allowed to leave the house.

These permissions and restrictions were at the whim of Caesar, Nero our Emperor.

Epaphras and Timothy quickly found a suitable house to rent for Paul on the small Via Lata, next to the Corso, the ancient race track. The place was centrally located, near the Capitoline Hill. A small fountain on a wall opposite the front door gave a constant flow of water for thirsty pedestrians as well as horses.

Along with Epaphras and Timothy, Luke and Aristarchus moved in with Paul. Before long, Tychicus, from Asia, arrived in Rome bringing latest news from Flavia that the church in Ephesus continued to grow in solidarity, which we were glad to hear. Somewhat later, John Mark came from Jerusalem. He is a son of one of the Marys, friends of Jesus, and a cousin of Barnabas, another of Paul's earliest associates. Both Mark and Luke were making notes and drafts for separate accounts of the life and teachings of Jesus—truly inspiring objectives.

Once settled into his Via Lata house, Paul began again his long-delayed work. His disciples went out daily, visiting the Christian churches and further evangelizing among the Gentiles. Restricted as he was to his quarters, Paul made the most of his long hours by writing to his churches and answering the many letters of well-wishers that soon came to him from throughout the Empire. But, more than that, a constant stream of Romans began calling at the house, some with adulation and curiosity, many with reasonable questions about the Way of Christ.

Paul needed help.

I became a sort of receptionist, spending many hours at the house. With most of the men out on their rounds, I was the one to separate the unworthy callers from the worthy. For the worthy ones I made morning appointments at a certain hour, so that Paul could speak to a number at once, saving his time for his own work. But even the doubters and troublemakers I sent away with a quieting message.

On the third day of Paul's captivity, he sent for the Roman leaders of the Jews. He explained to them the reason for his presence in the city: the persistent unwarranted charges of the Jews of Israel against him had forced him to appeal to Caesar. Paul did this to avoid similar persecution in Rome. But these Roman Jews contended that they had heard nothing of evil from Judea about him, neither by letter nor from travelers' conversation. Yet they did wish to hear what he thought of Jesus, for they knew the sect of Christ was spoken against everywhere.

Paul arranged for the day, and a great number of Jews came to hear him speak of the Way of Jesus. They stayed, and argued, from the morning into the evening. Some were convinced that he was right; others could not believe. So Paul sent them off disputing the facts among themselves, telling them that the Gentiles would listen.

After that, Paul concentrated his work on the Gentiles.

Later we learned that Peter, whom Paul called Cephas, was also in Rome, although in a different part of the city. Probably Peter preached primarily to the Jews, as they had agreed between them many years before—although certainly he would have included Gentiles too. Whether the two met in Rome I never knew, and I have to suppose they did not, even though their relations had been cordial. Rome, then, became the principal center of Christian activity, although Jerusalem remained as the formal headquarters.

Let no one believe that these days, which superficially appear to have been easy, were that, in any way. The presence of the Praetorian Guard in the house was a constant reminder of the coming trial before Caesar. We could not know from one day to the next which would be the last.

Our fear increased when we heard more and more about the change in Nero's nature. After the death of his stepfather, Claudius, the people of Rome had welcomed the young Emperor. Even when it became known that Nero ordered the murder of his own mother, Agrippina, the Romans shrugged their shoulders. Hadn't Agrippina plotted the assassination of Claudius, her husband, to put her son Nero in power? It was possible that Nero had discovered a plot by her to get rid of him, too. That was a family matter.

But when Nero sent his young wife, Octavia—his stepsister—into island exile in favor of his mistress Poppaea, the Romans were angry. They loved the beautiful and innocent Octavia. Then, when at the behest of Poppaea, Nero ordered Octavia's beheading on a false charge of adultery, the people's cynicism turned to hate. And when rumors spread that Octavia's head was brought to Rome to prove her death to Poppaea, the Roman citizens feared a monster as their Emperor.

Before this depraved man, Paul was to be tried for sedition.

Two years went by—two years during which Paul was not disturbed. With passing time, we dared to hope: could Nero have forgotten?

The Praetorian Guard reminded us—making each day a day of foreboding.

The dreaded blow came suddenly.

Aquila and I had just finished our morning meal. I was picking up the dishes and Aquila was about to go to his workroom, which he had built behind the house. We heard a rapid knocking at the door.

We looked at each other. I put the dishes down—I remember everything so clearly—I went to the door, already feeling the fear.

Epaphras was there. Immediately I saw him, I knew.

"Yes." His voice trembled. "They have taken him."

Everything swirled around me, seemed to be turning dark. . . .

Aquila came up behind me, put his arm around me, a hand on my shoulder. "When? How?"

"They came soon after dawn, a squad of soldiers and the centurion," Epaphras managed to say. "They took him off—with his arms bound across his back."

"Oh, Paul," I know I cried out, "how could they do it this way?"

"I was afraid it would happen soon." Aquila spoke in a low voice. "Now I am afraid—"

"I came because I thought you should know at once," Epaphras said huskily. "It has happened before, as it did in Corinth and Ephesus. We must pray it means Paul's release."

"Please, God," I said.

We grabbed up our mantles at once, and went with Epaphras down to the house on the Via Lata. On the way, Epaphras told us that Aristarchus, the oldest of our group, had gone with Paul, after the centurion gave permission. Just keep out of the way, the centurion had cautioned. It seemed the centurion knew the story of Paul, and what it meant. He had treated Paul as deferentially as his orders would allow.

Paul was being taken to the palace of Caesar on the Palatine Hill.

I cannot remember our walk through the streets that morning. I could only think of Paul and what he must be feeling. Paul, my Paul, the kindest and most gentle of men— O Lord Jesus, I prayed under my breath, grant he may be released, to continue his life for Thy sake. . . .

Those of us in Paul's group spent the day in silence and prayer. We were interrupted by callers who asked for the master. We took turns at the door saying that Paul was away that day, please come back another day and Paul would welcome you—it was hard for us to say that much in cheerful voices.

This was the longest day in our lives. We waited in the front room—waiting, waiting for the door to open with Paul shouting, "I am free!"

None of us ate or drank. We prayed to our God Almighty in Heaven—praying almost in desperation—but knowing in our hearts without saying it aloud that God's Will would be done. What would be his Will . . . we dared not think.

Not until late in the afternoon did Aristarchus return—alone. He opened the door, stood looking at each one of us with head low, arms limp. There was a long pause as we stared back. Several of the men stood up slowly; the rest of us remained frozen as the truth sank home.

I turned away and cried out, "Oh, God, no— please, God, no, no, no, no!"

Aristarchus came into the room, closed the door behind him. Tears filled his eyes.

"They have taken him to the Mamertine Prison." He hesitated. "Paul is condemned to death. As a Roman citizen, he will be beheaded, not crucified."

No one spoke for a long time.

Then Aquila asked in a hoarse voice, "What were the charges against him?"

"The centurion did not know. He told me that Caesar was in a bad mood today." Aristarchus hid his face in his hands. "As they led him away down the hall, Paul turned and smiled at me!" Aristarchus broke down completely, his legs gave way, he collapsed onto the floor, sobbing beyond control.

23

The next morning, I did something that, within all reason, I never should have done. I went to see Paul in prison.

I knew the danger I faced. So much so that, before I left the house, I stole to the door of Aquila's workroom and watched him at his work. How could I tell him what was in my mind? He would never have allowed it. But I could not be sure I would ever see my husband again. All my love went out to him, and I was sure he would understand if I did not return. I blew a silent kiss to him from my fingers.

I had dressed very carefully, for I knew I had to face the prison guards and authorities. I wore a simple gray tunica reaching below the knees, and a mantle to match. I wound up my hair in its usual coils, with a plain scarf over my head. I refrained from any facial makeup. The impression I wanted to make was of demure innocence.

Quietly I left the house. Aquila would think I had gone to market. I did go to a fruit stand, and bought the fruits I knew Paul liked—a certain kind of red-purple grapes, pomegranates, and green figs. I placed all in a special basket. Oranges were out of season.

In all of Rome, the Mamertine Prison was probably the most feared place—the death place of hundreds if not thousands of political enemies of the Caesars, captives of wars, criminals. When people spoke of it they lowered their voices. Situated above the far end of the Forum, beyond the temples, the prison was carved out of the solid rock under the Capitoline Hill, facing the palaces at the other end of the Forum.

I found it easily, and came to the huge iron gates that barred its entrance.

A guard stood inside. "What do you want?" he asked suspiciously.

"I wish to speak to the commander."

"Why?"

"I wish to see the prisoner Paul."

The guard raised his eyebrows. "Have you a permit?"

"No, I only wish to give him my fruit."

"Sorry, no one can see Paul without a permit from the Caesar's palace. Those are my orders."

"I want the commander to tell me that."

He hesitated. "You come here at great risk to yourself. I will see that the fruit goes to Paul."

"No, please, the commander—"

He looked at me carefully; I smiled back with confidence at the young man in full armor.

"One moment." He disappeared into the darkness behind the gate. I could make out by a torchlight in the wall that he talked to another guard.

This second one came to the gate and spoke to me through the bars. "The commander does not wish to be disturbed," he said roughly. "If you go to the palace for a permit—"

"Please," I begged, "I have only my fruit."

This man also examined me carefully. "You seem harmless enough," he said, and turned to the first guard. "Let her in. I will take her to the commander." But he quickly turned back to me, saying, "Young miss, I must warn you first. I can take no responsibility for you. You may regret this very much."

I smiled again. "I will take the risk."

He shrugged his shoulders.

The first one unlocked the gate, let me in, and locked it after me.

The second one beckoned me to follow him.

The horrors of that prison! It was dark except for the torches along the walls. Little daylight came in. The place smelled of blood and death.

I followed the man to the rear of the prison room. He knocked at a small door. A voice commanded, "Come in."

Beyond the door was what could only be called a cubicle. A bearded man sat at a table, and looked up as we entered. He had on a mantle of the official purple; under it a metal breastplate gleamed in the room's torchlight. A long sword lay on the table, which was otherwise covered with papers. "What is this?" he demanded.

"The woman asks to speak with you," the guard said.

The commander stared at me. "What about?"

"Sir, I wish only to ask your permission to speak with your prisoner Paul. See, I have brought fruit for him."

"What? See Paul! No one can see Paul without permission from the palace. Do you have it?"

I put out my hand to him. "You know I cannot get that. Please, sir, for a few minutes. Paul is my friend, and my master."

The commander gasped with disbelief. "Do you know what you are saying?"

"Sir, please, I do this out of love, before—" The tears in my eyes were of real desperation.

He leaned back on his chair. "Are you one of these Christians?"

"Yes, sir."

He kept staring. "You are either very brave, or very, very foolish, I do not know which. Do you know that I should arrest you at once for coming here and saying these things? What the judgment of the court would surely be, I do not like to tell you."

"If need be, I would die with Paul. Our God would be with us both."

The commander scratched his head. "You Christians, you and your God. I have heard much of you. There is something you Christians have beyond understanding."

He stood up and came around the table.

"Miss, you are much too beautiful and sweet to be in this place, especially down where Paul is. You will not like it. Does it really mean so much to you?"

"My life."

He sighed, and spoke to the guard. "Show her how to go down," he ordered. "But only for five minutes, understand? And watch them both. Keep your mouths shut, all of you out there. You know the punishment, otherwise."

The commander turned back to me; his voice was gentle now. "Go, take your fruit to your Paul. But I must tell you—do not come again." He paused. "There will be no need."

My hand went to my mouth. "So soon?"

"Yes. Now, tell no one what you are doing, no one, understand? It would be the worse for you, for me, and all of us."

With the most rending emotions, I took the commander's hand. "Our God will bless you," I said. My voice choked.

"Your God must have power I do not know," he replied. "I am sure he will bless you."

I will not describe the horror of the dungeon below the prison floor. The guard put down a ladder into the dark hole lit by one flickering torch. He held the fruit basket as I climbed down into the darkness. Then he followed and gave the basket to me.

I turned around to see the figure of a man rising up from his seat on a stone. The guard did not move.

"Prisca!—Oh, Prisca!"

"I brought you some fruit," I stammered. "Oh, Paul—" I threw myself into his arms, dropping the basket.

"Prisca, you should not have come. You have put your life into the greatest danger."

"I had to come—" Beforehand, I had made up my mind I would not cry in front of Paul; I would control myself and have no tears. My resolution fell apart.

"Prisca, let me tell you," Paul said slowly. "I am glad it is over." His arms quivered. "You remember the races at the Isthmian games? My race is won. My wreath is not one of withered oak leaves, but a wreath of the eternal glory of God. So it will be with you, my dearest and most faithful one, but not for a long time yet."

211

I could not say anything.

"Weep not for me, Prisca. Although I go in the body from you, I go to our Lord Jesus and to the Father in Heaven, where I shall always be. I am satisfied with what I have done in following the orders of our Lord. . . . I am at peace."

I raised my head. "I am not crying," I said with tears running down my face.

He smiled. "Listen to me, for they will not allow much time. You must take care for yourself, as you will be among those who have faithfully followed my teachings. Now it must be for you, all of you, to carry on the Way of the Lord that it may endure in the world forever. Wolves will come among the flock and try to destroy all who believe. Men of evil will do their worst to pervert the meaning of Christ. There will be persecutions, and terrors . . . and death. Be on guard, you may have to stand alone—not alone, for God will be with you."

Even in that dim place I saw the light in his eyes, the intensity of purpose. I remember it so well.

"The Way of the Lord must never cease." Paul's great shoulders moved forward; his jaw jutted out. "This will be in the hands now of all of you whom I am leaving: you, Prisca, Aquila, those of my associates, all those everywhere who believe in Christ Jesus. If I cannot see even one of them, carry that message to them."

"I will tell them, all of them."

He looked at me again, his eyes softened. "You have been my strength, my helper, the dear one of my life. I knew it when I first saw you—"

"In front of our house in Corinth," I exclaimed. "Do you know, I was afraid of you at first."

Paul laughed. "I was a weary, dusty traveler. I do not wonder."

"But, that night, you told Aquila and me you were bringing a great new faith to all the world, the faith in Christ. I saw it in your eyes. I understood then that I would always be a part of it."

The guard by the ladder said, "It is time; come now."

"One more thing, Prisca, which you must always remember," Paul said. He took hold of my hands. "If ever you hear my voice, believe and obey what I say. It will not be only my voice, but the commandment of God through me. Will you remember that?"

For an instant I wondered if Paul's mind was slipping. How

212

could I hear his voice again? "I remember what you once told me in our atrium in Ephesus," I said. "That when you prayed for me, the Lord would hear."

He nodded. "This is even more. Do not forget, even for my sake alone."

He put his hand on my head.

"The Lord bless and keep you, my dearest Prisca. Do not attempt to come again. You have already risked your neck once more."

"Come," the guard ordered. "You heard the commander."

I leaned forward and kissed Paul's cheek. He took me in his arms; I felt his body shaking. I turned and left him without looking back. The guard helped me to climb blindly up the ladder; every nerve of mine quivered. The commander of the prison himself helped me to my feet. He held my arm as I walked to the prison gate. There he turned and left me without saying a word.

The guard at the gate unlocked it. As I passed through into the bright daylight he murmured, "The peace of Jesus be with you, sister."

I never thought of what I had heard him say until much, much later. I stood on the pavement, dazed by the sunlight. Slowly I walked along the side of the prison wall until I came to a steep flight of stone steps that led up to the top of the Capitoline Hill. I knew that half-way up there was a lonely terrace, a lookout over the long stretch of the majestic Forum and the rooftops of Rome. Often I had been brought there as a child to see the glory of my great city. I found the place again.

Now I sank down on a stone bench and put my head on the parapet. There I sobbed and sobbed my heart out, for my beloved Paul, whom I would never see again in his brown robe. . . .

After a long, long time—hours, perhaps—something came into my mind, almost like a voice from afar. It was a quotation that Paul had once repeated to us in our Corinth home, something that had been told to him by one of the apostles in Jerusalem.

"Woman, why do you weep?"

Jesus, risen from death, had asked that of Mary Magdalene as she stood outside his empty tomb.

I stayed at home the next day, unable to leave the couch in my room. I sent Aquila to the market, telling him I had a terrible headache. I could not eat, I felt a numbness through my body, and could not even think. I was as if paralyzed.

At noon the following day, Epaphras came once again to our house. His face was gray. "This morning Aristarchus finally received official permission to see Paul in the prison," he told us in a flat voice. "He went there; it was too late."

"I know," I said.

"You know? How?"

"I saw Paul in the prison. . . . I talked with him there."

Aquila gasped. "You did not tell me this."

"The commander of the prison ordered me to tell no one, that if I did it could be worse for everyone. He told me it would happen soon."

"The commander—" Epaphras was stunned. "You could have been arrested, it would have meant prison, torture—or—"

"I knew that."

The three of us stared numbly at each other. Then I asked, "Where did they take Paul—" I could not finish the question.

"Outside the walls of Rome, on the road to Ostia."

"Paul, oh, Paul—" I cried out.

But I did not weep. Paul was with our Lord.

24

One morning, Aquila pulled off the blanket and leaped from our couch. I remember the day: the nineteenth of July, in the hot summer.

I came awake slowly as he rushed downstairs. Then I smelled the smoke too—strong, pungent. Pulling back the curtain at the window onto a dark, murky dawn, I saw the unnatural grayness. In the sky, low clouds drifted.

Aquila found nothing wrong in our house and came up the steps again. Then he saw through the window whirls of smoke blowing down the street.

"A fire, an enormous fire," he cried. "Dress quickly! We'll find where it is."

Our house was on the far side of the Esquiline Hill, in the eastern part of the city. As soon as we stepped out onto the street the acrid fumes of smoke stung our eyes. Hastily we made our way to the top of the hill, where we could overlook Rome, toward the Palatine and Capitoline hills. What we saw was terrifying.

Columns of black smoke drifted upward from the neighborhood of the Circus Maximus and its many shops and warehouses. Flashes of giant yellow flame appeared from collapsing buildings. Swirls of smoke swept around us, making us cough. Hot ashes were falling, and still-burning embers carried by the wind passed above us.

"The whole area beyond the Capitoline is burning!" Aquila said in awe. "Look, there's more smoke to the right. It must be reaching all the way to the Tiber! It's unbelievable."

As we watched, other people came to see. The shock showed on their faces. Suddenly a new flame burst up to the left of the main fire.

"That's close to the Aventine," Aquila said. "The whole of Rome seems to be afire!"

From the new fire another column of smoke rose up in twisting, vicious eddies.

"It can't come our way, can it?" I asked Aquila with alarm.

He pointed to a blazing piece of ash blown by the breeze over our heads. "I don't know."

"Those poor people down there," I murmured, and clutched Aquila's hand.

A small crowd had gathered by that time, gazing down in silent horror at the holocaust.

"Go back to the house," Aquila said. "I'll see if I can find Epaphras."

"No!" I said. "You might get caught in it. No!"

"We ought to find what is happening; there's something strange about this."

"Then we'll go together. We're not going to be separated."

We walked quickly through the narrow streets, eyes smarting from the smoke. Hysterical inhabitants stood outside their houses,

215

not understanding what it was. Women grabbed at Aquila's elbow. "What is it, what is it?" they demanded.

"Be calm," he assured them. "The fire is not near us; there will be time."

"How could it happen so suddenly?" I asked Aquila. "We've had fires in Rome before, but nothing like this."

"That's what I mean by something strange. Rumors in Rome say Nero wants to rebuild the city, with broad avenues and new buildings. He'd like to replace all the wooden houses crowded together. *Say nothing; someone might hear!*"

"You don't think—"

"Shh! I don't believe even an Emperor could start this."

We could not find Epaphras. He was not at his boardinghouse. He had left early in the morning and had not come back.

Meanwhile the fire continued to spread into other areas. The streets not affected by flames were filled with refugees escaping to anywhere away from the heat and smoke. We, while walking, learned to lean over, closer to the street where the air was fresher, to avoid inhaling the fumes.

In the afternoon we returned to our house, which up to that time appeared to be in no danger. Our neighborhood was quiet. All the same, we took turns watching and listening at the window.

Since Paul's death, we had closed the house on the Via Lata. All his associates had gone back to their posts in various cities of Asia, Macedonia, and other places. Only Epaphras was still in Rome, and he planned to leave for Ephesus and Colossae—his own town—soon. Meanwhile he had been boarding in a small house near the Corso.

Much else had happened in Rome. The terrible news spread through the Christian community that the apostle Peter, whom Paul always called Cephas, had suddenly been taken by soldiers and crucified on the west bank of the Tiber. No one could find out why. There had been no formal charges, or trial so far as could be ascertained. This tragedy, so soon after Paul's execution, could have been another of Nero's ghastly whims. But the suspicion was growing that Caesar had become alarmed at the proliferation of the Christian sect among the Roman population. Indeed, there were now many thousands of us in his Imperial City.

Even the highest and lowest of citizen ranks called Nero a madman for his arrogant dismissal of Roman law, his orders for unreasoned executions and assassinations, his sexual excesses in nighttime maraudings which made the streets of the city unsafe after dark. The whole city had become uneasy.

No one knew when the Emperor might suddenly turn against the Christians.

Toward evening, Epaphras came to the house. His face was streaked with soot, his clothing reeked of smoke. He was exhausted.

He had spent the day trying to find out the cause of the fires—he said there had been several—and what they might mean. His landlady had wakened him in the early morning, terribly frightened, for the Corso area was already covered with smoke. He hurried outdoors, found the origin of the first fire had been in the wooden warehouses and shops at the western end of the Circus Maximus—the same area we had seen burning during the morning. Epaphras had gone as close as he could to the blazing inferno. He was astonished to find that no attempt was being made to stop its progress.

A group of fire fighters were standing idly at the end of one street with the flames approaching, through building after building, from the other end.

When he asked one of the firemen about this, he was shown a group of men down the street busily pulling out merchandise of all sorts from threatened warehouses.

"See those men?" the fireman replied. "They will not let us approach; they say they have orders. Orders from whom?"

Epaphras, already suspicious about the speed of the fire, went farther. In one of the poorest sections of the city, where houses were closely interlocked, he saw a building newly burning and separate from the main fire. Three rough-looking rowdies were walking fast away from it.

Later, he found two other fires, more remote. Of course, burning embers could have caused them, dropping onto flat, tar-covered rooftops—but Epaphras thought his suspicions were confirmed.

As he moved about the streets, he talked with a number of by-

217

standers. He learned that the Emperor had already rushed back by chariot from his summer villa at Antium, down the coast, and was reported to be in his palace on the Palatine. Caesar had opened his private gardens along the Tiber for refugees, of whom there must have been by then hundreds of thousands. Remarkably, so far there had been little loss of life, due to an efficient warning system —suspicious in itself.

One man said to Epaphras, "I cannot understand it; it's very strange."

"You mean, this was planned?"

"I can't say that, but—"

"Nero?"

The man looked at him. "I haven't said anything, nothing"; then he quickly walked away.

Epaphras went at once across town to the villa of Rufus Calpurnius, at the foot of the Esquiline, on the far side from us.

Rufus, leader of one of the largest Christian congregations, knew Epaphras well. He was very concerned. "Right or wrong, the Romans are going to blame Nero for this," he told Epaphras. "So he will have to put the blame somewhere else. I have good friends in the palace, who have told me before now that Caesar would like to destroy the Christians. There is grave danger here for us. We are sending out word to all Christians to keep out of sight for a time."

This was the warning Epaphras brought to us. We kept him with us for our evening meal—a sparse one to conserve food for an anticipated shortage after this catastrophe. Aquila urged him to spend the night with us, but he was worried about his landlady and felt he should return. If the fire changed in the night, then her house might be affected.

We walked with him as far as the top of the Esquiline Hill once more. From there we saw that the great fire had reached the Palatine. The huge, tall imperial palace was ablaze all through its interior, like a giant torch against the night sky. The home of the Caesars for years. . . .

"Nero's own palace!" I gasped. "He couldn't have planned—"

"Hush!" Epaphras pinched my arm; people were standing nearby.

"He will build another one for himself," Aquila whispered.

218

The fire of Rome lasted for five days. At the end, most of Rome lay in charred ruins. Our section of the city was one of the few that survived.

A short time had passed when I was awakened in the night. I sat up straight. The earliest light of day came through the curtains of our room. I heard a voice.

"Prisca! Prisca!"

I clutched the blankets. I shivered.

"Prisca, you must listen to me. Remember the things I have told you. You are in the greatest danger. Wake Aquila, and leave your house at once, even well before the sun rises. Go from Rome by the nearest gate, take the country roads south to Brindisi. From there a ship will carry you to Corinth. Take nothing with you. You and Aquila go at once."

I heard the voice. I heard the instructions. "Paul!" I cried out.

There was no reply, but my call awakened Aquila. He looked at me sleepily. I told him what had been told to me.

"You had a dream," Aquila scoffed. "We have had no further warning from Epaphras. He would have told us. Go back to sleep."

"No! No, Aquila, I know it is true! Paul told me before, twice, that he might speak to me. I promised I would obey—believe me, Aquila!"

He left the couch, glanced at me as if I were out of my mind from a nervous nightmare, and sighed.

"Put on your old gray chlamys, that one you use for work," I urged. "Your worst sandals. I have a worn gray tunica also. We shouldn't use mantles, the weather is too warm."

"What about the house?" he asked, scratching his head.

"Leave it as it is; we will never be here again. Hurry, Aquila, the sun will rise—"

We left the house without touching a thing, taking nothing. The sun had not risen. As we closed our door I glanced up the street.

In front of the house of Linus, a dozen or so doors away, a group of soldiers stood at attention, swords drawn. Linus and his wife were members of our own church congregation. Even as we looked, we were horrified by a woman's scream from inside the house . . . a prolonged scream of terror which echoed against the line of houses and reverberated in the morning air.

"Livia!" I choked as I spoke the name. "We must help—"

"No, come, don't stop for anything. There is nothing we can do against the Roman soldiers." Aquila held me for a moment. "Now I believe Paul did speak to you. Come, but walk slowly. Don't attract attention."

We walked in the opposite direction, then turned a corner away from our street. We went through block after block, avoiding the larger avenues. When we went through the Nomentana Gate, in the wall around Rome, we held our breath. The soldiers on guard did not turn to look.

On the open road that led into the countryside we moved faster.

After a time an empty grain wagon with two horses caught up with us. The driver pulled on his reins, pointed south with his finger.

"Yes," Aquila said quickly, "we are going the same way."

We climbed into the back of the dusty wagon. The horses started up and the walls of Rome vanished beyond the open fields.

Aquila took my hand without speaking.

I smiled a little, in spite of my thoughts of the horrors we left behind.

"Paul lives!" I said.

AUTHORS' NOTES
AND
ACKNOWLEDGMENTS

One may ask, Another book on St. Paul? What more can we add? This story we have written probably never has been attempted: to see Paul day by day through the eyes of a woman.

Priscilla, wife of Aquila, surely knew Paul during the most critical years as no other woman did. He lived in Priscilla and Aquila's home at Corinth, in Greece; the couple accompanied him to Ephesus, in Asia Minor, where they established Paul's church in their own house; and, again, they had a Christian church in their Roman home during his two tragic years in the Imperial City. Priscilla and Aquila were tentmakers, like Paul, and he worked with them in their shop, at least in Corinth. Prisca, as Paul affectionately called her, certainly had with him a relationship of closest friendship and confidence.

Of the six times Priscilla and Aquila are mentioned in the New Testament, Priscilla's name appears before Aquila's four times, contrary to usual custom, indicating that her personality and activity made a greater impression than her husband's.

Fiction ordinarily has the advantage of giving writers freedom to take certain liberties or make surmises with historic persons. But with a personality as revered and honored throughout Christianity as Paul's, no writers can preserve their integrity and make assumptions without justifiable reasons. We have endeavored to re-create as authentically as possible every event, action, and conversation used, except as noted below. If things did not happen exactly as described, we feel the actualities were close.

We have not directly quoted Paul from his writings except in a few instances. After careful study of his letters for his beliefs, his attitudes, and for the way his mind worked, we have used what we believe he would have said under the particular circumstances. Critics may have honest differences of opinion here, but we wish to make clear that we are not attempting in this book interpretations of theological questions.

Scholars of religious history will find one major deviation from fact. When Paul made his second, brief, emergency visit to Corinth to straighten out the crisis there, he was reviled and insulted by members of the congregation. He returned to Ephesus, and presumably from there wrote a very severe letter to the Corinthians which effectively ended the crisis. That letter has never been found. For our story, we have Paul quelling the revolt in person while still in Corinth.

In Ephesus we have used three events not specifically recorded by Luke in Acts. These are Paul's imprisonment, his illness, and the thunderstorm episode. But Paul in his writings of Ephesus intimated he had been in prison in that city, that at one time he came near death, and that somewhere Priscilla and Aquila had "risked their necks to save my life." We believe our three events are justified explanations, and indeed their equivalents have been suggested by authorities on the New Testament. Other Ephesian episodes are factual, according to Luke: visit by Apollos, the silversmith riot, the exorcists, book burning, Paul's healing ability, etc.

We have brought into our story many names of people mentioned by Paul and Luke, including Paul's associates. Other characters have been created to interpret the actuality of the life and times of Corinth and Ephesus. Among these are Alcesta, the slave girl of the pagan temple; Dino; Antonia and Cyrus and their friends, including Druda, in Corinth. Flavia and Actius, in Ephesus, are fictitious. But, for each one of these, counterparts existed.

There has been only one ancient description of Paul himself, and that not reliable. He apparently explained to no one the "thorn in my side"—to our knowledge, not even to Priscilla! What we have used seems most fitting for this great and powerful man who preserved the Way of Jesus Christ for all time to come.

ACKNOWLEDGMENTS

The primary source of information for our novel has been the Epistles written or dictated by Paul and the relative narrative by Luke in Acts of the Apostles, Chapters 7–28. For this research we have used five separate published versions of the New Testament: King James English version; Standard Revised (Thomas Nelson); New English Bible (Oxford University Press); Jerusalem Bible as translated from French (Doubleday); and the Interlinear Greek-English New Testament, translated by the Reverend Alfred Marshall from the Nestle Greek (Samuel Bagster and Sons Ltd., London). All these differ in text but not content. We found that the literal translations of words from the Greek in many cases suited our purposes best.

We acknowledge with thanks permission to quote from the R. C. Jebb translation of Sophocles' "Antigone" as it appears in GREEK DRAMA, edited by Moses Hadas; copyright © 1965 by Bantam Books, Inc.

For a most complete understanding of the times and Paul's relation to them, we give credit to Professor F. F. Bruce's perceptive analysis in his *New Testament History,* as written and annotated (Doubleday-Anchor Book).

Other books used for research include *I Corinthians,* William F. Orr and James Arthur Walther (Vol. 32 of the Anchor Bible, Doubleday); *Interpreter's Bible with Commentary* (Abingdon); *Jews, God and History,* Max I. Dimont (Signet, New American Library); *Basic Judaism,* Milton Steinberg (Harvest Book, Harcourt, Brace and World); *An Archæologist Follows the Apostle Paul,* James L. Kelso (Word Books, Waco, Texas); *The Greek Stones Speak,* Paul MacKendrick (Mentor, New American Library); *The Meridian Handbook of Classical Mythology,* Edward Tripp (N.A.L.). Still other books, too numerous to mention, are on the shelves of the New York Public Library. Our thanks are hereby expressed to their authors and publishers, and to the New York Public Library.

Much of our research was accumulated for two previous books, written by us for the same era, including St. Paul to a somewhat lesser degree than in the current work. This earlier research was primarily done in Rome, Italy, with gratitude for the co-operation of the Vatican Library and the American Academy in Rome.

225